SOMEWHERE ON ST. THOMAS

SOMEWHERE SERIES, BOOK 1

TOBY JANE

CHAPTER ONE

I never expected a spelling bee to be the apogee of my life, but the night of July thirtieth, 1983, turned out to be exactly that. I was one of two finalists competing for a major college scholarship, and I needed to win or I was going to be stuck on our tiny island of Saint Thomas in the Virgin Islands, cleaning hotel rooms.

Blinded by hot stage lights, I clutched the old wooden podium and stood listening to my competition recite, "Succedaneum." Thank God they didn't also require a definition. Sweat prickled under my armpits.

My competition, a tall gangly boy with thick glasses and an accent that marked him as from the nearby French Antilles, made it through. Modest applause followed his effort.

"Antediluvian," the proctor said. Oh, this felt like cheating because I knew it so well. My parents had come to St. Thomas to do religious work, stayed on past their allotted stint, and made a niche on the island managing vacation rental homes for off-islanders.

"Antediluvian," I stated. "Of, or pertaining to the period

preceding the Great Flood referred to in the Bible. A-n-t-e-d-i-l-u-v-i-a-n."

More applause than the other kid got. I was showing off a bit, but I was tired of proving that red hair and big boobs meant bimbo. All I had to do now to prove that to the world was get off this rock, go to college, and become a lawyer in the big city.

"Xanthosis," the proctor said to the gangly boy. The kid's Adam's apple worked as he blinked behind his glasses. I could tell it was over.

"Xanthosis," the kid repeated. "Z-a-n-t-h-o-s-i-s."

The buzzer marked his shame, and sympathetic clapping escorted him off the stage. I felt bad for him, but he was younger and there would be other chances. This was it for me, and if I could get this word right, I'd win a golden ticket out of here. And oh, how badly I needed to get out of this palm-tree studded, nowhere paradise. There was nothing for me here—except my family, of course.

"Pococurante," the proctor said to me.

The lights blinded me. I clung to the podium and I shut my eyes. I could feel the prickle of sweat under my arms penetrating the green fabric of the dress Mom had told me to wear to enhance the color of my eyes. I tried not to hyperventilate. I pictured myself as the lawyer I hoped to be, making a confident plea to a jury.

I knew what this word meant, but I wasn't sure of the spelling. I sucked in a breath, blew it out, and went for it.

"Pococurante," I said. "To be indifferent to something. And I am certainly not p-o-c-o-c-u-r-a-n-t-e to winning this scholarship. I want it more than anything."

Huge applause broke out as a bell marked the end of the competition. My dad ran to the front of the stage and I hopped off and into his arms.

"I did it!"

"I never had a doubt, Ruby," he exclaimed, blue eyes extra-bright with excitement. "You're going to get your dream, girl!"

Mom, Pearl, and Jade were right behind him, and we mass-hugged in the narrow area in front of the battered wooden stage. I had the best, most loving family: Mom, sturdy and tall with her auburn hair and hazel eyes; ten-year-old Jade, who shared my green eyes but had Mom's hair, and Pearl who had Dad's blue eyes and curly blonde hair, already so beautiful at fourteen that she should wear a bag on her head.

Yes, this was the night I found out for sure I'd to be able to go to Northeastern University, where I've already been accepted. With this win, I'd be leaving in two weeks.

"Got a nice dinner planned," Mom said. "Lobster and fish. Hope you don't mind we invited company on your special night —he brought the main dish."

"Who is it?" I frowned a little. Mom and Dad were hospitable to a fault, always inviting ex-pats or the transient workers they hired for cleaning and yard work over for meals.

"New yard and coconut trimming guy." Dad hefted Jade up like she was two, and headed for the door. "Sailor. Seems to have some ocean skills." Dad liked guys with ocean skills. I usually found them not that bright.

Mom winked. "I think you'll like this one, Ruby."

"Hah. I'm out of here," I snorted. Mom knew how focused I was, so she liked to tease that I was going to fall in love, marry a local, and end up staying on Saint Thomas. I followed the family out of the church hall where the spelling bee was held, shaking hands with the geeky kid who'd lost and wishing him best of luck next time. I piled into the station wagon with my sisters for the drive back out to deep-armed, crystalline Magen's Bay, where we lived.

"You smoked that guy," Pearl said, grinning. She snuggled against me on one side, and Jade on the other. I felt warmed by their support. I knew I'd have felt very differently on the drive home if I'd lost that spelling bee.

"That kid didn't need the win as much as I did. He'll have other chances," I told Pearl.

We drove up the windy two-lane road out of Charlotte Amalie, with its red-roofed, Mediterranean-style houses and palm trees. I looked back down at the capital of Saint Thomas, waiting to feel sad that I'm leaving so soon—but all I felt was excited. The life I'd worked so hard for was going to happen in just a couple of weeks.

I was setting the long table out on the screened porch with its view of an aqua sliver of Magen's Bay when Mom came into the doorway, holding a string bag wriggling with lobsters. "Ruby, this is Rafe McCallum. He brought some fish that need cleaning. Can you take him to the outside sink? I have to get these lobsters into the pot."

"Sure," I muttered, dropping a handful of forks with a clatter. "Hi."

Mom turned, her eyes sparkling, and left. Rafe walked into the breezy space that doubled as our dining room. He was holding a canvas bag that smelled strongly of fish and was clearly heavy, if the knotted muscles of his bronzed arms were anything to go by.

"Hi. Need to clean these. Your mom said you have a sink?"

At least six foot three, topping me by a foot, he had eyes the color of deep open ocean. I didn't think I'd ever seen that color before. We stared at each other for just a little too long, and I felt the blush I'd suffered from my whole life prickle up my chest and heat my cheeks. I had that fair skin redheads do, with an ebb and flow of blood that betrayed my every mood.

Spooked, I headed for the side door. "Sure. Come this way."

I was still wearing the dark green dress I'd worn to the spelling bee, a fit-and-flare style that hugged my figure in a way I'd thought was attractive but modest, and now felt was entirely too revealing.

He followed me down chipped cement steps and around the lawn on the side of the house to the outdoor sink, a cold-water, galvanized affair with a hole that drained out onto the ground and a built-in wooden cutting board.

"Want some help?" I asked, pulling myself together, reminding myself I had one foot out the door. Guys like Rafe were a dime a dozen in the Virgin Islands: handsome, pleasure-seeking young men, rootless, with no more future on their minds than the next wave or sailboat or high. I mocked them with my friend Jenny. "I'll never date a surfer or sailor," I'd sworn, long ago. "Hot bodies and no brains."

"Could use a knife." Rafe dumped a couple of large, colorful parrotfish out on the board. I could see marks on them from his spear, and I imagined him swimming underwater in nothing but a pair of trunks. "I'll do it. You should keep your pretty dress clean."

I turned and hurried back into the house, going into the kitchen and taking the big filet knife in its plastic scabbard out of the drawer. Mom was dropping the lobsters into a pot on the stove.

"Cute, isn't he?" she said.

"He's a sailor, Mom," I said. "Probably surfs too." Surfers were the ultimate time wasters, in my not-so-humble opinion.

"He does surf, that's not a sin. And ocean skills are handy. Look at these lobsters and fish. But never mind," Mom said. "He's too much man for you."

"Not too much for me," Pearl piped up from where she was

chopping greens at the counter. Pearl was definitely precocious in the man department.

Mom bumped Pearl with a hip. "Give Ruby a chance to maneuver."

"I'm maneuvering right out of here." I hustled off, knife in hand.

I drew up short halfway to the sink, and gulped. Rafe had taken off his shirt. Late evening sun gilded a torso that could have been in the Louvre.

What's wrong with me? I've seen hot men before. I forced my legs to move, and Rafe turned from rinsing one of the parrotfish at the tap. I thought I saw a little red around his ears as he saw my hesitation. "I didn't want to get fish guts on my shirt," he apologized. "That knife sharp?"

"Oh, sure. Of course." I circled around to the other side of the sink to hand it to him, but now I had a view of chiseled chest and the kind of lean and supple abs that come from working and playing hard. I handed him the knife in its scabbard, noticing some sort of tattoo on his shoulder. I made myself look down at the fish. "You go spearfishing a lot?"

"Yeah." No elaboration. He plonked the fish down on the cutting board, and using quick, confident strokes, slashed the meat off in large filets. "I like this way to prep them. It's quick, and you don't have to deal with bones or scales." He flipped a filet, sliding the knife between the meat and scaly skin, slicing it off. He slanted a glance at me from under dark brows and caught my eyes on him. Long, chocolate-brown, sun-streaked hair framed a rugged, interesting face I'd been too busy gawking at his body to notice.

He was older than me, from the sun-crinkles beside his eyes, and definitely, totally, not my type. Probably hadn't finished high school and had an IQ of 80, though with that body he wasn't going to have any trouble getting women to chase him.

"Well. I'll leave you to it." I started to walk away, but he called me back.

"Ruby. Can I get a bag for the guts and such?" He held up the stripped carcass of the fish. It had taken him about three minutes to prep the filets. He definitely knew what he was doing with his hands.

"Okay." I had to go back in the house again, and I could feel his eyes my back. "Get a grip, Ruby," I growled at myself. "You have places to go, people to meet. Intellectual people, with good prospects. The last thing you need to do is get distracted by some pretty-boy surfer."

I managed to hang onto that resolve, keeping my eyes on my plate or my family members through dinner, only breaking from that during my father's toast to my spelling bee win. Rafe, across from me, met my eyes with his and my glass with his wine goblet as me and my sisters toasted with grape juice.

"Congratulations," he said. "I hope Boston is all you dream it will be."

"It's going to be awesome," I said, almost defiant. He shrugged, and sipped.

He had long, graceful hands, and he gestured when he talked, mainly with my parents since I wouldn't participate. They discussed the things he'd studied on the boat he'd crewed over to the Virgin Islands and the interests they had in common. He'd read everything from the Bible to Socrates, and he was learning astronomy and art history on the boat in his spare time. This trip was part of his "personal mission" to go everywhere, see all he could, and do what he wanted to in the moment.

Forking up a bite of sumptuous lobster, I considered that if I hadn't been the daughter of former missionaries and pure as a lifetime of Bible memorization could make me, I might have had a little fun with someone like him before I left for college. But as it was, on the eve of my long-awaited departure, I wasn't going to be derailed by anyone. No matter how handsome and interesting.

Rafe came to church the next Sunday. I stood a few rows behind him, appreciating the breadth of his shoulders, the wide column of his neck, the blond-streaked curling brown hair touching his back. That hair had a lively, rebellious quality to it, haloing his head as if to express impatience with the rules and all that was mundane and usual. The tattoo I hadn't got a good look at was peeking out of his shirt. I kept staring at his arms, trying to see what it was.

He had a great voice and belted out the choruses of our weary old tunes in the dog-eared hymnal with an enthusiasm I couldn't help but like. On the way back out, he hurried to catch up with me in the aisle.

"What are you doing after this?"

I turned my head, surprised. He was so tall I was looking at his collarbone. "Nothing in particular."

"Want to go for a hike? I hear there are some good trails around here."

"Okay," I said hesitantly. "I'd better ask my dad."

He grinned. "Tell him my intentions are honorable."

I blushed, that awful flare, and I saw him notice it by the widening of his nostrils, the expansion of his pupils as he looked down at me. I had to force myself to remember I was standing in the doorway of the church. I held my Bible over my cleavage like a breastplate.

"Never mind. I don't need to ask Dad. It's just a hike. You know I'm leaving in two weeks, don't you?"

"Like anyone around here could forget it. You're the boss's daughter, the smartest girl on the island. Leaving paradise and going to Northeastern University." He pronounced it in contemptuous tones. "I just want to go on a hike with someone who knows the trails around here."

"Okay, then." I was so embarrassed by my self-important words that I could hardly get down the steps fast enough, but he was right behind me. "Let me get into some hiking clothes. I'll take my bike and meet you at the park."

"Bring extra water," he said, lifting a hand in farewell. "You're going to need it."

I felt my heart speed up with excitement as I got into the family station wagon for the short drive home. "What was Rafe talking to you about?" Pearl asked, pouting.

"Nothing." I didn't want to deal with my siblings' teasing or questions. "I'm going for a bike ride."

Saint Thomas, in the non-resort area we live in, is rural and green with steep, jungled mountains made of the bones of the ancient volcanoes that formed the island chain. I hurried into the house and changed into shorts and a tank top, bundling my hair into a ponytail and rubbing down with sunscreen as I headed into the kitchen to fill up a plastic water bottle.

"Where are you going?" Mom was at the kitchen sink, washing something.

"I'm eighteen. Do I have to tell you everywhere I'm going?" I exclaimed, and filled the water bottle under the cold artesian stream of water.

"She's going somewhere with Rafe," Pearl said loudly.

"Am not!" I screwed the top on. "Just taking a bike ride."

Mom's hazel eyes crinkled at the corners. "Too much man for you," she whispered.

I didn't dignify this with an answer and flounced out. I hopped on my old bike with its three speeds and the wire mesh basket in the front. That bike was how I usually got anywhere from our tiny town on Magen's Bay.

Rafe met me at the seed-tufted soccer field in the middle of what passed for town. He was driving a rusty old red truck that looked like it had been around since the sugarcane days fifty years ago. He wore shorts and a black T-shirt with the sleeves cut off. The tattoo I'd wondered about was a bald eagle pouncing, with claws extended.

He looked dangerous, poor, and way too attractive.

I was having none of the above, no matter how my skin prickled at the sight of him. I was going to Northeastern University. Danger and poverty were not something I was interested in.

At all.

Rafe was chewing a stem of long grass, and he used it to point to the rugged dark green mountain rising directly ahead. "I want to climb that."

"Good," I said. "Because that's where we're going."

He opened the door for me, unexpectedly gentlemanly. I got into the truck and he slammed the door. Rust sprinkled down from under the dash onto my feet.

Rafe got in and turned the key, glancing at me with that wicked smile. Maybe it was the blue of his eyes in his tanned face, the white of his teeth, the fact that he knew good and well he was having an effect on me. Whatever it was, that smile scared me. I pulled my floppy hat down over my hair. The truck rattled and groaned reluctantly into life.

Dangerous and poor, I told myself forcefully.

"Look at you, pasted up against the door. I bite a little, but only when I'm invited."

I stared out the windshield, clutching my small canvas knapsack filled with a water bottle and a couple of mangoes. I pointed. "It's that way."

I directed us down a narrow road that turned to dirt. We bucked through ruts and potholes. "We've officially left the tourist zone," he said.

The truck hit an especially deep pothole and it threw me against him. His skin felt hot. I scooted away, fumbling in the crack of the bench seat for the seat belt.

"No belts," Rafe said. "You're gonna have to take your chances with me."

The dirt road dead-ended at a cow pasture. On the other side of the pasture, the long arms of ridges ran down from the steep mountain.

"The trailhead's on the other side of the pasture," I said.

"I never would have found this without you," he said as we swished through bunchy grass.

"You're welcome."

"So why are you so eager to leave?" He made an arm gesture encompassing the jewel-colored mountains, the deep blue sky with its feather-bright clouds, the velvety field trimmed in ornamental orchid trees.

"It's boring here."

He laughed. "You just haven't lived anywhere else."

"Where are you from?"

"California. Talk about a place with a lot going on. But I used to think it was boring, too." He told a few stories about a family home in a place called Red Rock, where Saturday-night excitement consisted of driving back and forth in cars packed with friends on Main Street and lighting bottle rockets at a drive-in movie theater.

"We don't have a Main Street, or even a movie theater of any kind except in Charlotte Amalie," I complained, jumping over a cow patty. "I've had it with this place."

"What about water sports?"

"I can do all of them." I waved a disparaging hand. "Surfing. Diving. Fishing. I've even been learning windsurfing, that new thing with the sail attached to a board. They're all fine. Probably the best thing about living here. But I want things that have to do with the mind."

"What about the body?" He turned those deep blue eyes on me. "You seem fit. For a girl."

11

I snorted. "Maybe I'll join some sort of sports team when I get there. There are no teams here, so I figure if I have a base of fitness, I can learn to play any sport."

"Any sport, huh?" We were approaching a giant fallen log at the edge of the pasture. He pointed. "Let's see you get over that."

"No problem." I reached up and grabbed a branch near the top. I hauled myself up to stand on top of the log, then jumped the six feet to the other side. I ran when I hit the ground, full speed, across the rest of the pasture and into the jungle on the other side. I'd show him how "fit for a girl" I was! I dodged and wove through trailing vines and towering trees, finally flattening myself against a mango tree draped so heavily in vines I was able to slip in under them as easily as hiding behind a curtain.

I heard him running, crashing through the brittle branches on the ground.

"Ruby!" he yelled at last. When I was born with red hair, my dad, in a poetic fit, named me Ruby Day Michaels. It was hard to live down.

"Boo," I said from behind him.

He whirled, and for a moment I was frightened by the intensity of his expression. He took two steps and loomed over me, and as suddenly as if we'd had a mind meld, I knew he was annoyed and aroused and amused with me all at once.

I could even see how I looked to him: my green eyes the color of the jungle leaves, the red hair I was named for bright as flame in the gloom, my skin flushed and lightly tanned as a perfectly done marshmallow. My body was an hourglass with amazing legs and a tight, round ass. His hands itched to heft me up against him. He wanted to explore every inch of my flushed skin in the dusky light of the jungle.

It felt terrifying and wonderful to so completely know what he was thinking and feeling. I wondered if he could read my mind, too, and my face heated up even more.

"You're a brat," was all he said. "This the trail?" He pointed into the greenish murk. Mosquitoes swirled around us.

"Yes. It's lighter up ahead on the ridge." I slapped at my arms.

"Okay. Let's get out of these mosquitoes." And he broke into a jog, leading the way.

I kept up with him for a mile or so, but by then the trail was switch backing heavily uphill, and though we'd left the mosquitoes behind, now we were in the sun, which ratcheted up the humidity and made my redhead's skin even pinker than usual. But I wasn't going to ask for a rest.

Instead I reached around into my knapsack and grabbed my water bottle, drinking some and pouring a little into my hand, splashing it onto my face and chest. He must have heard me because he stopped abruptly in the shade. "Let's take a break."

"You read my mind," I panted, rubbing the water into my neckline. I could feel it trickling between my breasts, wetting my shirt. I held his eyes, daring and naughty, and poured another handful, splashing it on my face, hair, and chest.

"Oh damn," he muttered, and turned away, pretending to focus on the view. The front of his shorts bulged.

The sight did something to me it had never done before.

I knew about erections. Until now, knowing that I could affect boys had been an uncomfortable mixture of embarrassing and disgusting. To be honest, I thought less of men for reacting to my body, to women, that way. It seemed to reduce people to animals.

But today, seeing how I affected Rafe brought an answering rush of blood, loosening my knees. I was beyond nervous, and yet I had an urge to keep provoking him. I took a long drink of water, wiping my mouth on the back of my hand, and lowered the bottle to see Rafe staring at my shirt. He turned away with a wrench of movement.

This whole thing was a bad idea.

I had a dream, and it was to get off this miserable little piece of paradise and go somewhere that was all about the intellect. I wasn't giving in to my hormones without a fight.

I had to keep moving. That was the answer.

I screwed the top on the bottle, stowed it in my knapsack, and passed him to hit the trail at a run, leading the way.

Of course, that meant Rafe was looking at my ass the whole time, and I could feel him doing it.

We were both exhausted and dripping, conversation impossible, when we crested the highest point of the ridges above the town. I sat in the lee of a boulder, panting, and looped my arms around my knees as I took in the huge vista. After a moment of hesitation, Rafe sat beside me, leaving a good two feet between us.

Magen's Bay swooped before us, cobalt toward the horizon and turquoise inside, the white beach so bright it hurt my eyes. The fringe of palm trees around the bay looked like lace from this distance. Belatedly, I remembered my sunglasses in the knapsack, took them out and put them on.

We both sipped water. Mine was gone first. He'd been right. I should have brought extra water.

"So. Why did you pick Northeastern University?" He still said the name like it was something bad.

I shrugged. "It's where I got a scholarship. And it's the farthest I can get from here."

"I think you might get a little homesick," he said softly, "when it's blowing sleet and snow off the Charles River, the sky's a flat gray ceiling, and there is nothing but buildings all around."

"You sound like you know what it's like."

"I've been there. Went to college in Boston. It was enough to make me take to the ocean full-time."

I didn't want to hear that.

There was no water left, so I took out a mango and my trusty

Swiss Army knife and used it to cut lines around the fruit, stripping off the skin in a few economical gestures. I handed the peeled mango to him, and saw he'd taken out a Buck knife with a carved horn handle.

"Mine is bigger than yours." He grinned, taking the sweet, slippery fruit.

I smiled back. "I won't hold it against you."

I stripped the skin off my mango and we ate companionably side by side. He cut slices off and ate them off his knife. I did the same, sneaking a glance at his large, capable hands holding the mango, the flash of the blade, the shine of his teeth as the fruit disappeared between his lips.

He'd taste like mango if I kissed him.

I pictured licking the fragrant juice off his sculptured mouth. Fortunately, he was gazing out at the beauty of the view below and the crystal turquoise of the bay and didn't see me staring. He had a mouth that looked perfect on his face, but might look too hard on someone else—the top lip a full, arched line, the lower one wide and mobile. His jaw was a stubble-roughened angle, his brows made secret caves over the blue of his eyes. That long blond-and-chocolate hair waved back from his brow, damp with the sweat of the hike.

He glanced at me, and I looked away. I took another bite, but butterflies were fluttering around in my belly so wildly my appetite was gone. I offered him the rest of my mango, holding it out mutely.

Instead of taking it, he leaned over and sucked the juicy tips of my fingers, his eyes sparkling blue mischief as he drew them into his mouth.

I gasped at the feel of his tongue on the sensitive pads of my fingers. The sucking sensation, his mouth so hot and slick, seemed to go straight to my breasts. I could feel my nipples

TOBY JANE

tighten, hard as acorns. My whole body seemed to light up, and I felt a rush of heat between my legs.

It was totally unfamiliar, yet as if my body had been designed for this, knew what to do, and had been waiting for a switch to turn it on.

That switch had just been thrown.

I couldn't seem to move. Rafe's tongue flicked my fingers, traveling between them, his mouth taking them all the way in, sliding back out, his tongue flicking the sensitive nerve endings at the tips again and again.

In, out, in and out.

His blazing blue eyes held my hypnotized green ones.

I couldn't breathe or look away as he made love to my hand with his mouth. I leaned inexorably in his direction. Finally, he encountered the mango on my palm and took it, sitting back with it between his teeth and taking a bite. "Thanks."

I realized my hand was still extended, as if in supplication.

Take me, that open, trembling hand seemed to beg.

So did the rest of me, yearning toward the source of these electric feelings.

I shot to my feet, flushed with humiliation and arousal, confused and terrified. I grabbed my knapsack and ran back down the trail.

I ran all the way to the truck and then stood there, dripping sweat and mortification. I looked back across the pasture. No sign of Rafe.

Well, hell if I was going to stand there and wait for that arrogant ass to meander down when he was good and ready.

Besides, I had nothing to say to him and he was as dangerous to me as kryptonite. Good thing I was in shape and it was no more than a few miles back to town. I set off at a jog down the sandy-dirt road. I could have used some water, but there was no help for it.

16

Rafe eventually caught up with me close to the park, slowing the truck down beside me as I ran.

"Hop in and I'll drop you off at home," he said through the open window, chugging along beside me.

I wouldn't look at him, still running, holding the straps of my knapsack. I didn't answer.

"Suit yourself," he said, and gunned it. The truck kicked up some bad-smelling exhaust and a little gravel in my direction. He drove on and turned left, going out of town.

"Son of a beehive!" I screamed after him, all the profanity allowed in my world.

I took a moment to wonder where he lived, what his place was like, if he wanted to try to see me again...and then I ran hard to punish myself for my weakness.

"That man is bad news." I muttered out loud, panting. "I just have to get on the plane and get out of here. That's all I have to do."

CHAPTER TWO

I managed to avoid Rafe for the rest of the two weeks until my departure. He made no gesture toward me, either, ignoring me at church and turning his back when we ran into each other at my parents' office.

This just made me want him more. I tossed and turned at night, waking myself up with sensual dreams, all starring Rafe doing things to me I'd only read about in the coverless paperbacks I picked up at garage sales. I was so distracted and irritable Mom was worried about me. "I hope you're not coming down with something. We've got the bonfire party tonight and tomorrow you're flying out."

"Like I could forget. I'll be fine."

I felt like I was living a double life. On the outside was the smart, good, virtuous daughter of missionaries who'd hardly been kissed, on her way to Northeastern University. On the inside was a tormented soul whose body had been switched on by the wrong man at the wrong time and now couldn't be turned off.

How I wish it could.

The bonfire going-away party was wonderful. My friend

Jenny, who was staying in Saint Thomas and going to community college, cried the most, hanging on to me and garlanding me with flowers. We sang songs around the fire to the strumming of guitars and beating of drums, and a wonderful potluck dinner filled my tummy with delicious island food.

Rafe didn't attend, though my parents had invited him. I'd noticed he wasn't there from the moment the party began, and was annoyed that I noticed, annoyed with myself, that it mattered. All of those feelings added up to annoyed with him.

Dancing around the fire with my friend Jenny, I realized I was going to miss this place, but that other world was so different I didn't know what to expect. Due to finances, I'd never been to Boston, and again due to finances, tomorrow I was boarding the plane alone.

The next morning was emotional. Getting ready to leave for the airport at Charlotte Amalie, I stood in the driveway for a last round of hugs from Jenny and my family. Both my parents were crying, and my sisters, Pearl and Jade, clung until I felt bruised.

I heard the distinctive rattling of Rafe's truck and looked up. He pulled up, parked, and got out of the truck as if his appearance were expected. He'd dressed carefully, I saw, in a patterned dark red shirt over black slacks. His long hair was still wet from a shower and combed neatly back.

"Hi, Mr. and Mrs. Michaels. Do you mind if I have a word with Ruby?"

My dad, open-mouthed, shook his head. My mom just stared, and I understood why: Rafe McCallum was indeed splendid to look at, with or without a shirt. Jenny wiggled her brows at me as Rafe took my arm firmly and towed me across the lawn to stand beneath a spreading Poinciana tree.

The pattern of the tree's leaf shadow fell around us and we were far enough away for privacy, but I was aware of watching eyes.

"What do you want?" I snapped, tugging my arm away, because my body was humming at being so close to him. I could almost smell the pheromones spilling into the air around us, an intoxicating scent of what could never be, hovering just beneath conscious awareness but powerful nonetheless.

"Just wanted to tell you—I enjoyed meeting you. And I'd like to keep in touch. Here's my address." He took my hand, set a little clamshell inside it, folded my fingers over it.

"You have an address? And it's inside a shell," I said.

He chuckled. I thought I could look up at the shadow of him towering over me forever.

He was still holding my hand, and then he pulled me close in a hug, socially acceptable in the circumstances. With his arms around me, my length pressed to his, he whispered in my ear, "You've gotten under my skin. I'm going to miss you way more than I should."

"It's the same for me," I whispered back, and he held me away from him as if using all his strength to do so.

"I wanted to see you every day since our hike, but I didn't want to be a distraction to you," he said. "And now you're leaving. I found I had to say goodbye."

"I wish you had come to the bonfire last night. I was looking for you." The words we said felt stilted but desperate.

"Time to go!" Dad bellowed.

Rafe took my hand and we walked back. I could feel my cheeks burning, conscious of my family and best friend watching. At the car he let go of my hand finally and said, loud and clear as a statement of intent, "I'll see you again, Ruby."

And he hugged me one more time.

I stared after him as he got into that funky old truck. The clamshell with his address in it was clutched in my hand, and I pressed that hand against my throat.

"Wow," Jenny said, appearing beside me and whispering into my ear. "I see why everybody's talking about him."

I flapped my free hand. "Just another surfer."

"Seems a little more substantial than that," Jenny argued. She traced a man shape, her white teeth gleaming. "I wouldn't mind finding out how substantial. Sure you want to leave that bone behind for me to chew on?"

I forced a laugh. "All yours. I'm off to the big city."

Dad and I got into the car after another round of hugs and turned onto the road for Charlotte Amalie and the airport.

"How well do you know Rafe?" Dad asked.

"Not well."

"You seem to have made an impression on him."

I thought of Rafe's mouth on my juicy fingers. Whatever impression had been made was mutual.

More hugs and prayers with Dad at the airport, his blue eyes emotional, and I got on the small prop plane and took off. The suitcase with all my worldly possessions in it was somewhere in the cargo area and the closed clamshell Rafe had given me was tucked into my pocket. I hadn't wanted to look at it until I was safely in the air.

I felt battered and torn and yet so excited I was guilty as the little plane climbed into the sky. Saint Thomas, cartoonishly beautiful, waved goodbye with its palm trees and blue water, dear family and forbidden lovers.

I took the shell from Rafe out of my pocket and opened the small white clam, two sides that made a heart shape when open. Inside was a tiny folded paper.

His writing was elegant, flowing, and the black cursive looked like it had been done with a fountain pen. *I think of you often. Let's stay in touch.* His address, care of general delivery at the general store in our village, made me smile.

"I think of you often, too," I whispered. And I dug my journal out of my backpack and started my first letter to Rafe, describing everything I saw from the air and my excitement about where I was going. In writing, I felt like I could talk to him, not like my tongue-tied stupidity and terrible blushes in person.

It took twenty long hours to make it to Boston. I arrived at night, when the city was a lacy shawl of colored lights around the harbor. The sidewalk outside the airport was warm in the early-fall night and smelled of gas fumes and the city, a whole new bouquet to get used to.

I hauled my suitcase with the broken wheel out onto the sidewalk and took my first cab ride ever, giving the address of my sight-unseen dorm to a driver with a turban on his head.

I had expected my dorm to be fancier than it was, Northeastern University being the upscale place I had pored over pictures to see, but by the time I located the right brick building in the dark (still towing the broken-wheeled suitcase), the simple room in the gracious old building looked like heaven.

I fell face down on the bare mattress and slept fully clothed.

CHAPTER THREE

Life at Northeastern University was colorful. Absorbing. Stimulating. Everything I'd hoped for. I was taking a general-ed slate of huge lecture classes and planning an eventual prelaw major. In French class I had a leg up because of our proximity to the French-dominated nearby islands and I was semi-fluent already.

On my second day I decided to adopt an imaginary persona as part of my Northeastern University experience. I'd be Juliette, exchange student from the French Antilles, and would speak with an accent. The red hair would throw everyone off and make me more intriguing, I hoped. It was a fun way to cast off my past and become someone new and sophisticated.

I shopped with my roommate, Shellie, a preppy girl from New York, at Boston's thrift stores to totally redo my look. I bought berets and scarves and old jeans with peace signs on the butt and a pair of boots with high heels. I liked the look of my red hair streaming out from under a scarlet or purple beret over the old navy pea coat I wore everywhere as the cold deepened outside and the leaves changed color.

I didn't have money because, even though I was on a scholarship, none of my living expenses were covered but the dorm room itself and a basic food plan. I got a job in the dining hall, serving students who didn't have to have jobs. I spoke to them only in French in reply to their English requests, a silly form of revenge. I was at Northeastern, but I still didn't feel like I belonged there. I might be smart enough, but one look at Shellie's wardrobe, shoes, and furnishings showed me I was out of my league in every other way.

I'd write Rafe at my desk using a feather quill pen in my persona as Juliette. I wasn't sure why I kept writing—perhaps it was because he was the only person who'd specifically asked me to keep in touch. At least, that's what I told myself.

The phone in the dorm was exorbitantly expensive, so I didn't call home. My parents called once, an ordeal during which Mom cried and Pearl demanded to know about all my boyfriends and my dad reminded me to stay chaste.

Because "Juliette" the flame-haired Frenchwoman was getting a lot of dates. I enjoyed the movies, ice-cream sundaes, swan-boat rides, and museum tours I'd been invited on, and as Juliette, I was able to shed my uptight missionary upbringing and affect worldliness. I even took to dangling a clove cigarette from scarlet lips, my beret cocked.

Under it all I still burned for Rafe. I worried because I hadn't met anyone to equal him. I kept an eye out for the mail like Snoopy dangling off of the cartoon doghouse, and Rafe's first letter arrived after a month. I closed myself into the bedroom of our suite with the STUDYING sign on the door so Shellie wouldn't poke her head in to see what I was doing.

I tore open the fat missive.

Dear Ruby. I'm picturing you in your purple beret as Juliette the girl from the French Antilles, and may I say it's brilliant? I know how hard you've tried to be your parents' daughter, but there's something dramatic in you, something wild…I glimpsed it that day we took a hike, and I think you glimpsed it, too, and it scared you. I stayed away the rest of the time you were still on the island because I could see I would be nothing but trouble for you, with the goals you had and departure on your mind. But it was hard, and I suffered more than I expected to, and I'm selfish enough to hope you lost a little sleep, too.

I'm glad you've found a safe way to let that wild side out to play, one that doesn't get you into too much trouble. But I do regret I didn't have longer to know that girl. You did something to me, and I've not been the same since.

I pressed my hand over my open mouth. It shocked me that Rafe understood me so completely, that he knew exactly what he'd been doing when he ate that mango off my hand, and that he'd been so bold as to tell me I'd affected him.

I love your letters! They are so full of all the adventure and experience you're having, all you are learning and seeing and doing. As for me, things are much the same in Saint Thomas. I work all day, keeping in shape climbing the coconut trees on all your parents' rental properties and cutting off the coconuts, working on the boat I'm crewing next spring back to California, and surfing every day now that it's the surf season. At night I have trouble sleeping, because I think of you and wonder what we might be to each other. Love, Rafe.

My hands were trembling as I folded the rest of the pages and stuffed them back in the envelope, afraid to read any more. Afraid for his hold on me to get any stronger, when his honest words affected me this way.

I needed to go out with someone else, I decided. Someone suitable, Northeastern University-ish, an intellectual. Someone more in line with the self I was inventing over here. Someone who could knock Rafe right out of my mind.

He came into my life that very afternoon, a tall young man who'd shyly struck up extra conversation each day as I served him behind the cafeteria line, my red tresses restrained by a hairnet and my curves packed into a long, tight white apron with the strings wrapped twice around my waist.

"Can we get together sometime?" he stopped the food line to ask me. He was nice-looking, with soft pink lips and a lot of black curly hair. The old-fashioned tweed jacket he wore had leather patches on the elbows like a professor. I knew he'd be a gentleman by the whiteness of his long-fingered hands as they brushed mine when he took the cardboard lunch plate.

Couldn't be more different than Rafe. Perfect.

"*Mais oui.* Call me." I took the ballpoint pen out of my apron pocket and scratched my number on his napkin. He retreated to a table with his friends. Much ribbing and backslapping went on over there while I went on serving, cool as only Juliette could be.

He called the landline in our suite that evening, and my roommate answered it since most calls were for her. She dragged the phone into my room. "It's for Juliette." She grinned.

I picked up my unlit clove cigarette and waggled it at her, taking the receiver. "*Oui?*"

"Juliette? This is Henry. The guy from the lunch line."

"Ah, Henri." I pronounced his name in the French way, and I heard how much he liked that in the smile in his voice as he said, "Can I take you for coffee tomorrow?"

"I'm studying, Henri, but I could meet you to do something at night," I said, making my roommate raise her eyebrows because she knew that I was an untouched virgin with wavering morals and a terrible fire in the belly. But not even she knew about Rafe. Telling anyone might make whatever was between us more real.

"Oh, excellent. I know a wonderful fish market I can take you to." We set up a time to meet, and I hung up, locking eyes with my roommate.

"I'm going to date this guy for real," I told her.

"Have fun with that. Just remember the first time can be

painful," she warned. "Tell me before you do it and I'll loan you some K-Y jelly."

"*Merde*, I didn't say I was sleeping with him!" I exclaimed, blushing.

"That's what serious dating means." She frowned. "And you must be the last virgin at this college. No one would believe it if I told them."

"That's what Juliette is for," I said. "So I can *not* be who I am."

I worried that I was, indeed, the last American virgin. While my morals had been wavering and I was eager to find out about sex, I knew I wanted my first time to be not only mind-blowing but with someone I was truly in love with, which meant it might be awhile.

Henry, with his earnest gray eyes and tweed jacket, was the first Northeastern possibility I'd met. He was a grad student and surprised to find out I was a freshman. I could tell he liked me too much for me to play around with his emotions, so halfway through dinner I broke character and told him I was Ruby Michaels and I was from the Virgin Islands.

"I'm so glad you told me the truth—but can you keep talking to me with that little accent and say my name that way you do?" Henry asked with a smile, and he picked up my hand and kissed my fingers very gently.

I was thrilled to feel a tingle.

"*Mais oui*, Henri," I said, and he kissed my hand again. The tingle I felt was nothing like the lightning bolt Rafe had zapped me with, but to my oversexed body, a tingle was great.

I liked Henry a lot. He was working on conjoint PhDs in psychology and music, and we talked about matters of the mind, which was what I'd come to Boston for. We went to dinners at a fish house, where he bought me my first Maine lobster, a Greek restaurant where I learned about falafels, and an Indian restaurant where I learned to love naan and more. Finally, he took me to his off-campus apartment where he lived with other grad students, and after he played a song on guitar he'd written, we kissed.

His lips were sweet from an after-dinner mint, and soft on mine. They seemed to be initiating a conversation—do you like this? Or this?

I found I did, and let him know. Our tongues touched. The tingle was very pleasant.

That evening, after he dropped me off at my dorm, I still had a ton of homework, but I was floating on air because I was finally getting over Rafe.

Just in time for more letters from him to arrive.

Damn you, Ruby. I'm trying not to think impure thoughts about you, but it's hard. You were so amazing that day we spent together. Sassy, smart, and you ran so hard you got my heart rate up in more than one way. I think over every moment of that day and wish I'd really savored it more. The way you looked when you stepped out from under those vines, like a wood nymph, that one strand of vine tangled in your hair, your cheeks red, those green eyes flashing.

And those breasts heaving, right there in front of me. God, woman. Because no matter that you're only eighteen, you're all woman. Your perfect tits, so round and full, always made me think of what it would be like to bury my face in them, nuzzle them, suckle them, and as I did so, work you with my fingers until you were screaming your release.

Because I know that's in you, my Ruby girl, a living flame.

I can't believe I was noble and just let you go, didn't take what I knew you were offering without knowing you were...but I also know that, woman though your body is, you're still a girl and innocent of what you're capable of.

I just hope I get to be the one to awaken that in you. Next summer I will be in California. Surely it wouldn't be that hard for us to meet. Because wanting you is driving me crazy. And you should know that your friend Jenny, while pretty and certainly willing, just isn't my type.

Until my next letter I'll be waiting for you. Wishing for you. Wanting you.

My hand had crept into the stretchy waistband of my sweatpants and found its way to my aching nubbin of pleasure as I read the letter.

Damn that man. I dropped the letter, threw myself back on the bed, and worked myself unabashedly to a shivering, pulsing, silent climax while I fantasized Rafe nuzzling, biting, and sucking my breasts while working me with his fingers.

That was the fantasy still playing in my mind as I kissed Henry in his room an afternoon or two later.

"Juliette," he whispered, and because it wasn't me, Ruby, he held in his arms, and because I couldn't have Rafe, I let Henry kiss his way down my neck with those soft, gentle lips of his.

He unbuttoned the black long-sleeved blouse I wore, gently undoing each button down to my navel and holding it open to gaze at my breasts in their black lace cups. The chill afternoon light fell across the expanse of creamy skin, my long hair tangling on his chest and across his legs as I sat on his lap, and even I knew the sight was gorgeous.

I shut my eyes and thought of Rafe, allowing Henry to set those soft full lips on the pulse point at the base of my throat, those lips that had spoken poetry to me and sung me Dylan songs on a guitar older than I was, and I welcomed his kisses.

"Henri, Henri," I moaned in my French accent, but it was Rafe's face I saw behind my closed eyes. Henry didn't take off his clothes, didn't touch me below the waist, but we kissed at length in my first make-out session.

In the secrecy of my mind, I was in Rafe's arms, and it was his hard mouth on me that took me over the edge.

I thanked Henry, as if he'd opened a door for me, which in a way he had. He walked me home through driving sleet under a big golf umbrella to my warm dorm. And in the shower in my bathroom, I cried.

I didn't feel in control anymore. Of my body, of what it needed, and who it had chosen. I cried because it wasn't Rafe I'd kissed for the first time.

I wrote Rafe that I had met someone. *His name is Henry, and he is the sort of man I should be with. Solid. Will have a steady life, with a good job helping people as a psychologist, and he'll fill a home with beautiful music he writes and plays. I like him and I want to more than like him. I let him take my shirt off and make love to my breasts.*

But you ruined it for me, because all I could imagine was your mouth on me, your hands on me, and in my mind it was your lap I was laid across. All I could think of was you, Rafe. Damn you for coming into my life when you did and doing what you did to me!

I folded the letter with hard, quick movements that made me slit my finger on the letter's edge. I didn't care that there was blood on the paper I stuffed into the envelope and addressed and stamped and ran out into the first snowstorm of the year to mail.

If he was going to torture me, I'd torture him right back.

The holidays were coming and I didn't have enough money of my own saved up to return to the Virgin Islands for Christmas. I was devastated when my parents told me they couldn't afford to bring me back, either, not least because now I couldn't see Rafe.

Henry got more serious, bringing me little gifts, trying to spend time with me every moment I would let him. I liked the company, someone to spend time with, and he was older, took charge of our activities and knew all sorts of places and things to do in Boston. I liked how much he cared for me, selfish as it was.

It was nice to have a boyfriend. But I never let him touch me, always having an excuse to leave, cutting things short after a few kisses.

I didn't want to lose control and have it turn into something it wasn't, with the wrong man.

Shellie felt sorry for me with nowhere to go for the holidays and invited me to New York to spend the break with her family. We took the train to New York City and I saw the Big Apple for the first time in my life, joining her warm and loving family in their big brownstone in Manhattan for three weeks.

Her older brother Sam was handsome at six feet with a build like a barn, light golden-brown eyes, and the blond hair and beard of a Viking. He was in his third year at Cornell, majoring in prelaw as I was.

"He's between girlfriends, so watch out," Shellie warned. She had an even older brother, Sean, who was in medical school and haggard with his residency work, his deep blue eyes hollow under black brows.

I was in no mood to watch out. In fact, I was more in a mood to get laid and leave my "Virgin Girl" nickname behind. I was fast losing my scruples and preferences of how that experience would go, and Sam, a football player and shot-put champion in the summer season, was just my physical type.

Shellie shrugged when I told her that.

"It's your funeral, Virgin Girl," she said. "Sam's a dog. Bangs anybody who's willing." But she must have said something to Sam about me, because though his honey-brown eyes heated when he looked at me, he was a perfect gentleman and never so much as hugged me the whole first week.

Shellie hated exercising, but Sam and I ran every day. We layered on winter exercise clothes and jogged the city sidewalks to Central Park, our breath puffing clouds of mist into the air. I never tired of craning my neck to see the soaring buildings sparkling in the low winter sun, the twisty black shapes of the leafless trees in the park, the sparkling white velvet of lawns covered in fresh-fallen snow, the sparkle of Christmas lights everywhere adding a festive feeling.

The same sort of physical competition sprang up between us that I'd felt with Rafe, something totally absent from my more cerebral relationship with Henry.

Sam dared me. Dared me to run across the ice of the frozen pond in Central Park. Dared me to run across the park benches and try a flip jumping off. Dared me to climb into one of the high branches of a bare-leaved oak in the middle of the park with no one around, and when I was twenty feet up, clinging to the tree and terrified the snow-laden branch would break, he joined me there.

"Oh my God," I breathed as the branch bowed under our combined weight. He grinned a daredevil grin, leaned over, and kissed me.

His lips were cold, but his mouth was hot, and my mouth opened under his, and our tongues tangled. He tasted like the hot chocolate we'd drunk before the run, rich and delicious, and he groaned. The branch was narrow and he lost his balance with a cry, but he turned as he fell, catching himself by his hands. He dangled from the bouncing limb and looked up at me.

"I shouldn't have done that," he said, and fell the rest of the way to the ground. I screamed as he landed in the snow beneath the tree, tipping over onto his side.

"Sam! Sam! Oh my God!" I climbed down as fast as I could and ran to him, rolling him onto his back in a panic. And that's when he clamped his huge, muscular football player's arms around me and hauled me down atop his Columbia jacket for more kissing.

"Dirty rat!" I exclaimed when I came up for air. "I thought you were hurt!" I smacked him and threw snow at him, and then we were pelting each other with snow, yelling and shrieking with laughter, and I didn't remember having so much fun since I had sand fights on the beach in Saint Thomas with my sisters.

That's how it was between Sam and me. *Fun. Laughter. Physical competition and daring exploits.* Like having a big brother but with a hot physical edge.

I didn't fantasize about Rafe when I was with Sam.

We took to running twice a day. I told Shellie I'd decided to join the track team and Sam was helping me get in shape. She quirked a brow and folded her lips together but was mercifully silent as we jogged off yet again toward the park.

Sam brought clip-on ice skates and taught me to skate on the pond. I was wobbly and tippy and he loved that, skating around me in circles and sneaking in to tickle me through my parka or push the backs of my knees, so I'd fall in a flurry of shrieks and laughter. He liked to grab me up and rub his bearded face in the tender skin of my neck, making me giggle, or give me piggyback rides halfway across the park to get his cardio workout.

There was pretty much nothing more fun than being carried around by Sam, my legs around his waist with his hands hooked under my knees, my arms around his shoulders. I'd breathe insults into his ear. "That all you got? Thought you were a football player!"

Sometimes I'd bite his earlobe to hear him gasp or laugh, and I never got tired of feeling the incredible vigor, vitality, and strength of his wide, strong body as he ran.

One day he even put me all the way up on his shoulders, and I clung to his head, pulling his hair, shrieking with delighted fright as he went out on the ice with me up there. It was an amazing feeling, like flying, as he pushed off and spun, and I shrieked with glee.

Then he stumbled. I flew off onto the ice and cracked my head on a protruding ice clump.

I must have been knocked out briefly because when I came around he'd unzipped my jacket and was feeling me all over, muttering, "Oh God, oh God, please be okay."

I kept my eyes shut and did a little moan to let him know that I was coming around, and he scooped me up close and felt the egg on the back of my head and said, "Oh God," again, and this time I reached up to touch his bearded face, smooth but rough at the same time, a wonderful sensation, and pulled him down to kiss me.

That went on for a while, with more roaming of hands on both of our parts. His bulk was considerable, hard and hot as a steel stove, and it warmed me, lying on the ice in my wet jeans as I was.

Finally, he stood up with me in his arms and made as if to carry me that way.

I kicked my legs and said, "No, I'm okay. Put me down, you big Neanderthal," but then I wobbled a bit, shaky, so we compromised and he piggybacked me out of the park.

It wasn't a short way.

He talked to me the whole time, apparently worried I had a concussion and was going pass out. He'd never talked to me that much before.

He told me about his first pet ("a wire-haired terrier named Comet, the best dog in the world"), his dreams ("making federal judge by the time I'm forty-five and designing and building my own house with my own hands"), and what he wanted in a woman: "hot, athletic, and lots of fun like you, but I always thought I'd end up with a blonde; everyone knows redheads are trouble."

"Redheads *are* trouble," I said into his ear, and bit it. He laughed.

I felt like I could fall in love with him, if only we had more time.

At the edge of the park he waved down a cab, and I rode home with my sore head cradled against his bulky shoulder and his arms around me.

Shellie took me Christmas shopping the next day, forbidding Sam to come. He moped like a kicked puppy, pouting exaggeratedly as he pumped a fifty-pound dumbbell and watched us leave.

"He likes you," she said as we strolled along, arms linked as we looked in the amazing shop windows that made Manhattan at Christmas the legend it was.

"I like him, too," I said, looking at an amazing display with full-sized trains looping through a replica of the Matterhorn. "Thanks so much for having me, Shellie. You can't imagine how different this is from Saint Thomas."

She wasn't distracted. "He wanted to come shopping with us. He never wants to come shopping."

"So? We have fun. We laugh a lot. We'd laugh a lot shopping, too."

"Has he tried to get in your pants?" She narrowed her eyes suspiciously.

I frowned, hands in the pockets of my ever-present pea coat. "We've kissed a couple of times, okay? But I don't feel any pressure for more. He's a real gentleman, actually. He likes to carry me around."

"Carry you around?" Shellie bugged her eyes at me theatrically. "You're not small."

I knew I wasn't small. I was slender but sturdy. "Gee, thanks, friend. I'm aware I'm not small. Which is why it's so cute the way he acts like I am. I told you I fell and knocked my head yesterday playing on the ice, but actually, Sam was skating with me on his shoulders."

"No wonder he was so freaked out! He's always been a daredevil, always breaking something and hurting himself. I can't believe you let him put you up there and go out on the ice!"

"It was fun, until he tripped. No, we just like to race and dare each other to do stuff." I told her about learning to do a flip off a park bench from Sam.

"I had no idea you had this side. You usually love doing your French beret thing and being so intellectual," Shellie said, taking my arm again. "Try that accent on Sam and see what he says." She sounded smug. "Play your cards right and you could be my sister for real, and there's nothing I'd like better."

"Ha, right. We're just friends," I said, feeling the hot blush sweep up my neck. "You didn't tell him the virgin thing, did you?" Virgin girl from the Virgin Islands—that was me. So embarrassing. It seemed like the longer you waited, the weirder it was to still be a virgin, like there must be something wrong with you.

"As a matter of fact, I did. I know what a horndog he is, so I told him the first day to keep his hands to himself and treat you nice, that you weren't experienced." Now Shellie was blushing a little. "I didn't want him to take advantage of you."

I stopped and put my hands on my hips. "Shellie Williams, I can't believe you'd embarrass me like that! Oh man. I'll never be able to look him in the eye now. He must think I'm such a loser, like nobody wanted me. It wasn't that. I grew up in a religious family."

"I told him that, too. And he promised he'd be a gentleman. Who kissed who first?"

"Well, it happened at the top of a tree and it was...mutual." Truth was I couldn't remember anything but wanting him to kiss me and then the fright when he fell out of the tree.

"Tomorrow's Christmas. We have some pretty fun traditions. One is a scavenger hunt." Shellie went on telling me plans the Williamses had, while I began to worry that with these exorbitant prices that I wouldn't be able to afford anything for the family. As if reading my mind, Shellie took me to an indoor mall with a Cost

SOMEWHERE ON ST. THOMAS

Plus imports store, and I was able to find fun token gifts for everyone.

♋

Sam unwrapped the little gift I'd got him, a key chain of a monkey made of jute with glued-on black bead eyes, a smaller monkey clinging to its back. *Fun in New York,* I'd written on a little tag dangling from it.

He laughed when he opened it. Sean, Shellie, and their parents all looked at the key chain in consternation.

"I don't get it," Sean said.

"Inside joke," Sam replied, with a broad wink to me. And right in front of everybody, he leaned over and kissed me on the cheek. "Thanks."

"Oh, for goodness' sake," I said, flapping a hand. I'd managed to make my meager gift money stretch far enough to buy a little token for each member of the family, but it was nothing like the nice things they gave me: a new, jade-green beret and scarf set from Shellie, a box of famous New York truffles from their parents, a T-shirt with a big red apple on it from Sean, and a pair of tiny silver ice skate earrings from Sam.

But I was really homesick for the first time, for my family. In Saint Thomas we did stockings, just because, but all our best gifts to one another were homemade: garlands of nuts, place mats of beaten copra printed with designs we made with cut potato stamps, necklaces made of coral and shells. Mom was known for making wreaths on a wooden circle with found seashells glued to it. We hung her collection of them all around the house.

I figured out the time difference and asked to use the Willams' phone for a long-distance call. "Merry Christmas," Mr. Williams said with a magnanimous wave. "Talk as long as you like."

39

So I did. They passed the phone around through the family, so far away, and I talked about the wonders of New York and all the things I'd done and seen. This was especially poignant with Pearl, who missed me more than she should. Finally, Mom took the phone back.

"Rafe's here for Christmas dinner," Mom said. "He'd like to say hi." And before I could do more than open my mouth to protest, I heard his voice.

"Ruby girl." He said it low like he was walking away from the phone, but I knew where it was tethered to the wall, an innocuous pistachio-green device with an extra-long cord. We used to step inside the pantry when we wanted privacy, and I could tell he'd done that by the cessation of noise. "I got your letter."

"Which one?" My voice came out high and breathless as my eyes scanned the room, frantic that anyone should catch me talking to Mr. Kryptonite himself.

"You know which one."

I was sitting in a seldom-used formal-looking parlor with cream-colored carpeting and the kind of shiny furniture that pushed you into good posture. I wound the cord of the phone I was on around my finger. "I've sent you so many."

"That one. About the guy. Listen." He pitched his voice low and intense, and I felt just the sound of it set up a throb between my legs. Yep, he still had an effect on me. He was still the man who'd switched my body *On*, and I still kind of hated him for it.

"Don't play with this poor sap Henry. He sounds like someone who could get serious about you, and you'll break his heart if you let it continue when you're not meant for him."

"Who am I meant for?" I could hardly breathe the words, couldn't believe I'd said them. Was afraid he'd answer them and was relieved when all he said was:

"Not him." Another long pause, then, "I want to see you again. Can you come to California when school is over?"

"I don't know. Money's really tight. I'm working at the dining hall, but all I make goes to living expenses. I don't know how I can afford it. It will be a miracle if Mom and Dad can even bring me home to Saint Thomas for the summer."

"I'll send you the money," he said. "Meet me in San Francisco. I'll show you around. It's a great city. You should see it with me."

"Okay," I said faintly. *He was going to pay my way out to San Francisco?*

"I better give the phone back to your parents or they'll think this was a marriage proposal," he said with a nervous laugh, the first I'd heard from him. "Keep the letters coming. Be honest. I like it."

And then I heard noisy chaos again, and talking and laughing, and my dad came on and I had to scramble my wits back into coherence.

After all that, I needed to be alone to sort through the storm of feelings the call had stirred up. "I'm going for a walk to the park," I announced, putting on my new jade-green beret and winding the matching scarf around my neck

Sam, who was assembling an elaborate 3-D puzzle of the Statue of Liberty with Sean and their dad, jumped to his feet. "Want to run?"

"No, just a walk for a little Christmas contemplation," I said, opening my mouth to ask him to let me go alone, but I couldn't bear to when he was already shrugging into his down jacket with alacrity.

We went down the steps of the brownstone and along the now-familiar sidewalk. I hunched my shoulders as the wind cut through my wool pea coat.

"You should get something heavier for these winters," Sam

41

said from beside me. "Here. I grabbed this out of the closet just in case." It was a heavy Gore-Tex parka. He put it on over my coat, tucking my arms into the sleeves. It was so big I knew it must be his and that's why it fit over everything I had on. "But keep that green hat on," he said, pulling the hood up over my head, "because it looks amazing with your hair."

"*Ah, mais oui. Vous êtes un gentleman.*"

His hands stopped pulling the hood tight under my chin. "Is that French?"

"*Oui. Je suis Juliette. Je vive en les isles des Antilles.*" I batted my eyes.

"No. Anything but French. Don't do this to me." He pulled me close by the cords of my hood, making me stumble so I landed against his chest. "I have a thing about anything French." And then he was kissing me. His mouth warmed me all the way to my frozen toes in my too-thin boots, and pretty soon I was pressed up against his solid width. It felt like climbing the side of a building. Both of our faces disappeared inside the voluminous parka hood.

Ah, Sam's kiss. It was rugged, and thorough, and beardy and delicious and lighthearted at the same time as being earnest and hungrily sexual as his tongue played with mine, imitating the act in such a way that I found my fingers digging into his down parka just so I wouldn't fall to the ground.

"Get a room!" I heard Sean's teasing holler from the doorway and realized we hadn't made it fifty feet from the brownstone.

Embarrassment made me break away and run, and Sam caught my hand and we ran together until we'd gone a block or two past the house. I slowed to a walk but still let him hold my hand.

"I was going to walk to clear my head and think about things," I said. "But now I'm all confused again."

"About what?" His light brown eyes had specks of green and gold in them, like the strangely beautiful toads that came out after the rain on Saint Thomas. What a strange thought to be having, right now in the winter in New York City, with this man from a privileged family. "Your eyes remind me of toads in Saint Thomas. *Que c'est beau.*"

He laughed and pulled me close to kiss me again. I didn't let him, instead running down the last few frozen blocks until we reached the park, rendered stunningly beautiful by last night's snowfall, and even on Christmas Day, full of people.

"Toads. You must mean something good by that," he said as we slowed, taking a meandering pathway under the barren trees.

"*Oui.*" I was still doing Juliette a little. "The toads on Saint Thomas come out after it rains. Hundreds of them. Sitting around in the puddles in the road and getting squished by cars. They have the most beautiful eyes." I stopped, took his square-jawed, handsome face in my hands. "They have flecks of yellow, bronze, green, sometimes even purple in them, and they're gold. Yours remind me of them. Remind me of home, somehow."

I felt my own eyes fill with the homesickness I'd been fighting all day, and when I closed them, fat tears rolled out the sides. I gulped back a sob.

"Aw, Ruby." He pulled me into his arms. My name sounded good in his mouth. The thickness of our winter wear had me feeling like I was hugging the Michelin Man. "God, you're sweet. I've never had such a nice compliment on my eyes before. If I were a chick, I'd be in heaven right now."

I laughed wetly and smacked him on the heavily padded arm. "I'm not such good company. I'm homesick and I spoke to someone on the phone at home. It was—confusing."

"A guy?" He'd taken one of my arms and pulled me in against him as we started walking again. "Come on. You can tell me."

"Yes, okay, a guy. Someone..." I shivered at the memory of Rafe's voice. "Older than me. Really gets to me somehow. He's impressed on me, like I was a duckling or something."

"He's older. Probably good looking." Sam's voice had steel in it now, and I remembered that in spite of his playfulness, one of his life goals was to be a federal judge. "But he's eight thousand miles away, and I'm here now. And I like you. A lot." He stopped, and this time he cupped my face in his gloved hands. "I never expected to meet a girl like you. Such a great friend. Makes me laugh. So pretty." He smacked his lips against my cold-pinkened ones. "Just an amazing body and a great mind, too. And you're brave and fun. You'll try anything. I've also discovered I've become one of those red-hair fetishists." He took my beret off and stripped the gloves from his fingers, stuffing the whole handful of winter gear into a capacious pocket. "It reminds me of flames," he said conversationally, sifting handfuls of my long, wavy hair so that it fell over the shoulders of my dark coat. "Or scarlet ribbons full of gold and cinnamon. There's a color in here like a nice cabernet, too."

"Waxing poetic," I murmured, but I didn't want to break the spell he was casting as he stroked his fingers through my hair again and again. It felt insanely good and I shut my eyes to feel his hands on my scalp, in my hair. Again and again.

"I can't believe I met you in winter," he muttered against my ear. "Because I want to see you in summer, all this white velvet skin getting a little color on it, and too many freckles for me to find and count, popping out all over you." He demonstrated with little kisses across my nose. "One, two, three, seventeen hundred..."

I pulled away. "I didn't expect this either, Sam. But since we're being honest, I'm also dating a guy back in Boston. Henry. He's pretty into me."

"Don't lead him on, then," Sam said. He put his face down in the warm hollow next to my neck inside the jade-colored scarf and rubbed me with that smooth-rough beard, sending shivers of delightful feeling through my body and straight south to the action zone. "Don't waste his time. Because you're going to be mine now." He kissed me then, in that conversational way he had, as if there was all the time in the world for him to invade my every corner with his big, bluff, warm, irrepressible self and persuasive tongue.

"I'll think about it," I said when I came up for air. For a minute those golden-brown Viking eyes blazed like a hawk's, and then he laughed.

"You're a tricky little virgin," he said, and squeezed my butt with a big warm hand. "I can see I'm going to have to bring my A game if I'm going to chase off these other guys."

I looked down and shuffled my snowy boots. "I'm not looking for a relationship. I'm at Northeastern University for the studying."

"Uh-huh." Disbelief permeated his reply.

We walked on as I tried to explain. "And the virgin thing. So embarrassing, but it's only because I grew up religious. I guess it still matters, because I want my first time to be—special." I kicked the snow ahead of my impractical secondhand boots. "I want to be in love. And have it mean something. But I'm not waiting for marriage or anything."

"In love. Meaningful. Special. It's good to have a dream," he said laconically, and I socked him again, and he made me chase him and then gave me a piggyback ride, and for the rest of the walk back we talked all about school, what we were studying and what our plans were for the next year.

Somehow I felt like something had been decided, and spoken, but I wasn't sure what it was.

The next week flew by. Sean went back to his hospital residency, a miserable-looking ordeal, and Shellie and Sam made it their business to show me all over the city, taking me on the ferry to Ellis Island, to visit the World Trade Center, to ride the carousel in Central Park, and to attend *The Nutcracker* ballet with the whole family. It was wonderful.

And in the back of it all, somewhere buried in my mind, was Rafe's voice. *I have to see you. Come to California.* Could I be so crazy as to listen to that voice?

We were taking the train back to Boston the day after the New Year, and on New Year's Eve the three of us watched the ball drop in person in Times Square, and I screamed with excitement as it became 1984, and at the turn of the year Sam kissed me so hard it split my lip. I didn't care, caught up in the revelry, excitement, and warmth, not to mention a few too many sips off of his silver flask of single-malt scotch. I was touched when he kissed the sore spot on my mouth until it felt better than any fat lip ever had.

But the next morning I felt like I was playing a familiar scene as Sam said goodbye. He had to leave for football team workouts and early strategy meetings at Cornell. He pressed his address and phone number into my hand and told me to write. "I'm serious. I want to see you when we can. Spring break, you're coming back to New York with Shellie, and we'll go on a real date."

I shrugged, trying for flippant. "Shellie tells me you're a player in more than one way, so don't make promises you can't keep."

He set a little silver box in my hand, his golden eyes as intent as they'd ever been. "Open this and see how serious I am."

I was terrified but I opened it, relieved to see a beautiful diamond-encrusted heart on a platinum chain, not a ring of any sort. "I love it. Wow."

He took the necklace out of the box, impatiently pushing my heavy hair out of the way and clumsy with the tiny clasp, but he eventually fastened it around my neck. My head bent before him and neck exposed must have proved tempting because he bit and sucked my neck, giving me a hickey that branded the mark of his mouth on the nape of it. I loved the feeling and arched back and rubbed my butt against him. He filled his hands with my ample breasts in the fuzzy red hand-me-down cashmere sweater Mrs. Williams had passed on.

"I want you so bad. I can't believe how much I want you," Sam said. Our bodies were kindling like sticks making a fire, and this was the first time we'd ever touched each other indoors.

Shellie opened the door a few minutes later to find us making out on the couch. She retreated with a squeal, yelling, "Sam, you're supposed to be going! Dad's waiting in the car!"

Sam kissed me one more time and said, "We have a date. For lots more dates. And more of this kind of thing, too. At spring break."

My beard-rasped neck and cheeks burned from his touch. I nodded robotically and said, "Uh-huh. Okay."

And he was gone, with one last pat on my ass and tweak of my hair.

I sat back on the couch and lifted the necklace from the collar of the sweater, dangling the sparkling heart from a finger in front of my eyes.

"Wow," I said. The platinum shone with the fire of real diamonds. I'd never had such a nice piece of jewelry before.

I rode the train back to Boston with Shellie, feeling more conflicted than ever the minute I was out of Sam's presence. *What am I doing?* All this romance stuff was horribly distracting from my studies, and I still had to deal with Henry, whom I really did like and knew I would miss. Were Sam and I a thing, after such a brief Christmas fling or whatever it was? Enough to break it off with Henry? And what the hell was I going to do about Rafe's invitation to San Francisco?

I needed to come clean with Shellie and get her advice.

I told her about Rafe finally and showed her the necklace from Sam. "And, oh God, I have to deal with Henry," I moaned.

"Oh, to have your problems," Shellie said.

I immediately felt bad for my selfishness. Shellie was adorable, a petite, stocky female version of Sam, with the same tawny brown-blond locks and bright brown eyes. She'd been dating, but nothing serious so far, and hadn't been a virgin since she was sixteen and did it with her then-boyfriend in high school.

"This situation's not that great, trust me. Very stressful. Rafe wants to see me this summer in San Francisco. Offered to pay my way out to California."

Shellie *pooh-pooh*ed. "Who is this guy? A surfer, sailor, drifter? A handyman? Sam's going to be a lawyer, like you, and the two of you get along great and have chemistry. Even Henry's got more going on as a boyfriend—he's going to be a psychologist. Kick Rafe to the curb. He's got nothing to offer."

Not a handyman, a Renaissance man.

There wasn't anything Rafe couldn't do if he set his mind and hands to it. Nothing to offer? Nothing but those amazing blue eyes, those hard, capable hands, that incredible promise of the pleasure he was able to give me, a fire he'd woken and could stoke with just a look, a touch, the sound of his voice, and those heart-felt letters I couldn't bear to tell Shellie about.

The letters were too intimate, too raw.

And Henry? He was sweet, and gentle, and his devotion, his quiet support, the way he sang me songs and read me poetry and even the way he worshipped my body—all of that was reassuring. I could handle Henry so much better than either of the others.

And then there was Sam. Big, bold, confident, playful Sam who made me laugh.

"You're right," I said. "Sam's amazing. What I can't believe is that he really seems to like me." I shook my head. "Talk about not having anything to offer. I'm the charity case here."

"I've never seen him like this before," Shellie said, her big brown eyes sincere. "And money's not a thing to our family. I mean, we have it, but we don't make a big deal about it. Everyone but Sam. Sam's a tightwad. Saves every penny for this mythical house he's going to build after law school. He's never done anything but sleep with my friends and break their hearts. I've certainly never seen any platinum necklaces before."

I wished that made me relax, knowing I meant something to Sam. Instead it felt like pressure, and it was scary now that he wasn't there with his playful bear hugs and piggyback rides to remind me that what I liked most about Sam was how fun he was, how he made me laugh.

The weeks went on. I dodged dates with Henry by pleading work and studying. I wrote Rafe secret, aching letters in which I told him what I wished for and wanted him to do with and to me in an ideal world where we didn't have to worry about how we'd make our different lifestyles work.

And Sam called. He called every week on Friday night, making a point of letting me know he could be doing something else, dating someone else, but instead he was calling me to talk. He'd tell me he wanted to be with me instead, and he'd share funny stories about the frat house he lived in and even stories about Shellie and how she was as a kid and a little sister.

Sam paid for our phone calls without a whimper.

"He's serious about you," Shellie assured me. "He always grumbles about long-distance phone bills. Never calls home."

I felt our attraction as Sam made me laugh, made me want him, and while he pushed me past my own comfort zone, he wasn't as overwhelming as Rafe.

Rafe's letters were totally addicting in a different way.

The letter he sent as he left for his month-long voyage to California contained a check for five hundred dollars wrapped around a poem. The note with the poem was simple.

Beautiful Ruby,

Come to California. I'll be there by spring break. Come to me. I can't wait any longer. Here's money for your ticket. Call me at this number. I'll be in San Francisco by March 1.

The poem was titled "First Night."

"First Night"

She comes to me in ivory
Not white, because she's Ruby
Even the skin of her secret places
Is a tawny shade of pale
Peppered with nutmeg freckles I want
To spend a lifetime counting.
She offers herself
Abundant and strong, sweet as honey and tangy as mango
And I use my tongue to worship her.
Every inch.
Every cranny.
Every place that's never seen the sun or
Known the touch of a hand.
Nothing is hidden from me, nothing is off-limits as I make her mine.
She's never known what can be felt and discovered, and every place I take her
I mark it mine
I take and I own
With kisses. With my hands. With my mouth.
With all of my body I worship her.
I teach her what has always been in her to feel.
I touch the nub of her pleasure until she explodes in cries of delight
And I'm surrounded
By her perfume
She's the garden of my discovery.

Only when she's boneless and begging
Will I move into her, sliding into that tight glove
Made for me alone
I'll take that "jade gate" by storm
I'll make it so good for her
She's ruined for anyone but me
Because this is only the first night
And there will be an eternity more.

"Oh God, oh God." I covered my mouth with my hand, and the check fluttered to the floor. "Oh no. What do I do?"

February 25 was the day I got his letter. Spring break started March 3, and Rafe would land the boat he was crewing to San Francisco in four days. Meanwhile, Shellie was making plans for us to travel together to New York, and Sam had a full slate of activities planned for the week of break.

Even Henry had been relentless lately, and I still didn't want to break up with him because it was so hard to hurt his feelings. I didn't know what was going to happen with either of the long-distance relationships. There were plusses and minuses on every front. None of them was perfect. Well, maybe Sam was a little bit perfect. But I was afraid to trust him, with his reputation and so little to go on as far as a relationship.

Someone knocked on my door, and Shellie stuck her head around the doorjamb, made a face. Henry pushed his way into my room.

He shut the door and put his fists on his hips. He wore a leather jacket that looked good with the red and black checked scarf around his neck. His curly black hair was dotted with snow, and he unwound the scarf and shook the snow out of his hair. His gray eyes were alight with a heat that set something off in me. I scrabbled up the poem and the check and stuffed them back into the envelope.

"Henry! What are you doing here?"

"This needs to stop," he said. "I'm sick of getting the brush-off. Are you seeing someone else?"

I felt betraying color sweep up my neck and suffuse my cheeks. "Not exactly."

"I can tell something's going on." He grabbed the chair from my desk and straddled it in front of where I was sitting on the bed. "You keep canceling everything. Just tell me if it's over." Hectic patches of red brightened his cheeks, and the forcefulness of his voice stirred me.

It occurred to me in that moment that I liked alpha, take-charge men. Up until now, Henry had been too mellow with me, letting me set the pace between us, and it made me lose interest. I moved closer and took his chilled face in my hands, kissed his cold lips. They quickly warmed and opened under mine, and his arms clamped around me and drew me close. The chair back became the only thing separating us.

"I'm sorry," I breathed. "There's this long-distance thing. I don't know what's happening with it."

"I knew it. I knew something was going on."

"I'd like you to wait for me. Until after spring break. I'll know more after. I promise. It will be on then, or off. For sure. Can you deal with that?" I held his jaw in my hands and gazed into his gray eyes. He closed them, as if he couldn't bear to look at me.

He had the longest lashes, ferny and black. I kissed his closed eyelids, thinking, *I could love this man, too.*

"That's it," he said, standing up. "You have until after spring break. And here's something so you know how I feel." He took a cassette tape out of his pocket and set it on the dresser. "Call me when you get back."

"I will. I promise," I said.

I picked up the cassette tape on the bureau and opened the plastic case. Taped to the cassette was a slim gold ring with the tiniest star on it and a moonstone like a dewdrop in the center. I peeled off the tape and slid the ring onto the third finger of my right hand.

It fit and looked lovely. *Special.* Like he made me feel. But not overwhelmed. Not scared of myself and of what could happen.

I put the cassette into my little boom box. It was a mix tape of Henry singing. Love songs, either solo, acoustic, or with his band. The songs were heartfelt and very good.

I wanted to cry.

Dammit.

I listened to the cassette and played with the diamond heart Sam had given me, as I twisted the ring on my finger around and around, and finally decided what I had to do.

CHAPTER FOUR

I got off the plane in San Francisco wearing my jade-green beret and scarf and the old pea coat. For once they were more than enough. March 3 in San Francisco was warm, the sky blue and depthless, the fog a far-off blanket on the other side of the city, and the hills across the bay green with spring.

I had left the suitcase with the broken wheel at the dorm and pared everything I brought down to my student backpack. In the baggage-claim area, I sat in front of a pay phone and fed in quarters. I dialed the number Rafe had given me.

It rang and rang, and as it did, I considered my folly.

Here I was, in an unknown city, with a hundred bucks I'd scraped together from the dining hall and a mouth sawdust dry from telling lies. Lies upon lies upon lies, for the first time in my life.

I'd told Shellie and Sam my parents had sprung for me to return to the Virgin Islands for spring break, and as much as it killed me to miss the time with them, I had to see my family. Sam had been crushed but pretended to understand. I'd told Henry the same thing, with a similar response, leavened by kisses of thanks for the ring. And then I'd told my parents I was going to be in New York with the Williamses, and we'd be traveling so not to bother calling their New York residence. I'd call when I could.

But here I was in San Francisco for the next week, no matter what happened with Rafe.

It had taken every cent of his check and more to buy the round-trip ticket out here. I couldn't change it without a fee, and I couldn't let anyone know where I was, and a hundred dollars wasn't going to last a week in the city.

I didn't have the faintest clue where to find Rafe or what to do next if he didn't answer the phone. I'd begun hyperventilating with panic when the phone was suddenly picked up. "Hello?" A woman.

"Is Rafe there?" I knew my voice came out breathy and thin.

"No." She sounded profoundly unhelpful. I wondered if this was a girlfriend.

"Um—this is his friend from out of town. He invited me here, gave me this number," I said, unable to think of a smooth story to explain my desperation. "I'm at the airport."

"Oh. You must be Ruby." Her voice warmed considerably. "He's down at the docks, but he told me you might come into town. Asked me to pick you up if you called. My name's Lisa."

"Oh, good." Tears of relief prickled my eyes. "I don't know my way around here. At all."

"What baggage claim are you at? I'll be there in fifteen. Look for a purple VW Beetle."

The purple Beetle was decorated with butterflies on the hood, immediately making me inclined to like Lisa. My first sight of her, hopping out with cornrowed hair clacking with plastic beads and a bright sarong on over leggings, felt like a hint of

SOMEWHERE ON ST. THOMAS

home. This impression strengthened as she hugged me with shiny ebony arms, enfolding me in the smell of coconut and jasmine.

"Welcome to San Francisco!" she said.

"You smell delicious," I said. "I hope you don't mind me saying so."

"Delighted to hear it."

I stowed my backpack in the back. "Where are we going?"

"I thought I'd take you down to the docks. You can surprise Rafe." Lisa's eyes, dark as chocolate, gleamed with anticipation.

"What did he say about me?" I asked, unable to resist.

"Well, that he had a friend from Boston who might be visiting. 'She's a cute redhead; you can't miss her,' he said. And he was right." Lisa smiled. She had amazing teeth that seemed to throw off light.

"Ha-ha. That's nice," I said, feeling my neck heat up. "So, are you roommates?"

"In a way. I run a boardinghouse. He has a room in it when he's here between trips on the boat."

I looked out the bug-speckled windshield, forcefully reminded of the difference in our lifestyles. *How could this ever work?* I didn't want to be with a guy who rented a room in a boardinghouse between boat voyages!

It didn't matter right now, I told myself. I was just here to see him. Just see what was what. Because I had to know something. About him, about me, about what we were together. So I could move on. So I could stop this ridiculous tug-of-war between men I liked.

It wasn't like we were getting married or something.

San Francisco was very different from Boston. For one thing, it was hilly. Very hilly, with ups and downs and a lot of totally confusing side streets. The buildings were smaller than Boston's skyscrapers. I loved the quaint rows of brightly painted little

57

houses, in every style from Art Deco to Victorian, that marched cheek by jowl up and down the slanting streets.

Lisa drove ruthlessly and confidently, weaving through the suburban areas to the waterfront.

"I take it you've been here awhile. You really seem to know your way around," I said, hanging on to the plastic sissy handle as we bolted through a changing light, dodging a homeless woman with a shopping cart filled with cats.

"Ever since I moved here from Puerto Rico," Lisa said. "I love the city. And I love escaping it back to the tropics."

"So has Rafe been boarding with you long?" I was hungry for tidbits about him, scraps of information that would help me get a clearer picture of this mystery man.

"Some years now," she said, and then glanced at me mischievously. "I can tell you some things, if you want."

"Yes." As we approached the waterfront, my nervousness increased. "Anything. We don't know each other too well."

"He's private that way," she said thoughtfully. "But he loves good music, plays some drums occasionally. Reads a lot. Works with his hands and is very good with them. I save up all the things I need fixed around the house until he's in port. He likes animals. I have a dog and he always brings home bones and scraps for her from eating out."

She pulled the Beetle up at the curb in front of an industrial-looking wharf. PIER 27 was emblazoned on it. "Go through the turnstile there, and his boat is the *Creamy Maid*."

"Okay," I said. I got out, my arms wrapped around my backpack. I looked back at her, scared to be abandoned in this strange place. "Will I see you later?"

"Sure." She winked. "Call if you can't find him, for some reason."

I watched the purple Beetle merge back into the hectic traffic and slung on my backpack, steeling myself.

I'd come on this crazy trip. There was nothing to do but go ahead and find Rafe. And hope he really had wanted to see me.

I approached the dock and went through the turnstile door. On the other side, rows and rows of boats stretched along the floating dock.

And there were three docks, each jammed with boats.

The air was redolent with the briny smell of the sea, the chime of metal fittings on rigging, and the intermittent squeaks of rubber bumpers hitting the boats as they jostled gently in their berths.

It was going to take me forever, walking up and down, to find the *Creamy Maid*.

I spotted a wiry old man, cigarette dangling from his bottom lip, winding rope beside a craft. "Do you know where the *Creamy Maid* is?"

"That way." He pointed with the cigarette down the middle dock.

"Thanks." I adjusted my backpack and walked forward. And walked. And walked, turning my head from side to side to scan the boats.

When I finally came upon it, the *Creamy Maid* was so big, so sleek and fancy, that the butterflies in my stomach multiplied. It was so enormous, it took up a whole arm off the dock.

I shouldn't be here. This was unbelievably awkward. Rafe wasn't going to be expecting me, and now I had to bug someone rich and important by visiting their boat?

I stood there, looking at the long, sleek shape of the *Maid*, her metalwork sparkling, her rolled sails snowy. I set the backpack down, in need of a drink of water and to figure out what to do next. I turned and bent over, rummaging for the water bottle I'd stashed inside.

"Ruby?"

I stood and spun around, holding the water bottle, filled with both mortification that Rafe's first view of me had been my bent-over ass in my best acid-washed Guess jeans.

"Hi, Rafe," I said.

Rafe stood on the high bridge of the boat, holding one of the lines. He wasn't wearing a shirt. He looked like a scrumptious pirate in a frayed pair of cutoffs, acres of tanned muscle and sinew shining in the early-spring sun. A bandanna held back long, sun-streaked hair.

"I'll be right down."

He slid from the top deck to the next one using just his hands on the smooth steel bars beside the ladder. He grabbed a navy blue shirt, hauling it on over his head as he tripped down the deck, slid down another level, and pattered down the gangplank toward me.

When he stood right in front of me, his eyes unbelievably blue, smelling like man and sunshine and the sea, I felt everything I'd gambled on coming together.

This isn't that crazy after all.

"You're really here," he said on an exhaled breath. He was as nervous as I was; I could tell because I could see the pulse fluttering under his jaw and his voice was husky. I felt better, knowing that.

"I guess I am." I smiled, and he scooped me in and lifted me off my feet in a bone-cracking hug. I squeaked even as I hugged him back, and he put his face into my hair and inhaled, knocking my beret aside.

"God, you smell good," he said. "And you feel even better."

"You, too," I murmured. That potent cocktail of chemistry that had always been between us swirled in the air. "I shouldn't be here. But I had to see you."

"I'm glad you came," he said simply. "No one else is on board right now. Can I show you around?"

"Yes, please. She's beautiful."

"She's a handful, is what she is," Rafe said, his teeth gleaming in that wicked smile I remembered as he looked back at me, towing me toward the gangplank. "But I've always had a way with wayward ladies."

I was blushing too hard to reply to this.

We went over the boat from stem to stern, and I *ooh*ed and *aah*ed over the gleaming galley, the shipshape staterooms, even the tidy little head he let me use.

I splashed water on my hot cheeks, looking in the mirror. My eyes had never been so green, and Sam was right. The jade-colored beret was great with my hair. I felt a little more confident coming out, but still amped up inside, as if there were too much wattage zinging around inside me to contain.

Rafe was wiping down the galley and turned to smile at me. "I still can't believe you're here," he said. "I'll lock up and take you to Fisherman's Wharf for some crabs. I know a place we can have a picnic."

"Sounds wonderful," I said, and my stomach rumbled loudly in agreement, making us both laugh.

We chatted as he locked up, news about Saint Thomas and about his trip crewing the boat back to San Francisco. I told stories about Boston, carefully avoiding any mention of Henry or Sam.

Before I knew it I was getting into another battered truck, this one black. "Different land mass but the same vehicle." I laughed as I slammed the door and felt the patter of rust on my boots.

"Gets me where I need to go." He shrugged. "Next stop, crab!"

This lighthearted Rafe, expansive with excitement, eager to show me everything he could about his adopted city, was new to me. And I know I was new to him, too, more confident, someone willing to take a chance way outside my comfort zone.

San Francisco lent itself to romance. Every view felt magical to me, glimpses of a steely dark sea, the soft shroud of approaching fog, the famous red struts of the Golden Gate Bridge appearing and disappearing between the buildings.

The stand with the crab was rustic, not a tourist attraction but a stout man in a rubber apron with a bubbling pot and a couple of ice chests full of crabs. Rafe haggled with the fisherman over a couple of fresh Dungeness and finally got the price where he wanted it. We bought a loaf of crusty sourdough and a plastic ramekin of melted butter, and he took me to Fort Point.

We ducked through a hole in a barbed-wire fence around the deserted, decrepit fort, and I panted a little as he tugged me up a crumbling stairway.

"Are we supposed to be here?" I asked nervously.

"Of course not," Rafe said. "That's why it's fun."

He spread a towel he'd wrapped around the food on the top of the roof, and almost directly under the Golden Gate Bridge, I ate my first Dungeness crab with my fingers and watched the sun set and the fog roll in, and finally, when it was getting dark and chilly, he picked up the leftovers and piled them into the paper bag the crabs had come in, then reclined on one elbow.

"Come here," he said softly.

I wasn't far away, but I scooted the couple of inches that separated us, lying on my back beside him. I was glad of my pea coat now. I pressed back against his chest, and the chill wind off the ocean passed over me and around me, and in the fog that muffled everything but the blowing of the foghorn, I felt magically surrounded.

He picked up my hand. "You've got some butter. Here." He drew that finger into his hot mouth, sucking gently. It was a replay of that time with the mango, and we both knew it.

"I think I see a little more butter." He frowned and drew two of my fingers into his mouth.

From my angle I could see only the side of his face, the tanned muscular throat, the cheekbone, the angled, rugged jaw.

A man's face.

Both Sam and Henry, for all that they weren't much younger than Rafe, were still boys. But Rafe was all man.

The touch of his mouth activated every electric nerve ending that had just been waiting for him. I surged up and pushed him over onto his back, straddling his body, filled with that relentless hunger he'd unleashed in me so many months before.

I tore the beret off, and my hair fell around his face in a lava-red curtain, and inside that curtain I leaned down and kissed him.

Oh, how I kissed him.

I plundered his mouth with mine, my hands wandering up and down his hard body, my thighs clamped around his hips. I snaked my hand under his shirt to feel the wide, smooth arcs of his chest, touching his tight nipples, my aching center sliding up and down his jeans-clad pelvis. I could feel the hard ridge of his erection beneath me, and its nearness drove me mad.

I was insatiably hungry, on fire, and clumsy with abandon.

He let me work him over.

He let me feel all I could feel through our clothes, kiss him roughly and kiss him softly. He let me show him all I'd learned in the months since I'd met him. And finally, I curled against his chest, panting, resting my head on his shoulder.

I felt a terrible need to cry.

Because this wasn't enough. It wasn't ever going to be enough, I was beginning to believe. And not only that, he wasn't taking it to the next level.

His arms finally came up around me then, gentle and slow, and he stroked me, from the top of my shoulders, down my back, smoothing over my ass.

And again.

And again.

"My Ruby one," he said. "My creamy maid." And he kissed my forehead and rocked me close and tender.

But he didn't take what I was offering. He didn't even slide a hand under my shirt to cup my breast.

I withdrew inside myself, ashamed of my overt assault, not sure how to react now that I'd made my intentions clear and he hadn't reciprocated.

"It's getting cold," he said finally. "We should go. Lisa has a couch you can stay on."

I was bitterly disappointed and tried not to show it as I rolled off and pulled the beret back on, wrapped the scarf around my flushed neck with quick hard movements, straightened myself, and buttoned up my coat.

"Sure," I said. "This was nice. I appreciated seeing this. Up here." I made an arm gesture.

"Ruby." He'd sat up, and he took my hand. I couldn't see his eyes in the dim light. The foghorn called mournfully. Lights from the bridge flickered on the side of his face. "I'm not going to have sex with you. That's not happening tonight, or anytime soon. Because I feel differently about you than I have for anyone, ever, and we need time. Time to see what this means."

Those words weren't what I wanted. I didn't want to get to know him. I didn't want to fall in love with him.

I just didn't want to be a virgin anymore.

I wanted "First Night." A week of "First Night," and all the variations on a theme that we could come up with. I wanted him to use me up, fill me, bang me senseless, and wear me out, and I had every intention of doing the same to him.

I wanted to do that with Rafe until I'd worked him out of my system and broken the strange hold he had on me.

And then I wanted to marry someone like Sam, who'd make me laugh and whose life goals were similar to mine. Or even Henry, who'd spend his life trying to make me happy and fill my life with music. I didn't want to be with someone who was a sailor, a surfer, a drifter, whose home was a boat on the sea and a room in a boardinghouse.

But I couldn't say that to this beautiful man with his beautiful words. I couldn't even put this whole shameful admission together in my own mind, but I knew it somewhere in my bones for a certainty.

"Okay. More time to get to know each other." I shrugged, trying to seem nonchalant.

"I know you're trying to figure things out, who to be with. I think we should go slow. Let's just have some fun while you're here, see the sights, get to know each other better. See where it leads."

"I guess." My cheeks burned with embarrassment. My idea of where it led had been to spend a week in bed with him, learning all the ways there were to feel pleasure.

"I can tell you had something else in mind." I could see his wicked grin, even in the dim light. "And believe me when I tell you I'd like to take you up on it, show and teach you everything I've been fantasizing about doing with you. But you have to trust me. This is going to be better."

I was tempted to run away from him like I'd done so many months ago. Run and run and run, away from my embarrassment, away from myself, away from what could possibly happen with him. I had a sense it was going to change everything.

Yet I couldn't run. I couldn't say no to what he was proposing. I had put myself in this situation, and now I was stuck in it.

Because I wanted what he was offering. Whatever he was offering. Even if it was less than the feast I'd pulled up to the table to partake of.

"Okay," I said, and my shoulders sagged, and he laughed as he got up and took my hand. We gathered up the picnic things without letting go, an awkward endeavor. And then we walked down the battered stairs and through the old abandoned fort.

Damn him for being a gentleman and holding out for something more than sex.

It looked like I was going to be the last American virgin for a while longer.

CHAPTER FIVE

San Francisco is one of the most romantic cities in the world, and I was determined to be done with my virginity by the end of spring break 1984, in three days.

That big, withholding bugger Rafe stood beside me, his muscled arms gleaming in the sun as we looked at the view of the city from Coit Tower. His elegant, capable hands dangled loosely off the railing as he looked out at the Golden Gate Bridge.

We'd been doing touristy things all week, each day something new. The zoo and the carousel one day, walking across the bridge another, picnics in the park and kites on the bluff, a walk along Ocean Beach.

Rafe became animated and articulate when he'd brought me to the de Young Museum, where he'd taken the time to explain the modern art period when I was baffled by a roomful of paintings that looked cartoonish to my untrained eye. It occurred to me that I'd never asked Rafe if he had a degree. The lifestyle crewing boats, trimming coconuts, and surfing when there were waves might have led me to an erroneous conclusion.

"Did you go to college?" I'd asked.

"I told you I did. Boston College. Mixed memories of my time there."

"Did you get a degree?"

"Of course." But he didn't say what it was in. I stared at his bronzy-brown, shoulder-length hair, fluttering in the breeze off the bay.

Of course? I thought he'd said he was on a mission to see and experience. That's what he'd told me when I'd met him in Saint Thomas. Back then, he'd seemed just like so many rootless young men traveling through the Virgin Islands before him.

"What is your degree in?"

"Why are you asking me this now?" He narrowed those cobalt eyes on my face.

"I'm not sure. I've just been thinking...I might have been wrong about you."

He cocked his head at me, his gaze full of secrets. "That's exactly what I was hoping for by putting us on time-out."

"Time-out sucks," I said. He laughed.

I'd employed all sorts of underhanded tactics all week to wear down his resolve not to do anything sexual with me. I took every opportunity to snuggle and rub against him. He'd pulled away like I was leprous. I flirted outrageously, licking everything from straws to ice-cream cones suggestively, and he'd just looked away. I'd even slid a hand into his pants one day and incurred wrathful flashing blue eyes and a forceful removal of my hand.

"Methinks the gentleman doth protest too much," I'd said, to which he did not reply.

I was so sexually frustrated that I wondered if it were possible to spontaneously combust, just start having a nonstop orgasm right in public. Right here at the railing. Eyes rolled back in my head, body twitching. I might be a virgin, but I knew about orgasms and knew when I needed one.

The thought made me smile. *That would fix him for holding out on me.*

He turned and caught my smile. "What?"

"I was just thinking that I'm so sexually frustrated right now I might just...start coming apart at the seams. Right here. Right now." I held his eye.

The color rose like the red in a thermometer under my redhead's skin as I blushed involuntarily at my own boldness, but I took a leaf from Meg Ryan in the new movie *When Harry Met Sally.* I began to pant.

To *moan.*

I arched my back, holding on to the railing, thrusting forward. I never broke eye contact with his hard blue gaze.

"Ohhhh..." I moaned. My breath hitched as I arched my back.

Rafe's eyes widened in shock, then darkened as his pupils expanded. His nostrils flared. His hands gripped the steel railing hard.

"Don't," he whispered hoarsely, and I suddenly knew he wasn't as indifferent to me as he'd been pretending all week, damn him for deciding to be a gentleman.

He was suffering, too.

Good.

Fellow park visitors stared as I continued my performance.

"Oh, oh...I need you," I panted huskily, and felt the flush of whole-body arousal tighten my nipples to diamond points and loosen my knees. Heat suffused and pooled in my lower abdomen. "Please. Please. I can't wait any longer."

What had started out in play had become a real confession.

Rafe grabbed me by the arm and frog-marched me away from the view and the crowd. I could feel his anger and arousal in every powerful stomp of his feet, in the way his long fingers bit into my upper arm and in the rigid set of his shoulders.

I might have provoked him a little too far.

I was terrified and eager to see if this outrageous ploy had worked. I had only three days left in San Francisco before I returned to college in Boston, and I didn't want to return to college still the virgin from the Virgin Islands.

He hauled me into a warm cranny beside one of the storage areas, pushed me against the wall, and bracketed his hands beside my head. His eyes, the color of the deep blue sea, promised retribution.

"Everyone tells me redheads are trouble," he ground out. "And I'm beginning to believe them."

He kissed me so hard I tasted blood, and I couldn't have been more thrilled.

I gave back as good as I got, pulling him in to me with handfuls of leather vest and T-shirt. All six foot three of him was rock-hard angles and chiseled muscles, and he felt exquisitely right against my body.

This morning, in a final and blatant attempt at seduction, I'd left both bra and underwear off for our walk on precipitous streets to Coit Tower. That couldn't have escaped his notice, because, even as his mouth ravaged mine deliciously against the warm stone, his hand tunneled under my shirt and traveled up my waist to cup my naked breast.

"Oh God," he whispered, and bent his head to bite me through the thin T-shirt. "I've wanted to do this for so long." His hand massaged the full round as his mouth dampened the shirt. His teeth connected unerringly with that incredibly responsive bundle of nerves that shot pleasure straight south.

I felt the first of what promised to be several very nice orgasms travel up my spinal column, lighting up pleasure points along the way so that I gasped, throwing my head back hard against the stone. My whole body rippled under his hand as heat dampened my thighs.

He lifted his head, eyes hazy with desire, cheeks as flushed as mine. "I can make you come this easily?"

"It would appear so," I panted, and he reapplied his mouth with determination.

I remembered this thrilling feeling. Rafe was able to take me to that teetering edge fully clothed, in public, against the side of the Coit Tower.

What more could he do to me, given a bed and a leisurely stretch of time?

I pulled at him and hiked one of my skirt-clad legs up to wrap around his hips. He ground against me, kissed and ravaged me up against that wall until the gasps and cries I emitted put Meg Ryan in her breakout role to shame.

"Yo! This is a public area!" someone hollered, and as suddenly as if ice water were doused over me, I remembered where we were—out of view, it was true, but only a few feet away from major foot traffic. I disentangled myself, peering around Rafe's bulk to see who was snapping pictures to send to relatives of the weird goings-on in San Francisco.

"Now you grow a sense of propriety," he said, closing and buttoning my jean jacket over my dampened shirt.

I pushed away from the wall. The knee-length skirt I'd worn was rucked up where I'd lifted a leg against him, and I smoothed it down. "Sorry. I got carried away. I'm feeling a little better now."

"Well, I'm not," he muttered. "I think it's time for a little relief for both of us." He towed me back down the sidewalk and along the steep hill to where he'd parked his old black truck. "You're going to pay the price."

"Oh, good," I said, bravado covering my thundering heart and stumbling feet. "Where are we going?"

"Not back to the house."

Rafe's room in a big old Victorian on the edge of the Cliffside neighborhood that a woman named Lisa rented out was a lovely high-ceilinged expanse at the back of the house. It seemed perfectly adequate for an afternoon of love to me, but apparently he wanted more privacy than we'd have there. I had been sleeping on a couch in a little sitting room, which, while perfectly comfortable, was not the place for my long-awaited deflowering.

He turned the key in the rusty old truck and I got in beside him on the bench seat. Bench seats always did something to me, and today was especially bad. I really wanted him to take me on the bench seat. If not today, maybe next week. Or any day, for that matter.

Rafe put the car in gear and set his hand, that long-fingered hand I so admired, with the slightly rough, calloused palm, on my smooth, bare thigh.

I gasped.

He took the hand briefly off my leg to shift gears, but other than that, without missing a beat, he slid the hand up under my skirt and between my legs.

"I could tell you weren't wearing panties, naughty girl. I can't wait to see this up close. See if the hair is the same color as the hair on your head. It must be so beautiful."

My cheeks were flaming. I tugged at his arm in embarrassment, to no avail. I gasped and wriggled, trying to get away and get closer at the same time. He glanced at me and grinned. "I've got a little education in store for you. You pushed me too far today."

I clamped my legs shut, but too late as he located a spot that made me twitch and gasp.

"Aha," he said with satisfaction, as if checking something cooking on the stove for doneness. "You're going to have to shift gears." We'd approached a stop sign, and he put in the clutch, but he apparently wasn't going to remove his hand from where it was working some serious magic.

"Oh God," I yelped, writhing, and I worked the shifter as his hand worked me.

I came for the second time that day, two blocks from the famous downtown San Francisco Fairmont Hotel. I was still flushed and panting with the seismic upheaval to my nervous system, only dimly able to focus, when Rafe pulled up with panache beneath the portico of the venerable hotel.

It looked like the mission to lose my virginity was finally going to be accomplished.

I rolled my skirt down, smoothing it toward my knees. I made sure my jean jacket was tightly buttoned. My feeble preparations didn't help. I was intimidated by the valet in gold-braided uniform who approached the truck and opened my door. I glanced over at Rafe, astonished that we were going to such a classy place.

He winked as he blew me a kiss from the hand that had just been between my legs.

I was as shocked by that as by anything that had just occurred between us on the front seat of his rusty old black truck. It felt like everything we'd been doing was stenciled on my face and anyone who looked at me could guess, and my complexion couldn't have been pinker if I'd been dipped in boiling water.

I stepped out of the vehicle and stood awkwardly on the sidewalk. Chilly San Francisco wind blew up my skirt and fanned my bare ass. My hair lashed my cheeks. I wrapped my arms around myself for warmth and comfort. I was embarrassed, terrified, and yet determined to get what I'd come for.

"In for a penny, in for a pound," I muttered to myself, one of my mom's favorite sayings. She'd be upset to see me here now, about to do what I'd decided to do after lying to everyone to get here. I thrust the thought of my family firmly out of my mind. Rafe shut the door of the truck firmly and said something to the valet, who got into the vehicle and drove off without batting an eye.

"Are you sure you can afford this?" I took Rafe's arm and huddled against him, feeling seriously outclassed as we went into the famous lobby, sparkling with crystal and gleaming with wood and leather.

"I was going to bring you here for dinner. Now we'll just go up to the room early."

I was struck dumb by the splendor of the Fairmont. Rich carpeting, gold-framed art, refined lighting picked out seating clusters in the grand lobby. I clung to Rafe's arm as he checked in, cool as creek water. "Reservation for McCallum," he said. "And guest."

"Yes sir, Mr. McCallum." The voice of the concierge was respectful. *That's how classy this place is*, I thought. *They don't even allow the staff to discriminate against drifter sailors checking in with penniless college students.*

We went up in an elevator gleaming with walnut and burnished brass, an attendant in the hotel's uniform inquiring what floor we were on. I felt awkward shyness settling between us and stepped away from Rafe, losing my courage as I looked up at the changing lights above the door.

What am I doing? I'd surely regret this, and with Rafe who didn't fit with my life goals. I had escaped the Virgin Islands through brains and willpower, but this man, who'd worked trimming coconuts off the trees on my parents' management estate, was already rocking all my assumptions about life—and he had a hold on me I couldn't shake.

As if sensing my uncertainty, Rafe reached out and took my cold hand in his large, warm one. I felt every inch of his height and frame dwarfing mine, and it was thrilling and intimidating. He smiled down at me.

"Glad to be with you," he whispered into my ear. "Thanks for coming to San Francisco."

I stared down at my feet in their impractical ballet flats. There was a smudge on my freckled knee, and I rubbed at it, reflecting on my folly. It wasn't too late to tell him to stop the elevator, ask him to take me back to Lisa's boardinghouse until my departure. Because I knew Rafe was a gentleman. He was doing this with me because I'd said I wanted it.

I had no one to call to talk over my ambivalence, because no one knew I was here. *No one.* Not my parents, not my roommate and best friend, Shellie, nor her brother Sam. Not my supposed boyfriend Henry, who I was "taking a break" from.

The elevator door dinged open. "Fourteenth floor," the attendant announced.

I was highly conscious of our lack of luggage as we exited. All Rafe carried was a small black backpack, and I had my purse with a comb, my wallet, and a pair of underwear in it.

He grinned down at me at the door, a shiny black edifice. "The moment of truth," he said, and slid the key into the brass lock with a definite *snick*. He must have seen me shiver, because he encircled my shoulders and gave a reassuring squeeze as he pushed the door open.

"Oh," I gasped. "Wow."

The room was a suite, with an incredible view of the Marin headlands and the lacy red struts of the Golden Gate Bridge, the graceful skyscrapers of downtown providing an architectural counterpoint. The carpeting was cream, the seating an elegant distressed brown leather, and the bed, the very big bed—was a garden of Laura Ashley cabbage roses on fine sateen.

I walked hesitantly in. I'd never been inside such a fancy hotel room before. Rafe followed, setting his bag beside the door and making his way to the combination TV and music console against the wall as I walked to the sliding glass doors leading onto a tiny balcony.

The doors wouldn't open.

"Locked permanently," Rafe said. "Jumpers."

"Oh, wow," I said, stepping back, the charm lost on me at the grim reminder that all wasn't happy for some, even in a magical setting like this.

He opened the shiny burled doors of the console. "Hmm. Got quite a selection here." I came back to stand beside him, looking through a stack of CDs with everything from instrumental to classic rock. "I think a little mood music." He put on some Otis Redding, which I recognized from my parents' collection. "How about some wine?"

I wasn't about to remind him I wasn't legal to drink yet. "I'd love some."

He went to a silver bucket and took out a bottle of champagne. "I ordered this ahead of time."

"So you had this planned?" I paced back and forth in front of the sliding glass windows. I was feeling nervous and keyed up, all the confidence I'd pretended at Coit Tower evaporating in the light of Rafe's apparent acceptance of my challenge.

"I did. I know you're leaving in another day or so. Wanted you to have a special treat." He popped the cork. I watched the shine of the late-afternoon light on tumbled bronzy hair that fell to graceful, muscular shoulders. He was wearing a black tee that hugged his body, and I spotted his tattoo curving around his deltoid muscle. It appeared to be some sort of claw, and I remembered it was a fierce eagle pouncing.

"That's so sweet of you," I said.

He filled a flute and held it out to me. "Nothing sweet about it. Making memories to tide you over until we see each other again."

I felt an immediate wrench at the thought of leaving as I

accepted the glass. Our fingers brushed and his touch was electric as ever.

"You do something to me," I said. "I wish you didn't. It's confusing." I tried to swig the fizzing drink, which promptly went up my nose and down my throat, causing a burning cough.

He thumped my back. "You okay?"

I'd invented a taste for champagne in my playful persona as "Juliette," a French-speaking immigrant from the Antilles who smoked clove cigarettes, wore a beret, and favored sparkling wine. Pretending to be Juliette had helped me adjust to life so far from home, but the truth was, I didn't know one wine from another.

"It's fine." I sipped more slowly. "It tastes good."

"That's right." He drew me into his arms. "Come here."

I stiffened instinctively, and I felt rather than heard the deep chuckle in the solid expanse of his chest as I pressed against him. "Relax. We're not going to do anything you don't want to. In fact, we can leave right now if you aren't comfortable."

"No!" I exclaimed, pulling back to look up into his deep blue eyes. "I want to be with you. Really."

"I know you think you do." He tugged me over to the rose-patterned bed, and we sat on the end of it. "But I think you're confused, and now you're finally admitting it. I wanted you to have this week doing things with me, spending time, so that you could get to know me. See if you really wanted to be with me, or if you just had a case of hormones."

I felt the blush sweep up the pale skin of my neck. "I want to sleep with you," I muttered. "I came here for 'First Night.'"

He laughed. "I was inspired when I wrote that one. I want you, too, Ruby. You have no idea how much. But like I told you the first day, I care about you. Too much to just take advantage of what you're offering."

"Are you saying no?" I looked up at him. I'd been using that look to get boys to do what I wanted since I was two years old. I knew my big green eyes lined in dark, spiky lashes were hard to resist. Ever so gently, I licked my pouty lower lip.

Rafe let out a stifled groan, bent his head and set his lips on mine. The kiss started out tender but quickly activated the heat that had been turned down to simmer since our make-out session at Coit Tower.

His tongue, tasting of the wine, tangled with mine. He tilted my head for better access, bringing a large, long-fingered hand to cup my breast, loose beneath the T-shirt and jean jacket. He kissed me thoroughly as he massaged and circled the round, palming its weight and flicking the nipple, hard as an acorn, with his thumb, then switching to the other one. He lifted his head to gaze down at my flushed face.

"These feel like the most beautiful breasts on the planet," he said. "Can I see them?"

"Okay," I breathed. He eased me back on the acre or so of Laura Ashley and unbuttoned each of the metal buttons of the jacket. I could feel the heat of his gaze on my braless breasts in the thin, tight T-shirt I'd worn in my juvenile seduction attempt.

"I need this off," Rafe whispered. "Please."

Mutely, I shrugged out of the jacket and skinned the T-shirt off over my head, tossing the clothing off the bed. Lying back on the bed and looking up, I noticed the tasteful gilt-framed oval mirror on the ceiling for the first time.

It was a revelation to see myself lying topless on the bed. Long, flame-colored ribbons of red hair were spread across the bed, setting off pale, creamy skin dappled with tiny nutmeg freckles. The large, round breasts that had been both blessing and curse since I was twelve pointed dusky rose nipples straight up. The arc of my shadowed ribs and flat belly disappeared into the modest skirt slung low on the graceful swell of my hips, the slight rise of my mound the only configuration in the landscape of my body still hidden.

Rafe's brown-haired head bent over me as he kissed my neck, his fingers sliding down my body, learning its shape. I relished the sight as he pulled off his own shirt in a quick brisk movement. His large, tanned torso contrasted with mine as he leaned over me, a sight so beautiful I wanted to watch it all day. The eagle tattoo on his arm looked alive, the wings flying as he moved, and what it was pouncing on was me.

His body was pure poetry of form and power, the muscles sliding in rippling movements across his back and arms, the chiseled plane of his chest punctuated by small brown nipples, his belly lean and contoured. Twin columns of heavy muscle supported the tender knobs of his spine as it disappeared into the waistband of his jeans.

I wanted to see it all, touch it all, kiss it all. But for now just gazing at him was a feast. I could look at him all day and never get enough. I relished the fact that he didn't know about the mirror yet.

I saw and felt at the same time as his hot mouth come down over the sensitive tip of my breast. I arched beneath his mouth with an involuntary cry, watching and feeling his hand slide down the valley of my waist, over the slope of my hip, and back up again.

It felt exquisite, tingling sensation following his explorations, every movement awakening something new in me. I moaned and tangled my hands in the length of his hair. The experience of both seeing and feeling him touch me was so arousing I felt the nervousness that had resurfaced in the doorway of the room disappear.

I wanted this. All of it. All of him. For better or worse.

"Please," I breathed into his mouth, into his hair, and I slid my hands up his muscled arms and drew his face down to my breast. "More."

"As you wish."

Rafe sucked my nipple hard, tonguing it at the same time. I gave a cry as that oversensitive bundle of nerves set off a chain reaction of combustible heat that pulsed, begging for release. He switched to the other breast and kissed his way along my collarbone and down the dip below my sternum. I thrust my hips at him in unapologetic hunger.

"So passionate," he breathed. "So responsive. You're pure fire. I knew it the first day I met you." His hands went to my waistband and he undid the button and zip of my skirt.

I pushed up and he wriggled the skirt down. In the mirror above his head, I watched every line of his body go rigid as he gazed down at me, hissing through his teeth as he gazed at my naked, flame-haired mound.

I felt a wave of self-consciousness. "I'm sorry. I know I'm funny-looking," I said, transported back to the gym showers at school, where my odd coloring had provoked so much teasing from the girls I'd refused to go back, choosing homeschooling instead.

"Exquisite," he said. "You're gorgeous." He bent close and blew on me. The puff of air was a tantalizing hot caress that promised pleasure. I thrust up toward him, wantonly craving his touch. He cupped me, stroked me. I tried to open my legs, but he didn't let me. He chuckled a little painfully as his hands made swirling patterns over my hips and thighs.

"You're an impatient woman," he said. "Slow down. Be gentle with me. You're my first and only redhead, and I want to savor every moment of how amazing you are."

"Please," I panted. "I need you. Everything. All of it."

He just shook his head, and proceeded to awaken my body.

He smoothed me, petted me gently, exploring and arousing. He kissed me at my core, stroking, and the incredible sensations pushed me past shyness as he flicked me with his tongue.

It didn't take long. Sensation like a wave swept up from my

toes, broke over my whole body, and engulfed me in a storm of lights that exploded in my brain and washed me up on the shore of *after*, boneless and wordless.

He rolled my limp body over to lie face down.

I lay on my bare front as he rubbed his rough, hard chest across the silky, firm rounds of my buttocks, an incredibly good feeling of a different kind.

I turned my head, and in the mirror, I could glimpse him squeezing my butt between his hands, rubbing himself back and forth over my ass. Even I could see that the only thing better than my breasts to look at were the firm, high rounds of my creamy-white ass cheeks, set off by little thumbprint-sized dimples above my slim waist.

"Dammit," Rafe said, tracing my buttocks with his hands. "I can't wait any longer." He dropped his pants in a quick move-ment and hauled me higher on the bed, still face down. I could see in the mirror as he mounted me, his hard thighs clamping around my hips. I didn't have time to wonder what he was doing as he said, "This won't take a minute," and slid his huge, rock-hard shaft along my butt, rubbing up and down against me as his hands clenched the tops of my hips convulsively.

I saw and felt him come with a heart-moan, his back a vast arching of muscles I watched and longed for in the mirror above. I felt a wetness that slid like hot honey into the small of my back.

I gave a yelp of outrage. "No. That wasn't how it was supposed to be!"

I tried to struggle up from beneath him, but Rafe had collapsed over me with his full weight. He groaned.

"I'm sorry. I couldn't help it. And we were never having sex today. At least not the kind you had in mind."

I slid out from under him at last. "Why do you get to decide what we're doing?" I was furious and embarrassed. I stomped into the palatial bathroom.

My eyes were flashing and cheeks flaming as I glanced in the mirror at my swollen breasts, heavy and pink, blotched with hickeys. My hair was a snarled mess. I was marked with kisses and beard stubble, and there was something wet sliding down my back.

I'd had orgasms, and now so had he, but I was deeply disappointed.

"Total bummer," I muttered. I turned on the shower and got in.

Moments later he got in with me. I scrubbed my body furiously with soap and a washcloth.

"I'm sorry. I couldn't...I was going to explode. Now I can take my time with you the next time," Rafe said. "Besides, I didn't have a condom."

"You booked a room and ordered wine, but didn't have a condom? Besides, there won't be a next time," I snorted, but slowed my angry movements as he began working a fragrant lather of shampoo into my long hair, massaging my scalp. He washed my hair tenderly, rinsing each section of hair, sliding it over himself as if studying the contrast of the vivid color with his own hardened, tanned, hair-roughened body.

The anger gradually melted out of me under his gentle, tender touch.

He carried me out of the shower. Wrapped me in one of the huge bath sheets. Turned down the bed and tucked me in, blotting my hair with the towel.

I fell instantly asleep.

CHAPTER SIX

I woke up abruptly, overheated.

Rafe was sleeping next to me, one arm over me and one heavily muscled thigh holding down my legs. His face was beside mine on the pillow, and in this unguarded moment, I could study it.

His deep blue eyes were closed, fans of long dark lashes resting against high, slanted cheekbones. Stubble marked the planes of his cheeks, the firm jaw now relaxed in sleep. His mouth, with its thinner top lip and wide lower one, a mouth that could look hard or tender, was slightly open, and his breath mingled with mine.

I was tempted to kiss him, and even though I was too hot, I didn't want to wake him. A feeling swelled in me, an overwhelming tenderness. I sneaked a hand up and stroked the line of his dark brows. His breathing never changed.

I wanted to wake up in his arms every day.

The thought chilled me. Scared me. I'd not come all the way out here, lied to everyone who mattered to me, to fall for a guy who was so wrong for me.

Surfer, sailor, drifter. Rafe McCallum.

I wanted solidity. A career. To own my home and drive a decent car. Maybe have a few kids someday. I didn't want to be dependent on the whims and generosity of strangers like my parents had been. I remembered too well how they'd had to scramble to find work, how Mom cleaned houses and Dad did yards until they'd eventually built up their vacation-rental management business.

I'd come out to San Francisco because I wanted Rafe's body. I wanted to experience sex with someone who knew what he was doing, and his behavior confused me. First he seduced me with his letters and got me out here. Then he put on the brakes and said he wanted to get to know me. Today he'd caved to my sexual pressure and we'd ended up in bed, but even that was confusing.

On the one hand, he'd certainly known what he was doing with his mouth and his hands, but on the other—no condom? That clumsy grasping, pumping himself over me, leaving me no way to give back to him?

I didn't know what Rafe wanted from me. It almost seemed like he didn't, either.

All of a sudden the weight of his arm and leg felt stifling. I eased out from under him, sliding gently to the edge of the bed and out from under the sateen spread.

He slept on. I loved the shine of late-afternoon sun on his long, tumbled bronzy hair, the round of his shoulder marked by an eagle, the curled open hand that rested in the dent where I'd lain.

I looked around the gorgeous suite. At the open bottle of champagne, at the view.

This room was costing poor Rafe the earth, and the longer I stayed, the more it would cost, and worse, the more vulnerable I would be to the hold he had on me. A hold that had begun to feel suspiciously like falling in love.

It seemed he wasn't going to have sex with me, and that's what I'd come for. So what I needed to do was leave before things got any worse, before my heart broke any more at leaving him.

I needed to get back to school and figure out what the hell I was doing with Henry and Sam. Breaking up with everyone right now seemed like an excellent idea. It was about time I remembered I'd come to college to get an education in something more than sex.

I pulled up my skirt from the carpet, stepped into it, and zipped it up. Found my shirt and yanked it on. Dug my panties out of my purse and put them on. Buttoned my jean jacket over my loose breasts.

I found a little bathroom kit containing a comb and a rubber band, and in the bathroom I braided my long bright hair, still damp and fragrant from that memorable shower.

I splashed water on my face.

My cheeks were pale now. The flash had gone out of my eyes when I stared at myself in the mirror.

I had two more days here, and now I had to find a way to avoid Rafe.

I picked up my purse and sneaked out, closing the door gently. Out in front of the hotel, I hailed my first San Francisco cab and took it back to Rafe's boardinghouse.

Lisa, the innkeeper, met me packing my things into my backpack in the little sitting room where I'd been sleeping on a couch. "Where are you going?" she asked sharply, hands on her hips.

"Things aren't working out with Rafe." I felt my eyes fill spontaneously. "I need to find a place to stay until I fly out."

"Oh, girl." Lisa's warm ebony arms encircled me, and she drew me in to her remarkable bosom. "I'm so sorry. I thought he was really into you. More than anyone I've seen him bring home."

"Ha." I sniffled, grabbing a tissue out of a nearby box. "No.

It's just not happening with us. I don't want to see him anymore. It's too embarrassing. Can you tell me a cheap hotel to go to?"

"I'll take you to a friend's," Lisa said firmly. "I don't want you to end up in one of those nasty places in the Tenderloin."

"Thanks. But you have to promise not to tell him where I am. No matter what."

"Cross my heart," she said, with a gesture over her left breast. "Now come with me."

We got into her purple VW Beetle, and she drove me to another house made into temporary boarding rooms, this time with her friend Triad.

Triad was another gorgeous Puerto Rican woman. "Po' thing," she cried, welcoming me into the dimly lit hall of the house she ran. It smelled of cabbage and marijuana. "Come on to your room. We'll keep your mind off that man with movies, and I have chocolate ice cream."

Apparently, getting over Rafe wasn't a new situation for either of these ladies to deal with.

I wished the thought didn't make the tears well up and pop out of my eyes, but I was at least able to stifle the sobs until I bade Lisa goodbye with further promises from her not to tell where I was hiding.

Alone at last, I flung myself face down on the twin bed with its thin, pilly, paisley-print spread, and cried.

I spent the next day in the room without coming out, watching soap reruns on a tiny TV, VCR movies, and eating a pint of chocolate ice cream Triad dropped off.

In the late evening I finally pulled myself together enough to ask Triad for the number of a takeout place, and when the knock came on the door, I hurried to open it, expecting the Chinese food delivery I'd finally got hungry enough to order.

Rafe towered in the doorway. His face was dark with anger. He wore the same black T-shirt and jeans he'd had on before, and he was holding a white bag of Chinese food.

"Rafe! How'd you find me?" I exclaimed, snatching the bag out of his hand.

He stepped inside and shut the door with great deliberation. I didn't look at him as I dug in the bag for the little white food cartons, unloading the chopsticks, napkins, and containers on a little side table.

"I was worried," Rafe said, each word measured out and snipped off as if with scissors. "I thought you were maybe lost somewhere. I couldn't imagine where you'd run off to and what I'd done that was so wrong that you had to sneak off and ditch me like that."

I sat on the twin bed with the takeout carton in one hand and the chopsticks in the other. I knew my eyes were hugely puffy from crying and my hair, still in the braid from yesterday, was unraveling and matted. I'd never been a pretty crier.

Good. Maybe he'll be so repulsed he'll leave.

"Lisa promised she wouldn't tell you where I went," I said through a mouth stuffed with noodles. "I thought she was a friend."

"She's my friend first," Rafe said. "And she only told me where when I was going to file a missing-persons report."

I choked on the mouthful of noodles. "That would not have been good."

"No, it wouldn't."

"Well. I changed my mind about being with you," I said to the carton in my hand. "I don't want to be with you after all. I'm going back to school and I'm going to be single. No dating. Just focus on my studies."

"What I don't understand is why you couldn't just tell me that. And then I have to remind myself you're not even nineteen yet. Your brain isn't fully mature."

I looked up and glared, and he grinned at finally catching my eye. "Good. That's better. Now tell me what's really going on. Just spit it out."

"Fine." I pushed back from the edge of the bed and sat cross-legged with my back against the wall. "I came here to lose my virginity. And somewhere in the middle of all we got up to in that hotel room, I realized you had no intention of doing the deed with me." I picked up the noodles again. "I have no idea what you want from me, but if we aren't going to have sex, I don't want to be with you. There. Now you have the truth. I hope you're happy."

I tried to take a bite of noodles, but my throat had totally closed. Tears were pouring out of my eyes and giving lie to my tough words. I fumbled for a napkin to blot them.

"I thought we were having sex back in the hotel," Rafe said mildly. "There are lots of ways to do it, you know."

"I begin to," I said, flapping a hand. "But I don't understand why you're being how you are with me. What are you trying to do? Make me fall in love with you or something?" The question came out on a squeak. "Because I can't fall in love with you. You're all wrong for me. Long-term." The words came out in a rush. "And I have to get back to school and get away from you before...before." I ended the muddled speech by stuffing my mouth with tasteless noodles before I told him that *before* had already happened. It was too late.

I'd fallen for him.

More than for Sam, who was nearly perfect and great husband material.

More than for Henry, who loved me already and was a terrific boyfriend.

No. Every minute I spent with this surfer, sailor, drifter, I fell a little more inappropriately in love.

"Ah." He sat beside me, with a couple of feet between us. The space seemed to hum with that chemistry we could never get away from. "Because to be honest, I've been feeling confused, too. You aren't any more right for me than I am for you."

"At least we agree on something," I honked my nose on my napkin. I caught Rafe's eye.

He smiled, but it was a little sad. "And yet."

"And yet what?"

"I've been around a lot longer than you. Eight years longer. Long enough to know that this feeling..." He gestured to the charged emptiness between us. "This feeling doesn't come along often. It's unusual. In fact, I've never had it before. I can't stop thinking about you. Wanting to be with you."

"I like some other people," I argued. "I think I can get over you."

He nodded. "And I expect you to try. In fact, I think you're already trying to get over me."

"I am. Getting over you." I bobbed my head like a marionette.

"Okay. Well, because of my greater wisdom, I didn't want to have sex with you. Because you grew up the way you did, in the church and with the family you have, you can deny it all you like, but it's going to mean something. Something big. That I'm your first." He said it definitely, as if there were no question about him being my first. "I didn't want to make the breakup worse by having that experience with you, because I knew I wasn't right for you. We want different things."

I was still nodding, that puppet's movement. "Right. Different things entirely."

"So, I decided to just spend time with you awhile when you got here, see if we liked each other. And I found I really liked you. You're fun to be with. I enjoyed all of our time together."

"Me too," I admitted, thinking of the crab picnic on the deserted rooftop at Fort Point. Flying kites in Golden Gate Park. Riding the carousel on Pier 39. Walking through the zoo, holding hands and eating cotton candy. Picking up sand dollars on the great empty sweep of Ocean Beach. Yes, San Francisco was a romantic city indeed.

"But that other thing."

"The chemistry," I said in a rush. "I can't be near you and not think of being with you. That way." My cheeks flamed at this bold admission. "Which is why I had to get away. Before it got any worse. Any more painful. Like measles."

Rafe threw his head back and laughed. "But it didn't work, did it?"

"No. It didn't." And I set the noodles down on the little table and turned to him, and he hugged me close, awkward because of the angle. I wriggled closer, and his arms tightened around me. I leaned my head down on his chest and sighed at the wonderful sound of his heart beating against my cheek. It felt like everything in my off-kilter world was coming back into alignment.

"And that's why I think we should get married." Rafe's voice rumbled in his chest next to my cheek, and his words vibrated in the air above me like a plucked chord.

CHAPTER SEVEN

I couldn't scramble off of Rafe's lap fast enough. I jumped up off the bed and turned to face him, hands on hips. "You need your head examined. Didn't we just get done listing all the ways we're wrong for each other?"

Rafe spread his hands, pitched his voice low, and gave me a lot of sincere eye contact. I hadn't seen this side of him before: confident, persuasive, almost like a businessman.

"I'm operating from my greater experience, you see. I told you, I've never felt this way before, and the longer I'm with you, the worse it gets, just when I usually lose interest." He reached out, picked up one of my long red ribbons of hair. "Now that I've seen you, tasted you...all I can think of is getting more of you. And having you be mine, always."

"And you can have me." He wound the hank of hair around his fist, and I let myself be drawn closer. I could feel my breasts tingling with the anticipation of his touch. His passionate words were loosening my knees already as I sank to the bed and kept coming toward him as he drew his fist, wrapped with my hair, up against his chest. Inches from his mouth, I said, "You can have me. I'm yours. But we're not getting married."

He pulled me in, and the kiss was demanding, harsh and hard and hot. When I tried to pull back, the handful of hair he held tugged my scalp painfully. I wrenched my mouth loose, tears stinging my eyes. "You're hurting me."

Immediately, he loosened his grip and used his other hand to unwind the hank of hair from the hand holding it.

"I'm sorry. I'm not used to hearing no." Rafe smiled, one side of his mouth cocking up. "I'm not used to making marriage proposals either. You don't know what this means to me. But then, you wouldn't. I'm the one with greater life experience, who knows how special what we have is. And therein lies the rub." He stroked my cheek with the back of his hand.

"I leave tomorrow," I whispered. "We have tonight."

"God, you're beautiful," he said against my mouth. "But I want all of you, and not for just one night. Forever."

I pulled away again, and this time I walked across the room to get away from him.

"This is ridiculous," I said, hands on hips. "You're scaring me. You're asking too much. I'll never marry someone like you. *Surfer, sailor, drifter.* We want different things."

His cobalt eyes had gone even darker at my words, and his brows drew down. "You don't know anything about me, really," he whispered. "If you did, you wouldn't say that. But you have to come to me freely. I see I'll just have to change my strategy."

He slid to the edge of the bed and stood up with the grace of a leopard, walking inexorably to me. "Come to bed. Let me give you pleasure. So you'll know what you're saying no to, and so you'll remember me when you go back to Boston."

I trembled as he reached me, unable to look away from his gaze.

"Okay," I whispered, my whole body switching on at his

proximity, lighting up like a power grid as juice coursed through it. "I'm gross, though. I need a shower. I've been in bed, crying and eating ice cream, all day."

"And I've been sweating and going crazy looking for you." Rafe pulled me into his arms. His mouth on mine was tender this time, and he stroked the tears that started involuntarily with the balls of his thumbs. "Come to bed," he whispered, and I did.

He took each piece of clothing off me carefully, his eyes and hands and tongue kissing every revealed inch of my skin. When he had me naked, he just studied me as I sat cross-legged on the bed, dressed in nothing but my hair.

"I want to see you, too," I said. "I didn't really get to, yesterday. Except in the mirror."

"The mirror?"

"There was a mirror over the bed."

"Minx," he said. "Red-haired witch. I can't believe you didn't tell me."

I smiled, a distinctly cat-with-canary smile. "I enjoyed seeing your body so much. Seeing it against mine." I could see I was affecting him with my words as his nostrils flared and eyes widened, but I just put my hands on the broad planes of his chest in the black T-shirt and tugged. "Off."

He skinned the shirt off obediently and tossed it on the floor. His torso was every bit as amazing as I remembered.

"Off," I said again, tugging at the waistband of his jeans.

He slid out of them. Now he was wearing just a pair of black silk boxers. His erection distended the front of them, and like the first time on the hike on Saint Thomas when I'd glimpsed that evidence of his reaction to me, I felt a deep feeling.

A tender awe. A breathless anticipation, a kind of inner wonder.

I did this to him.

He stood before me at the edge of the bed, letting me look my fill.

He was magnificent from the top of his wide, tanned, contoured shoulders, down the broad chest roughened by hair in the center, across tapered, chiseled abs to narrow hips. His sculptured buttocks flowed in a clean line into heavily muscled legs.

I slid to the edge of the bed, feeling my own arousal heat me to melting. I hooked my fingers into the black silk boxers and pulled them down.

He hissed as the material caught on his straining erection. I looked at it inches away, feeling my mouth go dry.

There was no way this thing was going to fit all the way inside of me. The glimpse I'd had in the mirror hadn't done it justice, and it was downright intimidating.

I glanced up at Rafe's face. I saw him struggle to restrain himself and the conflict in his expression—hope that I'd find him attractive, warring with worry that I'd be scared away.

I could also see that he'd decided to let me examine him and take all the time I needed.

"You can touch it," he said. "You won't hurt me touching it. Though I can't promise I won't lose control like I did last time."

I tentatively wrapped a hand around the thick shaft. It felt unexpectedly warm, silky, and pleasant. He groaned above me as I slid both hands up and down the length of it, learning how it felt, like silk over steel. Tenderly, experimentally, I licked the smooth helmet-like tip.

The whole thing jumped in my hand, and I laughed.

"Thanks a lot," Rafe gritted.

"No. It's not funny. It's just kind of amazing the way it responds to me," I said, and put my mouth all the way over it.

It tasted a tiny bit salty, and I used my tongue to explore the seam on the underside.

Rafe moaned again, and now his hands came down on either

side of my head to clutch handfuls of my hair. "Unbelievable how good that feels," he choked out. "And you don't even know how."

I pulled back and looked up the vast expanse of his chiseled body to his cobalt eyes, vulnerable with need and something more. I could recognize the something more for what it was now.

Love.

Rafe McCallum loved me. It was amazing and scary and ridiculous, but it was real. I could see it in the transparent blue gems of his eyes.

"Teach me," I whispered. "Teach me what you like."

CHAPTER EIGHT

I learned to make a tight circle with my thumb and forefinger at the base and lick the length hard, like a Popsicle, and to flick the head with my tongue at the end of the stroke. I learned more creative things to do with my tongue, swirls and sucks and flips, and finally I learned how to draw it all the way in and use my swallowing muscles.

When he finally let himself come, I hung in all the way to the end. It wasn't nearly as gross as I'd imagined it would be when Jenny first told me about this kind of goings-on. I felt hot and achy with sexual frustration, but also triumphant. I'd learned to give head and apparently hadn't done too badly at it.

Rafe collapsed with a groan and lay like a giant felled across the tiny twin bed.

"This isn't how I pictured this would go," he muttered, face down across the bed. "I thought I was going to be the one working you over."

"Oh, I'm sure we'll get to that," I said. "We have all night." I couldn't believe I was saying such bold words.

I rolled him over so his back was against the wall, and I drew the thin spread up over us. I snuggled against his heat and tucked myself in under his arm. "So. Rafe." I cleared my throat. "Are we going to do it the—the usual way?"

"Not until we're married," he said. "You'll thank me later."

I pushed away and smacked him on the chest. "That's never going to happen."

"Just say the word and it will. The word is 'yes.'"

"I want to." I couldn't help turning to kiss the wide expanse of his muscled chest where I'd just hit him. "You can get me to say anything. But it wouldn't be fair to either of us. It wouldn't be true."

"You're the boss." His voice sounded sad.

"I didn't feel like the boss just now."

"We can take turns with that kind of bossing." He smiled. "When we have time. And I plan on having a lot more time." He pointed to the pearly dawn at the window. "Sun's up. When do you have to be at the airport?"

I looked at the digital clock on the nightstand. "Oh no! We have to go. My plane's in two hours!"

"Shower first, at least."

And in the shower, he soaped and kissed and rubbed the marks of his kisses. He teased me with his fingers and mouth until we were both delightfully, if temporarily, sated.

Rafe handed me my backpack at the check-in gate and kissed me goodbye one last time. He released me and took my hand. Looking into my eyes, he uncurled my fingers and pressed a small black velvet box into my palm.

"Open it when you're alone," he whispered into my ear. "And let me know your answer when you can."

I tried to hand the box back to him, but he'd already turned and was pushing through the crowd around the busy entrance.

I got on the plane feeling numb, as if my feet were miles away.

A sensation of rending opened within me, as if that charged space between us had been sundered. In the void where it had been, the dark vastness of space echoed back frozen emptiness. It felt utterly horrible.

I leaned my head against the window and shut it out by falling asleep.

CHAPTER NINE

I unlocked the door of our suite late that night, relieved to peek into Shellie's dorm room to the left and see that her bed was empty. Spring break was officially over tomorrow, so she was probably out partying or hadn't returned from New York yet.

Guilt twisted my gut. I'd been so busy with Rafe I'd hardly spared a thought for my roommate and best friend, whose house I'd told my parents I was visiting.

I flicked on the light of my bedroom and jumped back with a little shriek.

There was a man in my bed.

Sam sat up, my coverlet falling to his bare waist, his bearded face fuzzy and adorable with sleep. He pulled the coverlet back up to his chest, a wide burly chest I'd had occasion to explore during winter break spent in New York with Shellie and their family.

"Oh hey, Ruby," he said. "I was waiting for you and fell asleep."

"Oh, no," I said, dropping my backpack. "You have to get out of my bed."

"Sure you don't want to join me?" His golden-hazel eyes were alight with mischief and invitation as he lifted the covers.

He wasn't wearing anything under there. He was huge, and gorgeous. I didn't want to compare him with Rafe, but I couldn't help it a little bit. I decided I'd have to have them side by side for closer inspection to see whose body was better, but it would definitely be a tough call.

If I hadn't just spent a week with Rafe, I might have been happy about this surprise.

Might even have responded with enthusiasm to Sam's open, happy smile and naked invitation into my own bed. After all, I was trying to shuck off my virginity.

I didn't see Sam as the type to suddenly grow a conscience and refuse to sleep with me. He'd been a totally enthusiastic, kind, funny companion in New York, and even taken it like a gentleman when I canceled our spring break plans for my mythical trip home to the Virgin Islands.

"Sam." I came closer. Sam's wide smile faded. His eyes, those golden eyes that reminded me of beloved toads on Saint Thomas, swept over me and come to a stop at the hickey I knew was blooming like a big purple rose on the side of my neck where Rafe had been a little overenthusiastic. "I'm sorry, but this isn't going to work."

Sam swung his legs out of my bed and stood. I kept my eyes on his with difficulty, intimidated by the six-foot, angry, naked man standing in front of me.

"I should have known that story about going home to your family was a crock. You look like hell. You look like you haven't been out of bed all week because you've been banging someone nonstop. Who is it?" he growled, as big and hairy as a golden bear.

I felt sick and sad and miserable. I'd liked Sam so much. He made me laugh. He understood me. We'd been playful, sexy friends, and I knew we could have been so much more. Sam was so different from Rafe, and unlike Rafe, was perfect for me long-term.

"You don't know him." I dropped my eyes to my feet.

Sam scooped up his jeans from the floor and yanked them on. "I can't believe I wasted my time on you. I could have had a dozen girls since I met you, but I was waiting to be with you. I thought you were different." He spat the words at me as he dragged a long-sleeved polo shirt on over his muscular football player's shoulders.

"I'm sorry," I said. "I would never want to hurt you. Ever. I've been confused."

"Well, I'm not confused. You're obviously not who I thought you were."

He scooped his jacket off the back of a chair and left, slamming the door so hard the room vibrated and the picture of my parents fell off the wall.

Yes. I was a terrible person. And there was still Henry to hurt.

I was too keyed up after sleeping all the way across the continental United States and the upset of hurting Sam to go to bed, so I unpacked my meager belongings and got in a long, hot shower. I washed my hair and blow-dried it into a long, straight fall. I put on careful makeup and dressed in a turtleneck and jeans that hid the bruises, hickeys, and stubble rash left by two days of orgasms with Rafe McCallum.

I might as well get the rest of this terrible business over with.

I took off the little gold moonstone ring Henry had given me and taped it back onto the cassette of love songs he'd made me before I left for San Francisco.

I'd told him he'd know one way or the other when I got back, and it was going to be the other. I then sat at my desk and wrote a letter, pausing to get the words just right and brushing the feather quill pen "Juliette" liked to use across my cheek as I searched for the right words.

I thanked Henry for being a great first boyfriend. I thanked him for all the fun sights we'd seen, the dates we'd been on, the experiences we'd had. I thanked him for sharing his beautiful music with me. And I told him I'd met someone else and I needed to take a break from everything and everyone, and I hoped he understood.

I put the letter, the cassette, and the moonstone ring in a manila envelope in case he wasn't home. I put on my old pea coat and let myself out into the damp, chilly Boston spring night.

I walked the whole way to his off-campus apartment, at least ten blocks. The streets were empty, and my brisk walking felt a little like penance, like a punishment I deserved, and at the same time something I needed to do to clear my head.

Because I was planning to send much the same letter to Rafe tomorrow.

My gloved hand held the velvet ring box he'd given me in my pocket like a talisman. I'd been afraid to look at it on the plane today, too overwhelmed with feelings to deal with any more.

I knew Rafe wasn't going to accept a letter easily, but I needed to break things off with him, too. I needed time to refocus on priorities. To sort out my heart, body, and emotions.

I reached Henry's building. The old brownstone, where I'd had my first kiss in the chilly light of fall in the second-story window, seemed as slumbering as a turtle closed in a dark shell.

Taking the coward's way out, I thrust the bulky envelope into Henry's mail slot and turned and walked back.

And finally, after checking to make sure the street was deserted, I took the ring box out of my pocket and opened it in the golden glow of a streetlight.

I'd expected some sort of diamond, probably small—but the stone was a cabochon ruby so dark it looked like a drop of blood in the dim light. It was surrounded by tiny, fiery diamonds.

It was utterly divine.

"A ruby," I whispered aloud. "Oh my God. Where did he get something so perfect?"

I couldn't resist trying it on, and it slid easily over the knuckle of the ring finger of my left hand. A stray beam of light caught it, and I could see fiery gleams in the heart of the stone.

I turned it so the ruby rested in my palm and fisted my hand closed around it. I'd never, ever had something so valuable in my possession, and it scared me.

The way Rafe scared me.

Too big, too much, too demanding.

I ran and ran and finally arrived at my building out of breath but feeling like I was back in my own body at last.

This was me. An almost-nineteen-year-old who liked to run, who had dreams for herself that didn't include getting married at a ridiculously young age, and who needed to get focused on what she came to college for. A career in the law.

Something as far away and different from the life I'd always known in the Virgin Islands as I could get.

Shellie was in her room even though it was past one a.m. by now, and I barely got the door open before she was grabbing me by my coat and hauling me inside the entry area. She was so mad that her golden-green eyes, so much like Sam's, were shooting sparks. Her tawny curls bounced as she stomped her feet.

"You lied to me!"

I smelled alcohol on her breath. *Uh-oh.* Shellie was a light-weight, so she seldom drank, but when she did, bad things happened. So far she'd streaked in the quad, picked a fight with the resident assistant in our building, and dropped a watermelon out the window onto the sidewalk below our room, refusing to admit it.

Now she screamed in my face. "You broke my brother's heart, you slut!"

"I'm really, really sorry," I said. There was nothing to say, nothing to do. I was losing everything right now through my risky choice to run off to see Rafe.

Well, maybe not everything. The ruby on my finger felt like a tiny comforting nugget in my hand.

Shellie pushed me in the shoulder. "I can't believe you lied about going to the Virgin Islands. You're white as a ghost! You didn't get any sun at all. Sam was right. You went somewhere else, with someone else. Where would you go? And who with? It had to be that Rafe guy, that worthless bum you met working in your parents' yard business!"

She could be forgiven her demeaning inaccuracies about Rafe and my parents' business. I was a terrible person and I felt terrible about myself.

"I'm so, so sorry. I don't expect you to understand." I tried to get my door open, fumbling with the key. I now deeply regretted I'd ever told Shellie about Rafe and our letter writing, because she'd jumped to the right conclusion about where I'd been.

"You should be with that worthless drifter. You two losers deserve each other! You're not good enough for my brother!"

I'd had enough verbal abuse now that I'd finally got my door open.

"Let's talk in the morning, when you're sober," I said firmly, and closed the door in her furious face and locked it.

"Slut! Whore! Liar!" she yelled, and kicked the door.

I heard the hurt behind Shellie's hot-tempered words. She felt betrayed by my lies, by her brother's hurt, by disappointment in her own hopes for our relationship. There was nothing I could say or do right now that wouldn't make the situation worse.

I went to my bed and lay down on it fully clothed. I heard Shellie's furious voice on the phone in the room next door. She was probably ruining my reputation with her parents, with any of our mutual friends she could get hold of.

I deserved it.

What had I been thinking? I'd been so caught up in Rafe, Rafe, Rafe that it hadn't occurred to me who'd be hurt if my ploy to meet him in San Francisco was discovered.

I pulled my blanket up over myself and burrowed under it. I imagined I still could smell the fresh scent of Sam in my bed, and my eyes prickled with tears.

I really did like Sam. So much. And Henry, too. I hated having to end things with them in such a hurtful way to all involved. The only fair, smart thing to do was to break up with Rafe, too, take a total break from men until summer, as I'd decided to do.

I deserve to be miserable for hurting everyone.

I opened my hand to peek at the ring.

The light of my bedside lamp fell on the ruby. It was set in antique-looking reddish gold with tiny leaves etched on the shank. The ring of diamonds around the edge of the central stone caught fire in the light, and now I saw that the center cabochon was a star ruby.

The stone lit from within as light struck it. Rays played across the rounded, deep red surface, following me whichever direction I turned it.

It was the most beautiful ring I'd ever seen.

I took it off my left hand and slid it onto the ring finger of my right hand. I couldn't wear it on the left without accepting Rafe's proposal, but it couldn't hurt to sleep wearing it, just tonight.

Because the ring reminded me that at least one person in the world didn't hate me right now.

CHAPTER TEN

I waited in my room the next morning until I finally heard Shellie leave, slamming and locking the outer door extra loud. She was still mad.

Only when I was sure the coast was clear did I go out, unlock Shellie's door with the key she'd given me for emergencies, and retrieve the clunky black phone on its long cord, which was part of the suite's furnishings.

I dragged it to my side, locked the door, and sat on my bed with the phone.

I dialed the number for Lisa's boardinghouse, the only number I had for Rafe.

"Hello?" Lisa's rich voice with its hint of the tropics was enough to make my eyes fill.

"Hi, Lisa. It's Ruby. Is Rafe around?"

"Hey, girl. Guess you two aren't on the outs anymore?" She sounded hopeful.

"No thanks to you, telling him where I was hiding out," I said. "We're still figuring things out."

"He's an old friend, and when he didn't come home the other

night, I thought you two had made up. If you know what I mean." I could almost see her wiggle her expressive eyebrows.

Even three thousand miles away, I felt a blush heat up my cheeks thinking of all Rafe and I had gotten up to that night. "I just need to speak to him," I said firmly.

"Well, he's at the boat, but he said he's coming home this afternoon to do some errands. He's getting ready for another trip out on the *Creamy Maid*."

"Oh." I felt my stomach clench with something I wasn't ready to figure out. "Well, tell him I called and I need to talk to him."

"Will do."

I hung up and looked at the calendar across the room.

I had a shift in the cafeteria in thirty minutes and a class after that. It was time to get on with whatever would be my man-free life. I felt as miserable as if I'd been beaten all over.

I scooped a blob of mashed potatoes onto the tray and pushed it across the counter to someone, whose hand reached out to stop me.

I looked up into Henry's gray eyes.

They were his best feature, a light bluish silver with a ring of dark slate around the iris, and he had black lashes long as a girl's. His long-fingered musician's hands were his other best feature, and one of them, warm and firm with tiny calluses on the pads from playing violin, touched my hand.

"We have to talk," he said. Gently. Not angrily. I blinked to keep instant tears from welling over.

"Okay. Tonight, after class," I said. "I'll meet you at the coffee shop." We had a favorite hangout, a little greasy-spoon diner where they served inky coffee in thick white china cups at red-checked tables.

I made it through the rest of the shift and class, struggling with my concentration but diligently taking notes during Intermediate Composition class with four hundred other freshmen, and finally I walked down the gum-dotted sidewalk through a gleam of light rain to the diner.

Spring was finally coming to Boston, and I could see the swelling of tiny green leaves all over the shade trees punctuating the sidewalk in this part of town. An obvious spring was a new thing for me. We didn't really have seasons in the Virgin Islands, just periods with longer days and less surf, more rain and bigger waves.

I had really enjoyed the seasonal aspect of my school year here in Massachusetts. I was going to need to keep thinking about all I liked about Northeastern, now that I was living a man-free, friendless life.

The hole I was in right now felt so deep and black that it sucked the light right out of spring.

I pushed through the old glass door and went and sat in the vinyl booth Henry and I usually chose. I ordered french fries, realizing I hadn't eaten all day, and a cup of coffee.

I was dipping the fries into watery ketchup when Henry slid into the booth opposite me.

He was wearing a bright red scarf that set off his black curly hair and fresh pink cheeks, and his gray eyes were intent. "What's all this about?"

I set the fry down. "I need to take a break from men. All men. Total break."

"You said there's someone else."

"There is. And I spent time with him during spring break." I could feel my lips trembling, and I firmed them deliberately. "I told you I'd tell you one way or the other at the end of break, and

I thought I should return everything to you, so you don't feel any obligation to me or misunderstand. I'm dead serious about this."

Henry didn't unbutton his coat or unwind his scarf, but he did take my hands in his, and that's when I realized I was still wearing the ruby. It was on my right hand, it was true, but there it was. Big. Beautiful, and glowing like a drop of blood on my finger.

"Where did you get that?" The warmth, the understanding that had been in Henry's voice evaporated as he gazed at the ring. "It's a ruby. Looks expensive."

"Um. Yeah." I yanked my hand away, pulled the ring off and stuck it in my pocket. "It's not mine. Just borrowed from a friend. I'm returning it. It doesn't have anything to do with the letter I sent you."

Henry's pink cheeks got pinker. That was something I'd always liked about him. He wasn't as handsome or as chiseled as Sam or Rafe, but he was sweet and appealing in his way. Part of that appeal was that he blushed as obviously as I did.

"There's been something going on with you the whole time we were together," he said deliberately. "You aren't the person I thought you were." He got up from the booth and stood looking down at me for a long minute. "You're as fake as your French accent, Juliette," he said, and walked out of the restaurant.

I covered my face with my hands.

Henry had loved my pretend persona as the girl from the French Antilles. Juliette, with her clove cigarette and beret, could flirt so much better than Ruby the missionary's daughter. I could feel tears actually squirting out of my eyes. I held my breath to keep from sobbing out loud.

I felt queasy with the hurt I was dealing out and sick at the harshness that was coming back at me—and justifiably so.

"Here." I felt the waitress touch my shoulder as she refilled my coffee mug and removed the plate of fries. "Some extra napkins."

"Thank you," I whispered, and picked up a handful without opening my eyes and pressed them against my face.

Nothing to do but keep going.

I left an extra dollar for a tip, pushed back out the door, and made my leaden feet take me back to the dorm. I was going to have to face Shellie again.

She still wasn't back, which came as a relief, but the phone rang as soon as I'd unlocked the door to my room. I shrugged out of my coat and mentally girded my loins.

"Ruby. Are you okay?" Rafe's voice was jerky with alarm, and I realized we'd hardly talked on the phone before. Between the long-distance charges and his sailor lifestyle, letters had worked better.

"Rafe." I covered my throat with my hand to help stabilize my voice. "I need to break up with you. I'm taking a time-out from men."

A long silence. I could hear a faint hiss on the line, the sound of cold, empty distance. That charged space between us stretched too far to be bridged.

"What happened?" Just like with Henry, his voice was soft, worried.

"Oh, the shit hit the fan. I got home and Sam was in my bed. To surprise me. And I broke up with him. I never told you about Sam. And then I took a letter to Henry last night to break up with him, and Shellie called me a liar and a whore, and Henry called me fake..." I let out a gasping sob, pushing my fist into my diaphragm. "I didn't tell you that I lied to everybody here when I went to visit you. And now it's all caught up with me."

Another long silence. I dragged the phone to the bathroom and pulled some lengths of toilet paper off the roll to blot my eyes with. "So I'm sorry, but I can't be with you, or anybody."

"Okay. How long is this hiatus going to be?" He sounded perfectly calm and not angry. I was heartened by this.

"Until summer at least. I don't even know what I'm doing this summer, if I'll even have enough money to get home to Saint Thomas. But I do know I'm sick of this roller coaster and I need to get off."

"Sounds reasonable. Are you giving me back the ring?"

"Oh, Rafe. It's so beautiful and valuable. I should send it back insured..." I took the ring out of my pocket, watching the light roll around in the star ruby.

"Don't worry about that. Just put it back in the box and put it away somewhere safe. I'll get it in person."

"What?" I said, my voice going high with fright. "I told you, we're breaking up." I could never resist Rafe if he somehow showed up here.

"Don't worry. I accept what you're saying. But also know, I'm not giving up on us. I love you, Ruby." His voice was deep, rough. "And I have enough years under my belt to know what that means. I'll give you your space. We're taking the boat out for a while, so I won't be able to talk to you anyway. But I plan to keep writing. Goodbye, now."

"No, Rafe. No writing. No calling. Leave me alone, and I'll figure out how to send the ring back!" I cried, but found I was talking to a dial tone.

I put the receiver down, rubbing my sore eyes and thinking about his voice as he said, *I love you, Ruby.*

He loved me. He'd asked me to marry him. He wasn't going to give up on me.

The phone rang and I jumped. I stared at it like it was a rattler sitting in my lap, shaking its tail at me.

It was probably Rafe. Or, God forbid, Henry. Or Sam. Or maybe it was for Shellie. None of the options were good.

Finally the ringing stopped, only to start up again.

I snatched up the receiver. "Hello?"

"Ruby?" My dad's voice, tinny with the distance from Saint Thomas. "Are you okay?"

"Oh God," I said. "Hi, Daddy."

"We had the strangest message on the answering machine last night. It was Shellie, your roommate, and she said you were lying to us and had never gone with her family for spring break; you'd gone to San Francisco to have sex with Rafe McCallum. She sounded drunk." My dad's voice sounded quivery and uncertain. I almost didn't recognize it.

I'd thought things couldn't get any worse.

I wanted to vomit. I stood up and gulped to keep the french fries and black coffee down. "She told you the truth, Dad. I'm so sorry. I know I'm a disappointment to you."

"But, honey! Rafe McCallum? We loved that young man, welcomed him into our home, our lives! I can't believe he'd take advantage of our daughter like that!"

Righteous anger was replacing the quaver in Dad's voice. My parents had introduced us, and he'd worked for them as a groundskeeper for months after I left for college.

"No, Dad. He was very honorable. Asked me to marry him." I looked at the ring in my hand. "But I just broke up with him. It was a mistake. All a mistake. I'm so sorry. I'm fixing it now."

I endured a lengthy lecture, and he finally handed the phone to my mom, who said, "Rafe asked you to marry him?" in a hopeful tone.

"He did. But I'm not going to. I'm sworn off men. I'm focusing on my studies one hundred percent."

She snorted. "I couldn't concentrate either at your age. Way too many hormones. Well, I saw the way you and Rafe looked at each other, and I can't say I'm surprised. He has my vote."

She hung up with that pronouncement, to my extreme relief.

"This is 1984! People don't have to get married to have sex

anymore!" I exclaimed aloud to the empty room. But in my parents' world, they did.

And now I saw Rafe's behavior in a different light: the light of respect for my parents and their lifestyle, even if he didn't share it, and the relationship he had with them separate from me. He might not agree with that lifestyle, but he hadn't taken advantage of what I'd offered, even pushed on him. Out of respect, out of caring for them and for me.

"I love him," I said out loud, freed by his confession on the phone to admit what had already hit me on the head when I was alone in the room at Triad's. "This is terrible."

I took one long, last look at the ring and put it away in its box. I hid it in the hollow metal leg of my bedstead, where I hoped it would be safe from thieves.

I got up to get on with my man-free life.

CHAPTER ELEVEN

It was kind of a relief to immerse myself in the studies I'd been distractedly muddling through thus far. Shellie and I avoided each other, and while I knew I wanted to try to talk things through at some point, her harsh words had cut deep and I wasn't in a hurry to hear them again.

In class I resisted the temptation to write to Rafe and took notes instead. I did my shift in the caf, but as myself. "Juliette" and her berets had been retired permanently.

Still, the fun I'd had in the role gave me the idea to try out for a play the Northeastern Players would be performing the last week of the semester, in May. With no boyfriend and no one to hang out with, even after all my studying I had more free time than I'd expected, so I showed up at the tryouts with no idea what to expect.

They were reading for a musical rendering of *Oliver!*, a remake of *Oliver Twist*, and I stood with a group and muddled through the manuscript reading with the rest of a crowd of wannabes.

The crowd thinned out and I was asked to read again, and after that they asked me to sing.

I sang "Amazing Grace" a cappella, because that's what I knew how to do, and my cheeks were wet with tears on the last note.

Tears for the sweet, sheltered life I'd had on Saint Thomas and had left behind so eagerly. Tears for a life where right and wrong were easy and well defined and I had a place I belonged and a role to play.

All of it was gone now. I felt totally adrift in a gray new world. It scared me, and I didn't know how to get back to any certain ground. I was doing my very best at this moment, and it had to be enough.

And I cried because today was my birthday, and there was no one to celebrate it with.

There was a short silence after I finished the song. The light on the stage shone in my eyes, and I couldn't see into the gloom on the other side where the judges sat.

"We'll call you," finally came from the darkness, and I all but ran off the stage.

I was done with my studying that night and doing sit-ups for something to do when I heard Shellie return to the suite.

I hopped up and opened my door. "Shellie? Can we talk?"

She turned in the doorway, and I saw her face was streaked with tears. "Oh no! What happened?" I cried, instantly thinking of daredevil Sam hurting himself.

"Oh, nothing. Just got dumped. Again," she said. "Come in. I need a drinking buddy."

"Are you sure you should do that? It didn't seem to go that well the last time," I said.

"Yeah, about that. I know I said some pretty harsh things. Can't really remember what they were, but I seem to remember kicking your door." I realized Shellie had already been drinking as she caromed off the corner of her dresser on the way to the hutch where she kept an impromptu bar. She opened it and took out a bottle of tequila. "Care for a slug?"

"Never had tequila."

"Well, it's better with salt and lime, but it works just as well without," Shellie said, and handed me the squarish bottle.

"Ugh. Is that a worm?" I exclaimed, looking at the greenish thing in the clear liquid.

"I dare you to drink down to it," Shellie said.

"No way. But I'll try a slug. Without the actual slug."

I swallowed a big mouthful.

It tasted vile and burned my throat so that it closed down entirely. I coughed and Shellie laughed. "Let me show you how it's done," she said, and knocked back a respectable swallow.

"Ugh," I gasped. "Maybe more is the answer."

That's how we ended up dancing with her stereo on full blast to Madonna's "Like a Virgin," and after we were really drunk and my head was spinning, I told her what I'd struggled with all day.

"I'm nineteen today. It's my birthday."

"Oh shit," my best friend said, and belched. "I'm sorry I didn't remember. *Feliz cumpleaños!*" She handed me the bottle.

"I'll drink to that," I said, and did. "I've missed you so much. I'm so sorry you found out I'm really a slut. But if you can believe it, I'm still a virgin."

"What? I saw you after you got back from San Francisco. Talk about someone who looked like they'd just screwed their brains out for a week!"

"Well, I didn't say we didn't have sex," I said. "It was just a little more creative than I knew was possible." I giggled a little, remembering.

"Well, I've got news, too. Sam's moved on pretty easily, it appears. He e-mails me his stats each week, the numbers of girls he's been with. Asked me to pass them on to you. So I'm not worried about his broken heart any longer."

I felt a stab of very real pain. I put my fist against to my stomach. "Oh God. I think I'm going to be sick."

"So you do care about him."

"You have no idea how awful that whole situation was. I'm lonely now, without anybody, but it was horrible having to choose and not being able to. I couldn't…" I suddenly felt the ill-advised tequila making a return and barely got to the shared bathroom between our bedrooms in time.

I'd never drunk so much that I puked before. It was not an experience I ever wanted to repeat, but it seemed to bring Shellie and me together. She did better than I did, holding my hair off my forehead when I couldn't seem to stop upchucking, and trying to get me to drink water.

"Some birthday," she said. "I'll have to find a way to make it up to you."

The next morning was Saturday, so we got to sleep in. Shellie rendered first aid, apparently feeling bad about dragging me down Tequila Road with her. She brought me coffee and aspirin and told me to get myself together by noon so she could take me to a birthday lunch.

The big, clunky phone rang around ten, when I'd recovered enough to be coherent, and I got birthday wishes from my family. "You never answered the phone yesterday," Mom said accusingly. Their package hadn't yet arrived, but I felt heartened by not having been entirely forgotten about.

The phone rang again and it was the director from the play. "We'd like you to come in and read and sing again, for the role of Nancy," he said, sounding like it was something cool and important.

I racked my brain. I had no idea who that was in the play; I hadn't read the whole script, just the little parts I'd been pointed to.

"Okay," I said hesitantly. "Is it a big role?"

He snorted a laugh. "Only the biggest female part. Have you done any drama before? Sung publicly?"

"No. I grew up on Saint Thomas in a very small village. I sang in church," I said. I realized that, for the first time in my life, I felt kind of proud saying those words.

"Well, you may not be able to handle this role, then," he said briskly. "But I'd like to see you try. You have a great voice and natural presence."

"Thanks." My heart rate picked up at this. Finally, something good might be happening, along with Shellie forgiving me. "I'll see you Monday for the reading."

I hung up and jumped out of bed. That was a mistake, as my brain seemed to have stayed behind on my pillow. I moaned, clutching my head. "I hate tequila!" I exclaimed.

Shellie stuck her head in. "There's some sort of package at the RA's office. Want me to get it for you?"

"Please. I'll just be here waiting for the room to stop spinning," I said.

Shellie was back shortly with a cardboard box. It was covered with foreign-looking stamps and looked battered and stained.

"This looks well-traveled," Shellie said, handing it to me.

"It's a long way to Saint Thomas," I said, sitting up gingerly to peel off the tape.

The object in the box was padded in odd-smelling cotton batting, which I lifted off. Inside was a silver jewelry box on little curved legs.

"Wow," I said, lifting it out. I frowned because this just didn't have a look of something my parents would pick out. They were much more practical. I usually got new underwear and socks, along with toiletries or some sort of homemade craft.

I opened the shiny lid.

Graceful tinkling notes filled the air as music drifted up from inside the box. The inside was lined with deep red velvet and small origami folded shapes.

Rafe had sent this. He'd said he'd keep writing.

Shellie had grabbed the chair from my student desk and dragged it over. "Classy gift. Who's it from?"

"Rafe," I whispered.

"Oh," she whispered back. "I kinda see why you dig him."

"If you ever saw him in person, you'd totally understand," I said, and unfolded the topmost note.

Happy birthday, Ruby. I love you and miss you, he'd written, and a lot of other words that turned fuzzy to my tear-filled eyes.

"I thought you broke up with everybody." Shellie frowned. "Because I'm starting to hope Rafe is single and just might be the guy to help me get over Bryan." Before the puking had started, I'd heard all about Bryan.

"Rafe said he accepted that I needed my space but that he wasn't giving up on us. He asked me to marry him," I said. "He gave me a ring."

"Oh man," Shellie said. "No wonder you kicked Sam out of your bed."

"I never meant to hurt anybody, but somehow I ended up hurting everybody," I said, closing the music box on the letters, which I wanted to read later.

Alone.

"Well, let's get out of here and get that birthday lunch," Shellie said.

Life got a lot better once I had Shellie back in my life. I got the part in *Oliver!* and a crash course in drama through a heavy rehearsal schedule, so when I wasn't working in the caf or on my studies in class, I was at the theater working hard there, too, and making new friends.

I never wrote Rafe back, not having an address even if I'd wanted to, but I treasured the letters he'd sent in the jewelry box, reading and rereading them. He continued to write from ports all along the coast of California, then Mexico, then South America.

Reading one from Panama—a vivid description of the locks of the Panama Canal—I realized that the *Creamy Maid* seemed to be working its way from San Francisco to Boston. I got frantic.

"Shellie!" I exclaimed, bursting into her room and waving Rafe's latest letter with the postmark from Panama on it. "I think Rafe's coming here!"

"Panama is a long way from Boston," she snorted after I explained. She'd begun dating a new guy, Phillip, a thin, arty type with Fu Manchu whiskers. He was smoking a doobie in her room, and I thought he might make it to the weekend before she kicked him to the curb.

"The Panama Canal's part of that famous trade route between Boston and San Francisco," Phillip said with more enthusiasm than I'd ever seen from him. "It's the shortcut alternative to sailing around Cape Horn. Does he say anything about the ports they're going through?"

"No," I said, feeling my cheeks heat up at talking about Rafe, whom Phillip seemed to think was really cool. "He actually doesn't talk about the overall voyage much. I don't know where their destination is. He talks a lot about what he sees, the sea life and birds and such."

I didn't really want to share any of what he said in the letters. They'd changed from our early passionate exchange of fantasies to more like a travel journal, with little vignettes about crew members and stories of fishing and weather and his hours working on the deck. He seemed to be trying to share his adventure with me, and I'd come to love the raggedy letters that arrived every few days, postmarked from all sorts of South American towns I'd never heard of.

"He's really kind of cagey about that, come to think of it," I said thoughtfully.

But I knew what he'd promised to do.

Come and get the ring in person.

CHAPTER TWELVE

Things had reached critical mass with my stage production and classes were winding down to finals several weeks later. One evening at around nine p.m., I walked out of the backstage door onto campus, surrounded by laughing, talking new theater friends.

A shadow detached from the wall, and I felt a hand on my arm. "Ruby."

I turned. The exterior light fell on a familiar face. "Henry!"

"I've been watching rehearsals. I didn't know you could sing. And act! You're amazing."

"Thanks." I mopped my face as I walked with one of the rough towels we used for removing makeup. "I tried out on a whim, and it turns out I've got a dramatic flair. I learned that from Juliette, at least."

He fell into step beside me as we headed toward my dorm. We dropped behind my gaggle of loudly talking friends.

"I miss you."

"I'm sorry. I haven't changed my mind about breaking up being the right thing," I said.

"Ruby, I am not going to creep you out by hanging around the theater anymore, but you know where I am if you change your mind," he said, and then leaned down to kiss me.

I let him.

It was soft and gentle.

It was goodbye.

I broke away with a little wave and ran to catch up with my friends, still feeling bad I'd ever let Henry get that attached to me.

This must be the week for confrontations.

That was my thought as I opened the door of the suite and there stood Sam, his broad back turned to me as he talked to Phillip, who'd turned out to have a lot more going on than I'd initially given him credit for and seemed to be making Shellie happy.

I looked a mess, I knew, with my hair in twin braids for my role as Nancy the pickpocket and wearing a sweaty ragamuffin outfit I'd planned to wash that night. I stuck the key in my door, determined not to get into anything, but Sam's hand dropped to my shoulder.

"Hi, Ruby," he said. "Can we talk?"

"I'm really tired from rehearsal," I said. "How about tomorrow?" I kept my bare, greasy face turned to the door, my cheeks hot with anxiety. I wasn't tired. I was keyed up and antsy, but I didn't want a fight with Sam right now.

Or ever.

"Listen." He'd drawn close. His bulk felt like a solid wall behind me. "I was an ass, coming onto you in your own bed like that. I don't take competition well. I'm sorry."

I blew out a breath, sagging so that my forehead rested on the door. "Can I at least shower first?"

"Of course. I'll fix you a drink." He moved away, back to Shellie's side, where a party was in the process of developing.

I slipped into my room.

It was a mess from my crazy schedule. I took five minutes to throw the worst of the clutter and dirty clothes into the closet and to make sure there were some pillows and a chair for us to sit on. I didn't want to end up on the bed with him in any form.

In the shower, I ticked through my reasons for my man-free season: I'd messed up with everyone by lying, and people had gotten hurt. I had been confused, not sure who I wanted. I felt like I'd lost my way, forgotten who Ruby Day Michaels even was in all the drama.

I hung my head. Warm water streamed off the ends of my deep scarlet-red hair, now long enough to brush my hips after a year with no time in the ocean, which had always given me split ends on Saint Thomas.

What did I know now, after my season of being single?

I'd discovered new talents and creative passion through my theater work.

I didn't need to hide behind a persona anymore.

I liked both Sam and Henry, but I had fallen in love with Rafe. He was the only one who'd stuck by me through my wavering, through our breakup, through my experimentation with others' affections, through my rejection and confusion.

Yes, it was Rafe I'd fallen in love with.

But was he right for me in the long run?

I still didn't think so.

On that painful conclusion, I turned off the water and got out to hear what Sam had come to say. I couldn't imagine what he wanted with me, other than to make sure his sister was appeased that there was no awkwardness between us. Shellie's news about his promiscuity had gone a long way to assuaging my guilt in his regard.

I went into Shellie's room, where the music was cranked up and the room was packed with bodies and inebriation of various levels. Sam elbowed through the crowd toward me, a red plastic cup in either hand.

"Come in." I held the door of my room ajar.

I wore ratty old gray sweats, no makeup, and a towel turban on my head. I wasn't making myself pretty for him, and he seemed to get the message that was sent as his eyes skittered away from my face. He strode ahead of me into the relative quiet of the hastily tidied bedroom, sat on the chair and handed me one of the cups.

"What is this?" I asked.

"Mystery punch."

"Ugh." It tasted like cough syrup. "Shellie mixes this up only when she's feeling cheap and trying to make the vodka go further."

"I know. It works, though." Sam took a sip. He was wearing a black waffle-weave Henley shirt with an open button at the neck that showed a tuft of chest hair that matched his neatly trimmed tawny beard. Black jeans and dark, scuffed motorcycle boots completed the impression of a Viking on the lookout for some pillage.

"I appreciate the apology," I said, rubbing my wet hair with the towel. "As I said before, I'm sorry, too. I should have found a way to be honest with you. It's good if we can get along. For Shellie's sake."

"I'd like another chance." Sam's golden eyes were sincere. He stood slowly, as if trying not to spook me with his size. "I told you in New York I knew I needed to bring my A game to win you from these other guys, but that's not what I did. I called you on Fridays and felt virtuous that I wasn't banging other women. I was waiting to bang you."

"Try not to overwhelm me with your sweet words, kind sir," I intoned, in one of the English accents from the play.

Sam laughed. He looked adorable when he did, and I remembered the easy humor that had always been my favorite thing about him.

"Anyway." He now made a theatrical gesture and a showy bow. "I never did any of the things that were suggested to me by experts in the field of love. Send you flowers. Compliments now and again during our phone calls. A card, a gift, even a visit one weekend. Meanwhile, that pirate Rafe really was bringing his A game. Shellie told me about his letters."

My cheeks and neck flamed. "She shouldn't have!"

Sam shrugged. "She got sick of my bitching after the two of you made up. She told me anyone would have given in to the relentless romancing that guy was up to. He's employing some serious long-distance juju on you. And what was I doing? Acting like a spoiled brat. Ambushing you by lying naked in your bed and thinking you'd be happy to hop in with me." He shook his head. "Not a class act. I'm ashamed of myself. Truth is, I've never had to work that hard for anything I wanted. I couldn't quite believe you didn't just fall all over me like everyone else had."

"So did you really bang all those women and tell Shellie to pass the numbers on to me?" A hard note had crept into my voice. "Because I'm hearing a whole lot of disrespect toward women here. Using them for sex, throwing them away. And it seems like I'm only desirable because I'm the one who turned you down. You're acting like I'm something you can win as a prize—with your A game."

Red stained Sam's high cheekbones, and his golden eyes were hot.

"I said that about banging chicks because my pride was hurt. *I was hurt.* I wanted you to be hurt, too. And yeah, I've had a drunken encounter or two in the last couple of months, but nothing like what I said."

"You're one of those men who will someday cheat and tell his wife, "It didn't mean anything, honey. It was just sex," I said, furious. "I'm not your bone to fight over with Rafe or anyone else. I'm single by choice. I'm not playing any games, A or B or C."

We stared at each other for a long moment.

"Noted," Sam said. "I obviously have a lot to learn about having any kind of real relationship. But I'm willing to learn, if you're willing to give me another chance. I can't seem to get over you."

I was taken aback to see a shine of moisture in his eyes, and that more than anything about this stiff-necked, prideful, privileged man made me step toward him and put out a hand. He took it, turned it over. Kissed the palm. His lips were soft but firm, and that beard tickled deliciously and reminded me how much I'd enjoyed his kisses, his vitality, his laughter, his brute strength and playful personality surrounding a steely will.

"I'm a jerk. I know nothing about women. Teach me, your humble servant. You can start by putting me over your knee. And spanking me. Hard. Oh, so hard," he said, batting those lovely eyes.

I was the one to laugh this time.

"I'm not ready for anything right now," I said. I let him hold my hand, though, and now we sat on my bed, something I'd sworn to myself wasn't going to happen. "Why don't you tell me how things have been going this semester?"

We sipped from our red cups and tentatively felt our way toward something a lot like our old comfort with each other.

"I'm done already with finals," he said. "But I needed to see you, to try to clear things up. I know it's not a good time to be in your hair with your play and finals and all, but I'll be around. I'm going to be staying at the Alpha Chi frat house."

"I'm sure that will be a real hardship," I said. "All those parties to keep up with."

"Hey, I'm working! I'm helping with their applications for next year as one of the frat leaders from my school. The future freshmen visit next week, and we're supposed to help convince them they want to pledge our frat. Once they do, that's when the abuse can begin." He grinned evilly. "So what's up with that skinny dude Shellie's seeing? It's not serious, is it?"

"I don't know," I said thoughtfully. "Phillip's got more substance to him than I thought at first. I think Shellie needed someone to really adore her, and he does. He came along at the right time."

"Well, he better not hurt my baby sister," Sam growled. "I'll break him in half."

I couldn't help grinning. "You sound just like Shellie when she confronted me after spring break. She was ready to beat me up in the hallway for breaking her brother's heart. Called me a lot of names and pushed me around. Kicked my door, too."

Sam smiled. "You did break my pride, at least. And my heart, too, a little. If I'm totally honest."

"I'm so sorry," I whispered. "It hurt me to hurt you."

And next thing I knew, I was in Sam's lap and he was kissing my neck, that delightful beardy feeling sending shivers of pleasure to my entirely too-celibate hot spot. He nuzzled and moaned with the delight of rubbing his face on my chest, mashing my breasts against his cheeks with his big hands, a feeling like a delicious marauding that made me arch and moan.

Finally we were kissing, and Sam's huge arms seemed to fold me into his body, making me feel tiny and petite but also powerful. Because I knew without a doubt now that, somehow, Sam the frat-boy football player, Viking son of privilege, had fallen for me.

"I want you to teach me," Sam whispered, his rough voice

stirring the hair beside my ear. "Teach me how to be the kind of man you could love."

I pulled back and held Sam's face in my hands, stroked his bearded cheeks with my thumbs. The gesture reminded me wrenchingly of when Rafe had done the same thing to my face, wiping away my tears with the balls of his thumbs.

Oh, Rafe.

Could he really be sailing all the way from San Francisco to meet me? The latest letter I'd received was postmarked North Carolina, and that had been a week ago. I couldn't tell what I felt about the possibility of his arrival—a terrible excitement? A frightening joy, a sickening anticipation, a scared euphoria?

Everything was mixed up in my feelings about Rafe and always had been.

How I felt about Sam would always be simpler. Easier.

"You're already someone I could love," I said. "You big Neanderthal. You always were." I kissed him, and he squeezed me so hard my ribs creaked and my spine crackled, and he stroked his hands through my damp hair, growling puppy noises into my neck, and made me laugh.

CHAPTER THIRTEEN

I hit the top note of the last song with the rest of the cast, and the curtains whisked shut on our last performance of *Oliver!* At this moment in May of 1984, I'd just survived my freshman year of college, finals week, and my first acting and singing experience in a major production. And I was, regrettably, still a virgin.

Applause lifted around us in a rolling, enthusiastic wave, and my castmates and I grinned at one another, giddy with excitement.

I ran to my curtain-call spot. The curtains whisked open. We held hands and bowed, and then, in turn, each of us in major roles stepped forward.

I felt my cheeks flame to match my red hair as a rose bounced off of me when I stood from my bow, causing a ripple of laughter. I was almost sure I heard Sam's baritone voice bellow, "Yeah, Ruby!"

I scooped up the rose and stepped back. The curtains closed with a swish, and we turned to one another, hugging and hysterical.

It was a good while later when I came out into the lobby,

changed out of my greasepaint and costume and wearing my usual jeans and Northeastern University hoodie.

"You were amazing!" Sam, my not-boyfriend, swung me up in his arms, spinning me around so that my legs flew out. I squeaked with delighted surprise. "I had no idea you had pipes on you like that."

"I'm full of surprises," I said, and then Sam's sister, Shellie, was hugging me and pressing an armload of roses on me, along with their parents, who'd come down to help Shellie pack to return to New York for the summer.

The reminder of summer gave me a quaver of worry. I had no idea what I was doing this summer, and I was pretty sure I couldn't just camp out in the dorm.

The chaos of well-wishing went on awhile, as this was the last performance of the season, on the last weekend of school of the season, and on the way out of the lobby I even hugged Henry, my first-ever not-boyfriend, and thanked him for the silver rose he handed me shyly.

"For your pile," he said.

Sam looped an arm possessively over me, but I shrugged it off. "Thanks, Henry. Have a great summer."

I pressed on, past Henry and the rest, determined to get back to my room for a shower before the big cast party being held at the drama professor's house. Sam refused to be brushed off and followed me.

Meanwhile, my eyes kept searching.

Searching, searching, searching through the full lobby. Looking, whether I wanted to admit it or not, for a tall figure with shoulder-length, bronzy-chocolate hair, big shoulders, and cobalt eyes that could see for miles across an open sea.

I was looking for my most devastatingly attractive not-boyfriend, Rafe.

But Rafe McCallum wasn't there.

I turned to Sam with a bright smile. "I'll race you back to the dorm. Here." I thrust all the roses and flowers into his arms and ran out the door.

I used all the adrenaline from the performance and all the angst I'd felt in a disappointment I wouldn't even admit to myself, to power myself at top speed across the open campus, dodging around groups of people. Sam laughed somewhere behind me—impromptu racing wasn't unusual behavior for either of us.

I ran through the moist, cool night as fast as I could, trying not to feel crushing disappointment that Rafe hadn't seen my performance.

I knew I'd sung and acted better tonight than I ever had, imagining him in the audience. I didn't even know where Rafe was right now, except that he was somewhere on the ocean on the *Creamy Maid*, the yacht he crewed for, and it had seemed from the letters he'd posted along the way that the ship might be making its way from San Francisco to Boston.

I'd hoped it was. Wished it was. The last letter I'd had from him had been a week ago, postmarked from North Carolina. It had seemed possible that the *Maid* might have made it this far by now, but I was probably deluding myself.

I could hear Sam thundering along behind me, his laughing shout. "Ruby, you wild woman! Slow down. I can't see over all these flowers!"

Sam was my roommate Shellie's brother, and in the dating misadventures of Ruby Day Michaels, he was, along with Rafe, one of two guys I still cared about. I was single now and not dating anyone, but Sam had reappeared in my life after classes at Cornell let out and had been putting the moves on me all week since.

And meanwhile, I couldn't stop looking for Rafe, and I'd hoped he'd somehow make it to see my play.

How unrealistic is that? I berated myself. He didn't even

know I was in a play. I hadn't communicated with him since our breakup after spring break, and even though I still had the gorgeous ruby ring he'd given me stashed in the metal leg of my bed, I hadn't communicated one word that might cause him to come all this way.

Sailing his ship.

None of that had stopped me from hoping wildly, crazy conflicted fool that I was, that somehow he'd make it to see me before Northeastern shut down for the summer.

I reached the doors of our dorm and waited for Sam to catch up. "Sam, would you mind meeting me at the cast party in half an hour? I need to shower, change, and decompress for a few minutes."

Sam stood breathing hard. He looked hunky and adorable in the amber security light near the door, his arms piled high with my flowers, six feet of rock-hard football player with a neatly trimmed tawny beard and golden eyes that never failed to move me in some way.

He handed me the flowers.

I could see the disappointment in his face. It felt like kicking a Labrador puppy. But Sam had been crowding me a bit much this week after we'd supposedly set some rules for our relationship—i.e., that we weren't having one. We were simply spending time as friends when it worked out for either of us.

But the friendship I had with Sam had always been a sexy one, and he was having trouble keeping his hands to himself. Now that my arms were full of flowers, he took my face in his hands and I saw my green eyes reflected in his for just a second before his mouth came down on mine, all hungry, manly deliciousness.

I sighed out a breath into his mouth, leaning into him, the flowers crushing between us and releasing their scent in a heady wave. When he'd thoroughly plundered my mouth, he stepped back.

"Now I'll go," he said, and turned to lope off.

That was Sam. Steely will, physical presence, humor and friendship all in one complicated package.

But nowhere near as complicated as Rafe.

Surfer, sailor, drifter. Renaissance man. Someone who knew how to use his hands. And his mouth, too, and everything everywhere in between.

I pushed into the building, deserted tonight with all the parties and half the students gone home already. I clumped wearily up the stairs to the fourth floor, where our dorm suite was, feeling ninety rather than nineteen, the adrenaline buzz worn off.

I'd told myself I wasn't going to worry about anything until after finals and the play. *Then* I'd worry about this summer. Though my parents had saved all year to pay my way back to Saint Thomas, I wasn't at all sure home was where I wanted to go right now.

I didn't know where I wanted to go.

I pushed open the exit from the stairwell and stopped in my tracks. My jaw dropped at the sight of pure male magnificence on my doorstep. Rafe McCallum was leaning against the battered entry of our dorm room.

CHAPTER FOURTEEN

"Rafe!" I cried, and ran forward, dropping the flowers at his feet and flinging myself into his arms, leaping up onto him. He staggered back, laughing, having no choice but to heft me up against him as my legs crossed around his waist and my arms tugged his mouth down to mine in ecstatic greeting.

He shifted me higher, so our crotches were in alignment, and settled his hands over my ass to hold me up, as my arms clung to his neck and I kissed him in a clumsy frenzy.

"I'm happy to see you, too," he muttered between kisses.

"I thought you might be coming here," I gasped. "I hoped. From the route the *Maid* was taking. I told myself I shouldn't be hoping. I hadn't done anything but break up with you...But your letters..."

He wrenched his mouth from mine for a second. "They worked?"

"Oh, they worked all right, you pirate." I felt his hands, those clever, agile, hardworking hands, sliding along my ass crack to hold me up against him, and I loved the dark tension of the slightly painful grip he had on me. "And that jewelry box on my birthday. Oh God."

We kissed some more, and I thanked whatever impulse had told me to send Sam away. This would have been a very different greeting if I'd met Rafe with Sam in tow.

"Your performance was amazing." Rafe gazed into my eyes. "You're so full of passion, Ruby. Everything you do shines with it. You literally light up a room."

"Oh, you saw it, then." I felt the blush roar up my chest and across my fair skin to make my cheeks burn. Being a redhead had its downsides, and blushes were one of the many.

"Wouldn't have missed it."

"How did you even know?"

"I asked your resident assistant. He knew where you were, that it was your last performance. Can we go inside now?"

"Oh, jeez. I'm sorry." I dropped my legs, but he didn't seem in any hurry to let me down, still holding my ass tightly so that I was plastered against him.

"I couldn't forget how great you felt in my arms, but this is even better than I remembered," he murmured, and kissed me for a long while. I felt my whole body going soft, pliable and molded to his tall, chiseled frame. My hands stroked through his bronzy hair, even longer than usual and past his shoulders, wandered over the planes of his lightly stubbled face, around the tender curve of his ear.

Finally, he released me. I staggered and we laughed, and I got my key out and unlocked the outer door as Rafe picked up the flowers and followed me in when I unlocked the door of my room.

"Looks like a dorm room." He peered over the battered flowers at my humble surroundings.

"Looks like a bomb went off in here," I apologized. "I've had a crazy schedule with full-time rehearsal, work, and finals."

Rafe cleared off the one chair and sat on it. "What were you going to do before I waylaid you in the hall? I'm sure there's something you should be going to."

"Yes. A cast party. But I'd rather catch up with you," I said. "I just need a quick shower first."

My face flamed again, remembering the last time we'd showered together, and I saw in his unwavering cobalt gaze that he remembered, too.

"I could use a shower as well," he murmured. "Okay if I join you?"

"Oh God," I muttered, and it was a prayer. Was I really going to just jump on him, with Sam's kisses still on my mouth? I was right back in my terrible dilemma about who to be with—and the stakes felt even higher now.

"Much as I'd like that, we'd better not," I said. "I couldn't help how I said hi to you, but I'm still technically on a man time-out."

"So that's Sam. The big guy with the beard. I saw you together outside the building."

Rafe knew about Sam, but the last time we'd talked, I'd told him we'd broken up. Unfortunately, it had been a little harder to maintain than I'd anticipated, and if Rafe'd seen us outside the building, he'd seen Sam kiss me.

"Yeah, that's Sam," I said miserably. "Can you maybe find something to put the flowers in while I shower? We'll talk after."

He just nodded, and I went into the bathroom, locked the door, and leaned on it, shutting my eyes for a long, breathless moment.

"I'm really in the pickle jar now," I muttered. One of my mom's sayings. I longed for her with a sudden fierceness, her warm hugs, her strong arms, her certainty about right and wrong. What would Mom do?

"Rafe," I whispered. Mom had already told me who had her

vote. But she'd never been practical like I was. She was a dreamer, and that dream had led her to marry my dad and spend her life as an impoverished missionary in the Virgin Islands.

I was going to do different things and have different things. Like a career, and money, and security. I stripped off my clothes as I thought of how many things I wanted different from what my mother had. Things I could have with Sam but probably not with Rafe.

And Rafe had made things all or nothing by refusing to sleep with me until we were married and by giving me a ring that was totally over-the-top—an antique star ruby that was nearly irresistible.

It actually made me mad now, thinking of it, as I turned on the water of the shower. He shouldn't be able to hold out on me, tell me what kind of sex we could have and when, and use my lust for him to get me to marry him.

Emotional blackmail. That's what it was!

On a wave of that anger, I opened the door and stuck my head around it. "Your ring is in the hollow metal leg of my bed. Left side. You can take it out of there and take it with you."

Rafe hadn't moved from the chair directly across from the door, and his deep-sea eyes seemed to burn as he stared at me. "Did you know there's a mirror behind you?"

I turned my head to look. Rafe had a clear view over my shoulder of my bent-over ass, dangling breasts, even the tuft of bright hair between my legs. It looked like some porn-star fantasy pose. No wonder he hadn't appeared to register what I was saying about the ring while getting such an eyeful.

"Emotional blackmailer!" I exclaimed, and slammed the door and locked it.

I planned to fully explain that comment to Rafe in detail when I got out of the shower.

I washed my hair, fuming, shaved everything that could be

shaved, and even blow-dried, thinking sulkily about Rafe waiting outside and hoping to make him half as irritated as I was.

It was totally deflating to find the room empty when I finally came out. The flowers had been trimmed and arranged in a water bottle whose plastic top had been cut off. I wondered how he'd done it—probably with that Buck knife he carried around.

I spotted a note on my cluttered student desk, written with the plume-quilled pen I'd affected in my persona of Juliette, a French-speaking character I'd made up and pretended to be for a while, to help adjust to life in Boston.

Dear Ruby,

I know you have more to say to me on the subject of emotional blackmail, but you need not bother to explain further because I know exactly what you're referring to.
I'm not ashamed to say I'll use any means, fair or foul, to bind you to me. And if that means a long, slow seduction, so much the better.

I was hasty with the proposal and the ring, but I didn't want you to leave San Francisco without knowing how very deeply I feel and how serious I am about making you mine. I found the ring and removed it, but I hope you'll wear it someday, and someday I'll tell you why it's special.
There will be a "First Night," and a hundred thousand more.

I love you, Ruby, my creamy maid.
—Rafe

"Damn his poetic soul," I muttered, my hand against my throat, completely undone by the words in his elegant penmanship with the old-fashioned plume. My anger was completely gone, leaving nothing but sweet longing for him. I looked franti-cally for some way to contact him—a phone number? An address?

Nothing. Just the note.

The towel fell off, and I paid no heed, frantically picking up the bed by its leg to check the hollow leg of the bed—and sure enough, the little black velvet box holding the amazing ruby ring was gone.

He was gone.

I felt devastated. Hollowed out, furious, abandoned, and lust-ful, too, a volcano of sexual frustration. My body must have thought it was going to get some release soon, because my itch was back, worse than ever and compounded by the lack of outlet.

I wanted to scream and have a tantrum like a two-year-old.

I had no way to contact Rafe. I had to wait for him to contact me. More of his mind games. Now I saw it how Sam had seen it. I was being played by a master with an A game. *I'm not ashamed to say I'll use any means, fair or foul, to bind you to me.*

What would drive Rafe wild? Make him share my frustra-tion? Make him as miserable as I was?

If I could find a way to be sexually satisfied without him. I could choose Sam, and not Rafe, and sleep with Sam. But I cared about Sam too much to hurt him by using him that way when I wasn't at all sure if we should be together.

I hated the situation I was in, and I had no idea how to get out of it, and right this minute I was no closer to knowing who I really wanted. At least I'd shucked off Henry and didn't have one more complication. I promptly felt ashamed of thinking of poor Henry that way. And now I had a party to go to.

I really was a terrible person.

The buzzing of these unpleasant thoughts preoccupied me as I dressed all in black: black turtleneck, black jeans, black zip-up heeled boots. My freshly washed and blow-dried hair floated around me like an iridescent red cape.

I put the platinum heart Sam had given me at winter break on over the turtleneck. It glowed on its sparkling chain like a starry promise.

Maybe it was too much of a promise. I didn't want Sam getting the wrong idea.

I took it off and grabbed my purse and my old pea coat and hurried out the door.

The party was in full swing when I finally arrived. I did hugs and kisses and congratulations with my castmates, and we took photos, and finally Sam spotted me and joined me, looping a hand proprietarily around my waist. I removed it, still talking with the director.

"No, I'm not sure what I'm doing this summer," I said. "Either staying here in Boston and getting a summer job, or going home to Saint Thomas."

"I know which one I'd choose," the director's wife said. "But if you do decide to stay, I need someone to help me with child care now that the kids are out of school."

"Thanks for the offer," I said, smiling. "I'll let you know."

"Or you could come to New York and spend the summer with Shellie and me," Sam said as he tugged me away and bracketed me into a corner. "What took you so long?"

"I had to blow-dry my hair." I held up a drifting handful of the shiny red tresses. "It takes forever."

Sam was frowning, but his face softened as he ran a hand though it, thrusting his face into my neck and inhaling. "Mmm. I love that watermelon shampoo you use."

"It's cheap." I was still feeling agitated and not sure what to do with those feelings.

"Shellie said she saw a guy in the lobby at the play that looked a lot like what you said Rafe looks like."

Now I knew why there was a deep dent between Sam's brows and his eyes were narrowed.

"Yeah. We said hi." I was done with lies. "I gave him back his ring."

"You saw him?" Sam's voice climbed into a higher register, and he grabbed my shoulders. "He gave you a ring?"

"Let go of me."

He did.

"I have some unfinished business with him. But don't forget, I'm not with either of you right now. So stop acting all jealous. It's a turnoff." I could feel my mouth compressing into a tight line. "In fact, I'm going to enjoy my cast party with my theater friends. I'd appreciate it if you went to your frat house and tortured some freshmen or something."

Sam drew back. "You're being a real bitch right now," he said in astonishment.

"Yeah, well." I folded my arms. "Deal with it."

"I'll be in touch." Sam shouldered away through the crowd.

I needed alcohol and lots of it. I headed for the bowl of spiked punch.

My friend Colin, who'd performed as Oliver in the play, helped me back to the dorm on one side and Elise, one of the street vendors, held up my other side. I thought drunkenly, as they poured me into bed, that I'd probably lost my chance to get hired as the drama director's nanny after my drinking at the party.

And then I had no further thoughts on any subject.

CHAPTER FIFTEEN

The next morning came way too soon, and with it, Shellie pounding on the door. After I let her in, she handed me coffee. "Sam says you saw Rafe yesterday."

"I'm getting sick of the two of you spying on me and passing news back and forth." I sipped the coffee, feeling surly and bedraggled. "Sam's getting to be a real pain in my ass."

"He'd like to be a lot more of a pain, if you get my meaning," Shellie said, obviously making an effort not to be offended by my grumpy words.

"Like he'd let me forget that for two minutes," I grumbled. "I am trying to navigate this situation, and it's not easy, let me tell you."

"Well, I get it now that I clapped eyes on Rafe. Talk about a long, tall drink of Take Me Now."

I laughed, then clutched my head. "Yeah. And Sam's pretty delicious, too—not that I expect you to want to hear that about your brother. So I'm in a real situation here."

"Well, Sam is sincere in inviting you to New York with us, but I'm not sure that's a good idea," Shellie said.

I flapped a hand. "I agree. I need to either go home and spend time with my family on Saint Thomas, or find gainful employment."

"Well, I'm almost done packing. I feel bad just leaving you here with no plan."

"It's time I got one," I said. "Gimme a heads-up when you're leaving, will you? So I can come say goodbye to you."

"And Sam, too. He's coming back with Mom and Dad and me."

"And Sam. Double good reason for me to get out of bed and brush my teeth." I hauled my hungover carcass into the bathroom.

I could have used another cup of coffee or four, but at least I was dressed with my hair braided and a little mascara and lip gloss on when Shellie knocked on the door. "We're heading out."

"Okay." I helped carry some of Shellie's many boxes down to the U-Haul the Williamses had rented to transport her things back to New York. Sam was there, working hard and looking amazing in a skimpy black tank top and basketball shorts, but he barely looked at me and grunted in response to comments from his family.

Good. I didn't want to talk to him either.

It was going to be better to say goodbye and figure out my summer with all these distractions out of my hair, but I felt anxious and a little like a puppy being abandoned as I hugged Shellie and we finalized our plans to room together again next year, this time in an off-campus apartment.

The Williamses got into the SUV with Shellie in the back-seat and the U-Haul attached. They waved and drove away, but large and surly Sam was left standing beside me on the sidewalk.

I frowned. "Why didn't you go with them?"

"I drove here in my own car." He gestured to a red Camaro parked nearby.

"Of course," I said dryly. "Rich frat boys have their own cars."

Sam looked like Thor in a snit as he put his hands on his hips and lowered his brows. "Whatever. I invited you to New York and you didn't even have the courtesy to respond."

"Sam. You know that's a bad idea. Even Shellie didn't think it was a good one. I have to either go home or find a job, and I'm leaning toward going home." I glanced around at the already-deserted campus. "This place is a graveyard already."

"Well, I'm not leaving with us mad at each other."

"So you get to tell how it is, do you?" Sam's comment reminded me too much of Rafe. Rafe's rules. Rafe setting the agenda. Rafe deciding when and how we'd have sex. Rafe wanting to marry me. "I don't appreciate how you've been crowding me."

"I hate knowing that he's here somewhere. And he's going to make a move on you while I'm gone."

Yes, Rafe was looming large between us. I wasn't going to deny that.

"Sam." I put my hands on his thick shoulders and looked into his eyes. "You have to let go. What will be, will be. You can't make me do something. I know how you feel, how frustrated you are. Believe me when I tell you, I'm frustrated right now, too. I am trying to figure out what to do."

Sam stared down at me with those golden, long-lashed eyes. I noticed all the colors in them—green, and rust, and even a fleck of purple—and once more they reminded me of the toads I'd had such an affection for on Saint Thomas.

"I wish it was like the olden days and I could fight him for you," Sam whispered, his eyes intense, his voice rough.

My nipples tightened and I felt a zing at the thought of a bare-chested Rafe facing down a bare-chested Sam, perhaps wearing loincloths. Would they fight with swords? Or bare-handed? God, I'd love to see that, and be the spoils that went to the victor—or perhaps it would be a tie and we could all do it together?

I still found that damn sexy. I stepped up to Sam, hooked an arm around his neck, and drew him down for a kiss that showed him just how sexy I thought that would be.

Sometime later he detached himself. "We're alone now. You said you don't want to be a virgin anymore. Want to go upstairs? We can take care of business. I even have a condom."

He patted his back pocket, smiling like a Viking jumping off his dragon boat in front of a tasty village lass.

I found the words sticking in my mouth. "Wow, you're right. I did say that. And thanks for the offer. But I'm on a man time-out, remember? And if we had sex, don't you think it would be like we were together?"

I found I was having a hard time being casual about my first time now that I was on the spot about it. Here was Sam, offering me the perfect foil for Rafe's "emotional blackmail." Wouldn't it fix his wagon, as Mom would say, if I slept with Sam just to deal with the virginity thing?

It would be a blow I doubted Rafe would recover from.

"Would it be such a bad thing for us to be together?" I thought I saw a calculating gleam in Sam's eye.

He knew exactly what he was doing. He was trying to beat Rafe to get into my pants. He definitely wanted to get there first, but I wasn't at all sure it was for my benefit.

"No thanks," I said firmly, stepping back. "I won't have a phone number after the dorms close, but I'll call you and Shellie when I know what's happening with my summer. And I'll see you when I see you."

"Dammit, Ruby." He grabbed my hand and gave it a yank that pulled me against his broad heat. "That was crude, how I asked you. I'm a crude guy. But I mean it. There's nothing I'd rather do than spend the next few days here with you, getting to know our way around the bedroom. I promise I'd make it good for you."

"Sam. Thanks. But no." I tried to pull away.

"You know what? I think you've already made your choice." He let go and pushed away from me. "I've wasted enough time on you. I've been more miserable since I met you than at any time in my whole life."

He spun and walked away. I covered my face with my hands, feeling the blast of his hurt. I pretended not to hear his muffled curses, the sound of his boot kicking a trash can, and then the roar of the Camaro firing up and peeling out.

"It must be love if you're that miserable, Sam, and I'm sorry. Because I think you're right. I have made my choice," I whispered to the taillights of the sports car.

CHAPTER SIXTEEN

Back in the dorm, I went to the RA's office.

"Hey."

Kenny was a tall, geeky guy with the kind of patchy beard that should be dealt with some other way than being allowed to grow. He was packing up his office, a tiny closet at the end of the hall on the first floor.

"Hey, Ruby. Saw the play. You were awesome."

"Thanks. Listen, I'm wondering how long I get to be in the room before the building shuts down."

"Well, till the end of the week."

Today was Sunday.

"You mean next Friday?"

"Yeah."

He must have seen my expression because he said, "You got somewhere to go?"

"I'm sure I do," I said. "I'm just not sure where."

"Hey, did Rafe find you? The sailor guy?"

I felt an immediate heat in my cheeks. "He did, thanks. Did he say where his boat is berthed?"

Kenny straightened up, eyes twinkling. "You should see if they need another deckhand or something. That's what I'd do." I belatedly remembered Kenny was gay, and I grinned back at him.

"Not a bad idea."

"Well, he said they were anchored at the South Boston Yacht Club. I asked him some questions, you know, to make sure I wasn't siccing some psycho on one of our students."

"I'll bet." My cheeks were fiery now, but I winked back at him. "I think I might just do that. I'll be out by the end of the week." I waved goodbye and headed down the hall.

I didn't have time to wait around until Rafe decided to get in touch. I had to find somewhere to be by the end of the week, and I needed to talk to him first.

There are a lot of places to park a yacht in and around Boston, a fact that made me very glad to at least have the correct name of where the *Creamy Maid* was berthed.

It wasn't nearby.

I had to take the subway and two buses before I ended up at the waterfront where the large, intimidating structure of the South Boston Yacht Club building fronted the sparkling ocean.

I'd worn a hat because the sun was high and bright. I tried to walk around the building confidently and like I knew where I was going. The wind off the bay kept yanking at the hat, a straw boater style Shellie had given me that was more cute than functional. I had decided the look for a yacht club should be preppy, so I'd worn a kelly-green polo shirt, denim shorts, and leather boat shoes, but the same wind that yanked at my hat made me realize a parka might have been a good idea.

There were very few boats moored at the main dock, and I saw with a sinking heart that most of the bigger yachts were anchored far out in the bay. It was going to be a much bigger production to find and reach the *Creamy Maid* than it had been in San Francisco.

I finally worked up my nerve to approach a grizzled-looking older guy scrubbing the deck of one of the boats tied up at the dock.

"Excuse me. I'm looking for the *Creamy Maid*. Can you tell me how to find her?" It sounded funny to talk about the boat like that, but I was pretty sure that's how people discussed boats.

Like they were women.

"Ask at the yacht club information desk," the salty dog said, pointing, eyeballing me up and down.

"Thanks."

I felt more comfortable inside the venerable building than I had expected. It had the kind of old-world, shabby charm evident in a lot of the buildings on Saint Thomas, and I felt a pang of homesickness.

I approached the well-groomed blond teenager at the information desk. "Hi. I'm trying to get hold of someone on the *Creamy Maid*. Can you tell me how to do that?"

The teenager looked me up and down, much as the salty dog had, and clearly my preppy outfit was the wrong color or style or something. "We have a ship-to-shore phone directory," the kid said, pushing an old-fashioned logbook over. "You can call from that phone." He pointed a finger.

"Thanks." I looked through the book, which was simple. Recent entries were listed with a number beside them by the order they'd arrived. A date was entered when the boat left, and the number was reassigned. I steeled myself to speak to male strangers and explain my embarrassing mission to find Rafe. I felt like a hooker or a groupie, invading this male sanctuary.

Finally, I found the number and, copying it on a scrap of paper, saluted the teen. "Thanks."

He bobbed his head, going back to the Rubik's Cube he was working as I walked across the battered, luxurious Persian carpet of the main room. I dialed the old-fashioned rotary phone, my fingers trembling.

"*Creamy Maid*," came a brisk voice, and in surprise, I recognized it.

"Rafe?"

"Ruby?" He sounded astonished. "Where are you?"

"In the lobby of the yacht club." I put my hand on my throat to keep my voice from trembling. "Can we talk?"

A long pause. I looked out the bank of windows at the sparkling green water of the bay peppered with yachts, wondering which one was the *Maid*.

"I'm just thinking the best way to go about this," he said.

"I'm sorry to bug you at work. It's just that I had no way to contact you, and I have to be out of the dorms by the end of the week, and I don't know where I'm going or what I'm doing," I said in a rush, putting my hand up against my flushed cheek. "I wanted to—I don't know. I need to figure out what to do. So I wanted to talk."

"I understand." His voice was brisk, still in work mode. "I should have left you a number. I didn't realize you were on such a tight schedule. I'll be over shortly."

"I'm sorry," I said again, but I was speaking to a dial tone.

I hung the phone up and went to one of the comfy, saggy old velvet chairs clustered in groups around low tables filled with sailing magazines and newspapers.

I watched the boats through the window. I considered going outside, but I could see tiny whitecaps, and I knew I'd be standing on the dock, holding my stupid hat on my head, feeling and looking awkward.

A small white Zodiac appeared, bobbing over the whitecaps, and I recognized the shoulders and the whipping long hair.

Rafe.

I took the hat off as I walked out of the lobby, and my hair promptly whirled around my head like a dervish as Rafe drew the tender up to the dock and cut the engine. He hopped up onto the dock and tied the little boat off.

He walked toward me with that graceful stalking stride, wearing cutoff jeans and a black T-shirt with the sleeves ripped off.

He looked dangerous and poor.

I remembered thinking that when I first met him, and finding it scary.

But I discovered, my heart thundering as he approached me, that I didn't care about that anymore. I was more of a dreamer than I'd known. Because I wanted him anyway.

I wanted to be with him. Even if it meant we spent long times apart while he worked on yachts and sailed the world. I wanted to be with him, even if I had to keep working at jobs like the student cafeteria for the rest of my life.

I wanted Rafe, to be his and for him to be mine.

I wished there had been some easier way to come to this conclusion.

Two more long strides and he stood looming over me, just a little too close. I could smell sunshine, sweat, and salt on him. His eyes were a piercing nautical blue under his dark brows. He still intimidated me, but I knew now that I was as strong as he was, in my own way. I straightened my spine and looked him in the eye.

"Yes," I said.

"What?"

"Yes. That's it. No seat belts. I'll take my chances." He'd said I'd have to ride with him that way back on our first date.

He threw his head back and laughed. He was gorgeous and mesmerizing as he did so. And then he crushed me in a bone-cracking hug, lifted me so our crotches were aligned, and kissed me silly.

"Everybody's looking," I muttered. "I feel like a groupie, coming here."

"That's 'cause only groupies, sailors, and boat owners come here. But you're my groupie, so it's okay. Come inside. We have to talk." He took my hand, and we went into the yacht club building.

"Hey, Captain McCallum," said the teenager respectfully, looking at me with new eyes.

"Hey," he said, tugging me past as we headed toward the dining room. "You hungry? We can get some lunch."

I tried to tug my hand out of his. "Captain? I thought you were a deckhand."

"How do you think I got to bring the *Maid* all the way from San Francisco to Boston?"

I opened and shut my mouth a couple of times as we reached the dining room, thinking of all the millions of questions I'd never asked and he'd never told me. I felt very young and stupid all of a sudden. Self-absorbed, too.

To be fair, he'd never volunteered much either, even in all those letters.

The dining room was another place that reminded me of the gently worn, gracious old-gentry enclaves of Saint Thomas. We got a window seat, and I held my slightly greasy, laminated menu, staring at it without seeing.

It appeared my seat-belt-free, taking-chances ride had already begun. What did I really know about Rafe McCallum?

Rafe pushed down the menu to see my face. "You look pale."

"I feel a little sick. I can't believe I just told you I'd marry you."

Now he paled a bit. "Is that what that was? I thought—never mind."

"What? The offer was off the table?" I dropped the menu, scrambling to get up and flee.

"No, no, no." He grabbed my hand, tugged me to sit back down. "This is classic. I just thought you'd decided to ditch Sam and pick me. I can't believe you're ready to jump all the way into the deep end of the pool."

"I thought that was the only option you were giving me," I said. My eyes felt too wide, my lips were numb, and it was hard to speak. A waitress approached, but Rafe waved her away, keeping a hard grip on my hand as he gazed into my eyes with his deep-sea ones.

"Come to think of it, I guess it was," he whispered. "Will you marry me, Ruby Day Michaels?"

"Yes, I will, God help me," I said. I was terrified and excited and felt the color flame back into my face.

"Holy crap." He tugged my hand and pulled me from my chair around to his side and onto his lap.

We kissed for a good long time that way, and I felt the rightness of it all the way down to my bones.

Yeah, dangerous and poor he was. And now there would be two of us.

The waitress had returned, and she cleared her throat. "Did you want to order something?"

I made to get up, but Rafe kept me unapologetically clamped in place on his lap. "Yes. We'll both have burgers and Cokes. We just got engaged, so we're a little happy over here."

"Oh, congratulations!" the waitress exclaimed. "Well, carry on, then."

So we did.

CHAPTER SEVENTEEN

Much later we walked along the dock. I was in a state of euphoria so extreme it actually reminded me of the misery of leaving him in San Francisco. My feet felt too far away and I felt untethered, as if I would float away and be lost somewhere over the Atlantic—but as long as Rafe was with me, it didn't matter.

"Practical concerns," Rafe said, swinging one hand as I held the ridiculous hat on with the other. "I'm not gonna lie—this is a little unexpected. So I'm adjusting the sails, so to speak. I have to call your dad, ask permission to marry you. Then I think we can do something quick on board the *Maid* with one of my captain friends."

I stopped, turned to face him. "But I think my family will want to be there!"

"Do you really want to wait until we can sail to Saint Thomas for a proper ceremony?" He lifted my hand, nibbled on the tips of my fingers. "Because I don't think either of us can wait that long. We'll go there for a honeymoon and redo the ceremony at your church."

"You're being silly. The actual wedding's a technicality," I argued, even as pleasure sizzled down my nerve endings to melt my resistance. "I said I'd marry you. Let's just go—to bed." I knew my priorities.

"Yes, let's. As soon as we get married. I'll get you back to the dorm and you can pack your things." He turned me around and we walked briskly back to the yacht club building. I felt almost delirious, like I was going to wake up from a bizarre and fast-moving dream any minute, but Rafe was still talking in that unfamiliar brisk work mode. "I need to get on the phone, take care of some business."

That's how I came to be standing in the middle of my room in something of a daze as two sturdy sailors from the *Maid* threw my paltry possessions into boxes, hauled my meager furniture to the corner for campus recycling, and then set about cleaning and scrubbing with the same uncomplaining energy they'd already impressed me with.

I got back to the docks in short order after checking out of the dorm, escorted by the two sailors in the yacht club's truck with all my stuff. Not that there was much of it. What I had fit into a storage locker assigned to the *Maid*.

Rafe then put me in a hotel next to the yacht club for the night. "Don't argue," he said against my mouth. "I'll be back to get you in the morning. I'm sending something for you to wear."

I looked at my one suitcase with the broken wheel. All I'd arrived in Boston with and now all I was leaving with. There were so many unanswered questions, like what the hell we were doing, but I was scared to ask them. I felt swept along by a force greater than myself, greater than Rafe even, and it turned out I was enough of an adventurer to want to see where it led.

But that didn't mean I wanted to be abandoned in a hotel.

"Don't you want to stay? And, um...convince me this is a good idea?" I knew I sounded plaintive, but this so wasn't how I'd imagined it would be the night before my wedding. If I'd ever had such secret fantasies, they'd involved lots of bridesmaids and other silliness. It was going to be just me, alone in a hotel room, waiting for Rafe to come get me like a bundle of laundry he'd dropped off.

He stopped and seemed to really see me for the first time since he went into a frenzy of mysterious arrangements. He cupped my face, brushed my lips with his. "Oh, Ruby. God. I'm trying to do the right thing here," he breathed into my mouth.

"Don't. Just be with me," I begged.

He stepped back into the room and shut the door. "Maybe you do need a little convincing," he said. "A preview of coming attractions can't hurt."

My heart sped up to trip-hammer speed as he swiftly shucked off the long-sleeved crewneck sweater and jeans he wore. Clad only in those black silk boxers I thought looked amazing on him, he draped the clothes over a nearby chair. "But first," he said nonchalantly, "we need to call your parents."

"Oh God," I said, my eyes filling. "They're going to hate this."

"Not as much as they'd hate you moving into my cabin on the *Maid*, which is what I'm going to tell them is the alternative."

"I'm going to let you have fun with that, since this is all your idea," I said, sticking my tongue out at him. "I need a shower." And I went into the bathroom and turned on the water.

I was just soaping up when Rafe thrust the receiver into the shower. "Tell them you're okay and I haven't kidnapped you or something."

I would have laughed at his disgruntled face and tone if I hadn't known he was perfectly serious.

"Ruby!" My dad's voice was an alarmed shout I could hear a

foot away. "What the hell is going on?" Dad must have been really freaked out to use the word "hell."

I shut the water off, but now I was standing there stark naked, holding the phone and looking at Rafe with my father's angry voice vibrating between us. Rafe shut his eyes and handed me a towel, which I plastered against my front as I took the phone.

"Hi, Daddy. It's all okay."

"He asked permission to marry you!"

"It's legit," I said, smiling at Rafe. "He apparently really wants to."

"I told him you're a handful, and he said he was well aware."

I frowned at this. "I thought you wanted to see if I wanted to marry him, Daddy. I'm not sure whose side you're on."

My dad's voice had calmed down. "Well, honey, you know our values. I know perfectly well you'd never go along with something you didn't want to do. We want to be there to make sure you're happy."

"I'm happy," I said, and held Rafe's eyes as I said it. "I've never been happier."

Rafe stripped off his boxers and stepped into the shower with me, taking me in his arms, towel and all. He held me and kissed the top of my head as I talked to Mom and then Pearl, and finally, when everyone was reassured we were coming straight to Saint Thomas for a redo of the ceremony, which they could plan to a tee, I set the phone down outside the shower.

"I believe we were going to have a preview of the coming attractions," Rafe said.

"Yes. I think I still need some convincing you're the right guy for me. I've been really confused." I said it dead serious, and he tipped up my chin and looked into my eyes, his narrowed, and that's when I grabbed a tuft of chest hair and tugged. "I'm a little mad at your emotional blackmail. I mean, it worked. But I'm still a little mad."

"All's fair in love and war," he quoted. And bent his lips to mine.

We got started in the shower, a lengthy and delicious foreplay. My mouth on his nipples, his mouth on my neck. Slippery, soapy hands sliding all over each other's bodies. His hands on my breasts, hips, thighs, and finally, sliding deliciously around on my ass, mine stroking up and down his washboard abs, around the chiseled lines of his chest, over the tight rounds of his butt. And everywhere I looked, his hard length seemed to be. I was still a little afraid of it.

"I can't take this anymore. To the bed with you," he growled. I grasped him by that protruding member and tugged as I stepped out of the shower.

"I need to reacquaint myself with my friend here. Does he have a name?"

A short, charged silence.

Rafe sounded strangled as he followed me to the bed, my hand tight around the base of his equipment. "Um. Sometimes he answers to 'Captain,'" he confessed, and I laughed in delight at the sight of the tops of his ears turning red.

"Aye, aye, Captain," I said directly to his shaft, and dropped to my knees.

I ran through my repertoire of skills, which apparently seemed to still be working if Rafe's helpless groans and inarticulate exclamations were anything to go by. It felt terrific to be down on my knees in front of him, in such a subservient position, yet to know I held all the power. It felt amazing, and I knew I'd won our little battle of wills when he tried to detach from me before he came and couldn't.

"You slay me, woman," he said when he could string words together. "That wasn't how I thought things would go."

"That's the second time you've told me that," I said with a triumphant grin. "Get used to your new life."

He picked up one of the towels and wiped himself and my mouth, then tenderly rubbed my wet hair. I shivered with the sopping length of it against me, and he made a clucking noise. "I think we should get you dry before round two."

He hustled me back into the bathroom and into a robe, then plugged the hair dryer in. "Where's your brush?"

I pointed.

He turned on the hair dryer and applied it to my head, drawing the brush gently through the heating strands of my waist-length hair. Within minutes, I was purring like a cat as he blow-dried it, brushing it until it rose rebellious around us in a shiny, crackling cloud.

I hadn't felt so loved since I was a child and my mom used to do this to my hair, then braid it for school.

He turned off the dryer and set it on the counter. He buried his face in the abundance of my hair, his arms around my waist for a long moment. "I've wanted to do that for a very long time."

"You can do that every day if you like," I said hopefully.

He chuckled.

"Go to the bed, Ruby," he said, very definitely.

I went, a fine trembling beginning in the pit of my stomach.

"Take off the towel."

I did.

"Go and sit on the bed. Lie back against the pillows and wait for me."

I did, feeling that fire I was becoming familiar with stoke my belly, feeling the delicious anticipation he knew how to build in me.

"Close your eyes, Ruby."

I did, my legs together and hands crossed modestly over my breasts.

I felt the dip of the bed as his weight dented it, heard the slide of his body on the cheap coverlet, felt the heat of his breath above me.

I burned for his touch, but I waited. Because I knew it would be better if I did, and it was what he wanted.

I felt something drop onto my belly, something hard and heavy, and my eyes flew open. The star ruby winked up at me, held in the cup of my navel.

"It's yours to wear now," he said, and his voice was soft. "Put it on."

I picked up the gorgeous antique ring and slid it on the fourth finger of my left hand. "It's so beautiful, Rafe. It's too much for me." I looked up at his eyes. They were dark with emotion.

"It was my grandmother's ring," he said. "She wore it almost all her life and gave it to me when her arthritis got too bad for her to wear rings anymore. 'Give this to your future wife,' she told me when she gave it to me. I couldn't believe it when your name was Ruby."

I didn't meet the Captain that night. I wasn't surprised, but when Rafe wrapped his big, hot body around me and we both fell asleep, I knew I'd meet him the next day.

I finally felt ready for all of it.

CHAPTER EIGHTEEN

Rafe was gone when I woke up, but the pillow beside me was dented and still warm, so I knew he'd spent the night with me. In the chilly late-spring sunshine pouring through the window, I felt all my doubts return.

We hadn't even talked about school next year. I had no intention of quitting. All we'd talked about was this summer, of which the only plan was sailing to Saint Thomas for a redo of our wedding. I felt as unsettled as ever, with too many questions—but under that was also a rock-solid certainty: This was the right man for me, and it didn't really matter about the rest.

We'd figure it out together. I had no doubt he was already ten steps ahead of me on that front. That thought gave me the energy, in spite of my mild aches and pains from a night of excessive pleasure, to get up out of bed and face the day.

The first thing I saw was a big white box topped with a bow on the side table. This must be the "something to wear" he'd said he'd send.

He was so incredibly thoughtful and thorough in everything he did.

I opened the lid, feeling a pang of all that was missing from this moment—my friend Shellie, no doubt full of commentary; my mom, fussing around, my sisters, excited and proud.

"All that can come later," I muttered aloud to myself to quell the loneliness of the moment. I smoothed tissue paper away from an ivory silk dress.

I lifted it out. How could he possibly have had time to pick something off the rack that would fit a figure like mine, big busted and slim hipped?

The gown was simple in design, I saw to my relief. Ivory silk subtly patterned in something that looked like waves, tucked into a modest-looking sweetheart neckline with long sleeves. A tulle overskirt frothed over the narrow underskirt.

I turned the gown over, wondering how to get it on by myself. On the back was a row of tiny buttons, but hidden behind them was a long zipper with a length of ribbon tied to it.

In the bottom of the box were a pair of matching ivory satin low-heeled pumps and a set of underwear that included a lacy demi-bra, a thong, and a garter belt with ivory stockings.

He'd thought of everything.

"What guy does this? And it must have cost a fortune," I muttered, frowning.

I set the wedding clothes back in the box, feeling in great need of a cup of coffee. I threw on a pair of old sweats, ran down to the Ramada Inn lobby, and filled two Styrofoam cups with inky brew. Sipping double-fisted, I headed for the elevator.

"Hey!" Someone was hailing me. I turned, and a flash went off in my face. "Are you Ruby Michaels?"

"Yes," I said hesitantly, and the flash went off again. "Stop with the pictures. I don't even have mascara on yet. What's this about?"

"Are you secretly engaged to Rafe McCallum the Third?"

"I don't know that this is any of your business," I snapped, feeling cornered and apprehensive. The Third? I'd never heard he was a Third of anything. And who would care?

"Aren't you a minor?" the busybody reporter shouted into the door of the elevator. If both my hands hadn't been occupied with coffee cups, I might have flipped him off.

"I'm nineteen, thank you very much," I snapped. "And aren't you unbelievably rude!" The doors finally closed, and I rose, sipping and frowning and wondering what the hell kind of news story was made by a boat captain wedding a missionary's daughter from Saint Thomas.

The phone was ringing inside the room and I had to hustle, wrestling with the key and the coffee. By the time I got there it had stopped, but thankfully it started up again.

"Hello?" I said, gazing at the dress, feeling conflicted.

"Hello, love."

He'd never called me that before. My heart jumped like a fish on the line.

"Rafe! Oh, thank God. There was some jerk trying to take pictures of me in the lobby. Asking questions. I don't get it!"

"What did you say?"

"Not much. I told them to mind their own business. But I did say I was nineteen when the bugger pretty much accused me of being a minor."

A short silence, then a sigh. "I was hoping to have a few days before this hit the fan, but I guess it was not to be. Please don't answer the door or phone unless it's me. I'm sending the guys to get you at ten a.m. Be packed and dressed. In what I sent."

I felt a waft of anger. "Don't boss me around, Captain Rafe McCallum the Third. You might be in charge on your ship, but you don't get to bark orders at me."

Another sigh from his end.

"I'm sorry, Ruby. I know this is scary and hard for you to go through alone. I'm glad we spent the night together—aren't you?"

"Yeah." His kindness melted my defenses. Remembering how tender he'd been with me last night reminded me I had a lot more of that in store. "I just wish you were here now. And I didn't know you were a Third."

"Old stuff that doesn't matter, and it's bad luck to see the bride in her outfit before the wedding," he teased. "Besides, I'm neck-deep in details, trying to get everything ready for the ceremony and shipping out."

"I'm sorry. I feel useless." I sat on the bed and bit my cuticle, a bad habit when I was worried.

"There's really nothing you can do or need to do but be ready to go on time. We're sailing out on the tide. And don't talk to any reporters."

"I don't get why they are interested in us."

"I'll explain everything later. After the ceremony."

"You aren't a criminal or something, are you?" I laughed weakly.

"No. I promise you it's nothing to worry about. Just be ready, okay? Can you do that for me?"

I was the one who sighed. "It feels wrong doing this all by myself. But at least there's a cord to pull the zipper on the dress up. I can't promise it's going to fit, though."

"It'll fit. Just remember I love you, Ruby, and we're doing this because we love each other and want to be together." There was a note in his voice as if he were reassuring himself as well as me, and I frowned, looking down at the play of light on the star ruby on my finger and thinking of all the unanswered questions.

"I guess."

He laughed. "Just be ready at ten." He hung up.

I looked at the clock. It was nine. That gave me an hour to get into the dress, assuming it fit, get some makeup on, and figure out what to do about my hair.

At least I didn't have to wash or blow-dry it. Even now it floated around me, loose and silky from Rafe's ministrations of the night before.

"Onward, Ruby Day Michaels," I said aloud. "Hammer down that coffee and get ready for your wedding."

CHAPTER NINETEEN

I stood on the deck of the *Creamy Maid*, clutching Rafe's hand. The dress was on, and I knew from my endless checking in the mirror that it couldn't have fit better if it had been designed for me. I could see admiration in the eyes of the cluster of the *Maid's* staff that had gathered with us,

I'd messed with my hair for a few minutes and then just decided to leave it down, tying the ivory satin ribbon that had been used to pull up the zipper around my head. The brisk wind of the day before was mercifully absent. I sneaked a peek at Rafe, resplendent in a tux. The sailors wore dazzling whites, and the ship gleamed and brass glittered as if freshly washed.

In spite of all that, I felt the loss of my family and any female friends keenly, and looked down at Rafe's hand, clutched in both of mine, for reassurance. Why did everything have to be such a rush?

Oh yeah. We want to have sex, and Rafe won't do it without being married.

Rafe's friend who had a license to perform weddings, Captain Jock Huskins, situated us in front of him with gentle instructional murmurings. He was an imposing figure in dress whites with a lot of gold braid on them.

"Our ceremony today is to witness the marriage of Rafael Leland McCallum the Third to Ruby Day Michaels, this twenty-seventh day of May, 1984." Captain Huskins sent a glance around the properly somber group of the *Maid*'s staff. I hung on to Rafe's hand, unable to look up or at him because I could feel tears of emotion welling in my eyes and getting ready to pop out the way they did. I breathed shallowly so as not to sob.

"Do you, Rafe McCallum, take Ruby to be your lawfully wedded wife, to have and to hold, in sickness and in health, for richer or for poorer, until death do you part?"

"I do," Rafe said, and gave my hand a powerful squeeze. I looked up, and sure enough the tears popped out. He lifted a hand and wiped them away with the ball of his thumb, leaning down to kiss me gently. I drew a deep shuddering breath and felt stronger.

Huskins cleared his throat and said, "Do you, Ruby Day Michaels, take Rafe to be your husband, to have and to hold, in sickness and in health, for richer or for poorer, until death do you part?"

Somewhere off in the distance I could hear the approaching thunder of a helicopter, but now my eyes were fixed on Rafe's, green drowning in his blue. "I do," I said, and it came out clear and strong.

"You may exchange the rings."

I felt my stomach drop. I had no ring for Rafe! I started to look around wildly, and he squeezed my hands again as one of the sailors approached. He was holding the little silver music box Rafe had mailed me, and he opened it beside me. The sweet tinkling music lifted into the air as he opened it, and I saw a heavy gold band inside, battered and old-looking, along with a slim woman's band.

Rafe slid the plain band onto my finger above the ruby and whispered in my ear, "These were my parents' rings."

"Oh. Where are they?" I asked, feeling terrible for yet another thing I hadn't asked him about.

He just shook his head, avoiding my eyes, and I picked up the heavy masculine band and slid it over the thick knuckle of his finger, surprised to see how well it fit and feeling sad his father wasn't here to see what a magnificent son he had.

"I pronounce you husband and wife. You may kiss the bride."

There was some restrained applause from the sailors as Rafe swept me in for a good, hard smack full of promises. I heard and felt the thrum of the engines starting.

Huskins all but ran to the side to climb down to his tender, yelling, "Good luck!" as he did so. I could still hear the thrumming of the helicopter, and now Rafe circled my shoulders, glancing toward the helicopter.

"Let's get under the canopy." Our company moved deep into the shadow of the bridge. "Let's get underway." The crew dispersed like a well-oiled machine, and I stood in my dress, feeling ridiculous.

"Let me take you down to the cabin and you can change if you like," Rafe said. There was a frown line between his dark brows. "I want you to be comfortable."

"Are you coming down soon?"

"Of course. I just have to make sure we're on our way and on course."

I felt rattled and unsettled and generally like I wanted to work up to a major temper tantrum as he hustled me below to the luxurious cabin in the bow of the yacht.

"Where are we going?" The boat had begun to cleave the waves with a rolling sensation, and I thanked God I'd never been a seasick type or I'd be in hell right now, trapped down here.

"First leg of our honeymoon."

That told me a whole lot of nothing. I bit my lip and tried not to cry or yell at him as he shut the door firmly behind me and hustled off to do whatever he needed to do. I knew he'd be back, and I could let him have it then. In fact, I had the rest of my life to fight with him.

That thought was going to take some getting used to.

I had taken the ribbon that pulled up the zipper off to tie around my head, so now I couldn't get the zipper down. After some ineffectual contortions, I gave up and crawled onto the large, tidy, triangular bed dressed in bright navy bedding and built into the bow of the boat. I looked out the row of portholes on either side of the bow.

They were placed about five feet above the surface of the water and just a foot above the bed's surface, so I could lie on my side and look out.

It was beautiful outside. The boat purred through the waves, rising and falling with a rhythm like breathing. I loved the alternating blue-green of the sea with the purity of the sky. I would see an occasional gull, or a cormorant, and then, suddenly and magically, the portholes filled with dolphins, leaping and surfing the bow wave, just feet away from me.

Their silver bodies flashed and leaped, and I even saw one look at me, its smile totally contented, as if everything was right with the world.

"Rafe! Rafe! Oh my God!" I shrieked. I am not quiet when I shriek, and I wasn't surprised to hear the thunder of footsteps on the ladder and hear the door whack open.

I turned over to face him. "Dolphins, Rafe! Dolphins!" I felt my face fill with happiness.

I have always loved dolphins. They are everywhere in Saint Thomas, those emissaries of playful joy, and they'd always seemed to like me, too. I'd swum with them in Magen's Bay more times than I could count, and that they'd appear now brought more reassurance to me than anything else could have.

If I had a spirit animal, it was the dolphin.

The high color of alarm ebbed out of Rafe's face, and he looked out the window, a grin breaking over his face.

"Well, damn," he said. "Haven't seen any since we got into Boston. Nice escort." He shut the door, turned the lock. "It's time to be with my bride, anyway. They can figure out anything else that needs figuring out."

He yanked at his tie, but it refused to come undone. I hefted up my frothing skirts and crawled to the end of the bed. "Let me help you." I reached up and tugged the tie, undid the stiff collar. "I don't know why you decided to go all formal with these clothes," I said, gesturing to his tux and my dress. "It was just us."

His blue eyes smoldered. "I didn't want you to feel slighted. You deserve the best. And we'll use them again, for the ceremony on Saint Thomas."

I shrugged. "I would have been fine in shorts and a T-shirt."

"I wanted to see you in a dress," Rafe said. "And what's under it. I have fantasized about this for so long. You have no idea."

Now my cheeks heated up. "Oh." I had no words, since I was the latecomer to this rapidly coordinated party. "Well, I tried to get the dress off, but I can't get the zipper down." I gestured.

"Let me help."

I turned my back and watched the dolphins playfully leaping, entranced, as Rafe slid the zipper down, kissing the knobs of my spine as they were revealed.

He stopped with an intake of breath at the narrow ruffled strap of the G-string curving up my butt and over the top of my hips.

"You bought that," I said a little irritably, to hide how nervous I was.

"So I did," he said. And the zipper continued all the way

down to the top of my ass, and he peeled the dress forward and helped me take my arms out of the long, tight sleeves.

"We should hang it up," I fussed. He didn't answer, just swung me around, stood me up, and lifted the whole rustling garment away from my body so that it fell with a shushing noise and a gush of warm air around my feet, and left me standing there in the ivory underwear set he'd picked out.

His eyes looked glazed as he stood there staring at me. I took the ribbon off my forehead and shook out the mane of my hair so it covered me like a cape, and I struck a sassy pose.

"What?"

"I can't believe this moment is actually happening," Rafe said. "You, in front of me. Looking like this. Wearing this. About to be mine. And just to make it really over-the-top, there are dolphins jumping in the background."

"I expect bluebirds of happiness to start flapping around our heads any minute now," I said, and he laughed, and I did, too, and stepped forward to undo the black buttons of his shirt, tugging the shirt's tail out of the black slacks.

"But before we get too far with beginning official married life, I have some questions," I said, my hands coming to rest on his shirtfront.

Rafe rolled his eyes. "Of course you do. It so happens I knew you would. I have champagne to help this go better." He busied himself at the silver bucket on the tidy sideboard. I felt chilly in the fancy underwear, so I unzipped my battered suitcase and put on my fuzzy yellow terry-cloth robe. The dolphins had moved on, I saw to my regret.

Rafe turned, holding two bubbling flutes, and broke into a grin at the sight of me. "God, you're adorable."

"Good thing you think so. You're a lot more likely to see me in this robe than in the sexy underwear."

"I'm pretty sure my favorite outfit for you is nothing at all," he said, handing me the glass. "To us."

"To us."

The champagne was tickly and tart, and I smacked my lips. "Another acquired taste I think I can acquire. So, questions. Who the heck are you, Rafe, that we're hightailing it out of the harbor with helicopters after us and reporters are trying to get pictures of me in my sweats at the Ramada Inn?"

He took a long sip of his champagne, belched a little, and looked at me in appeal over the rim. "I think I'd like to do the deflowering thing first. I'm not sure this is going to put you in the mood."

"Oh God. Are you an ax murderer who did in his first wife or something?" I tried to laugh, but I could feel the color draining out of my cheeks.

"Bottoms up. Drink your champagne," he said. "We can't leave half-full glasses rattling around with the motion we've got going on." I tipped back my head and drank my champagne, and it immediately made me feel a little dizzy and warm.

Rafe set both empty glasses in the little metal sink built into the sideboard and crawled up on the bed beside me, pulling me into his arms. We stretched out, and he pillowed my head on his arm and stroked my body through the fuzzy robe. I put my ear against his chest so I could hear the thump of his heart and the deep rhythm of his breathing.

"I haven't been entirely honest with you," he said. "I want you to remember I didn't ever lie to you. I just didn't volunteer everything."

CHAPTER TWENTY

"Just tell me, please." I wriggled closer, because I was scared to hear whatever came next.

"I'm not who you and your family assumed I was. Yes, I'm a surfer and a sailor, and for a while I was a drifter, but that's not the whole story. During that time I met you in Saint Thomas, I was at a crossroads. I was trying to figure out what I wanted from life. I was fleeing a lot of things and working out some grief. Because, you see, my parents died."

I turned to him, pressing my face to the triangle of warm skin I'd uncovered as I'd begun unbuttoning his shirt. Just his presence was melting me like wax, and I kissed his chest. "I'm so sorry. How long ago was it?"

"Three years. They died in a plane crash. Their private jet. The rings we're wearing? They were old ones they'd upgraded. That's why I had them at all."

I lifted my head. "Private jet?"

He nodded. "The *Maid* is my boat. Lisa's house in Cliffside is my house. I'm actually annoyingly wealthy."

I felt my eyes bug out. "And you were going to tell me when?"

"Now was always when I'd planned to tell you. After we were married. Because I wanted you to choose me for me."

I had begun scooting away, and now my butt came up against the portholes. "You were worried I'd marry you for your money?" I snorted, feeling betrayed and insulted—and a tiny bit guilty, too, because I *had* judged him and I *had* wrestled with my goals and decided to pick him anyway.

Realizing I needn't have worried about it made me mad. So did the fact that he'd thought it would be a major factor in whether or not I chose to be with him.

It was a factor, but not a major one. More bothersome to me had always been that Rafe wanted me to make such a big commitment with so little to go on and at such a young age.

Rafe was still trying to explain. "It wasn't you. It was me. I was sick of the burden of being the only son of two powerful people with too much money. I loved my parents very much, but the pressure of managing everything after they died was just too much for me, I guess, and I wasn't at all sure I wanted to live their lifestyle, the lifestyle I'd been groomed for. So I farmed the companies out to management and took the *Maid* out on a trip around the world. Everywhere I went, I challenged myself to survive without my family's money. I went into each port wearing just the clothes on my back. I found work and made friends and got by, and along the way I began to find peace. I had a few trusty crewmates who've been with me forever who knew who I was; and, of course, Lisa knows."

I crawled to the edge of the bed and went and poured us each another glass of champagne. I handed him his and settled my back against a porthole. "Lisa. I thought she was a friend. I was so naïve."

"Well, you were, but adorably so. And like I told you in San

Francisco, she was my friend first. I wasn't deliberately hiding anything. I knew there were clues about me, but I decided to let the whole thing play out, let you make your assumptions about me and work through them on your own. I'd been burned by women who wanted Rafe McCallum the Third. Not for who I am—as you said so well, surfer, sailor, drifter, art lover." He lifted the flute in a little toast and we both sipped. "No, they wanted the position. The money. I was so devastated after Mom and Dad died that I didn't trust myself not to fall prey to someone pretending to love me. So I started my quest." He spun the fragile glass's stem. "I know how young you are, that you have lots of ideas about your life and how it will go. And I didn't want to mess up that process. At the same time, the minute I met you that evening in Saint Thomas, everything changed for me."

I eyed him though the bubbles. "I can't believe you let me think the things I thought about you."

"What did you think?"

"I thought of you as a pirate. Dangerous and poor."

"It turns out I am a bit of a pirate." Rafe set his glass aside. "I know a treasure when I see one, and I'll do anything to get it."

He crawled over to me and plucked the glass out of my hand, draining the last sip of champagne. "Do you have any more questions?"

"Yes," I whispered.

"What?" He opened the robe and set his lips on the fluttering pulse at the base of my neck.

"What is your degree in?"

"Business administration."

"Of course," I said. "But I bet you wanted to major in art history." I'd never forget his passion as he'd explained the modern period to me at the DeYoung. He raised his head and those dark blue eyes blazed down at me.

"You know me so well already."

"You could go back to school with me. And major in art history this time." I pulled his shirt off with hands clumsy with eagerness. "I want to see all of you."

"And I want to see those undies I had Lisa pick out."

I yanked my old robe closed. "Lisa saw this outfit?"

"I had her order the dress custom-made. She swiped some of your clothes for measurements. And I told her to pick out all the incidentals."

"When was this?"

"During spring break I told her I was going to marry you, and I had her start working on it."

"Oh my God," I said. "I'd be embarrassed if she weren't three thousand miles away."

He opened the robe and stared at my breasts in the lacy ivory cups. He was down to his dress slacks, and I let him peel the robe off of me and work his magic with his stroking hands, nipping teeth, busy tongue. I warmed and melted, heating up beside him, my own hands sliding hungrily over the hard planes of his chest, the sensitive nubs of his nipples, the bands of muscle around his belly and back.

I finally pushed his big, hard shoulder and climbed astride him, and he moaned as he played with the straps of the lingerie and the innocent ruffle on the G-string.

"I think it's time for your pants to go," I said. I undid them and slid them and his boxers off.

The Captain was at full attention, and once again he gave me pause.

"Don't worry. We'll go as slow as you need," Rafe said, rolling me to the side. "Let's get this underwear off you."

I hid my face in his neck, suddenly shy, as he unclipped the stockings and peeled them and the G-string away. Only my bra was left now, and he spent some time on my breasts, teasing and licking, finally sucking them hard so I cried out and arched against him.

"Yes!" I said. "Do it! Just do it!"

He laughed. "Not sure the crew heard that, love. A little louder." He sucked the other breast, and the sound I made was somewhere between a moan and a shout.

And still he didn't do it. No, he tortured me with pleasure, with mini orgasms, with total worship of my body until I thought he could stick a cannon in me and I'd do nothing but yell with happiness.

After my second orgasm with him kneeling between my thighs, I looked up and took his face in my hands. "Please, Rafe, I want you. All of you. I'm not afraid. I'm in all the way. No seat belts."

"Well, there is the condom. It's a kind of seat belt," he said with that wicked grin, and I even found the sight of him rolling on the condom sexy. I was in no mood by then for half measures, and I sat up and grabbed his hips and pulled him down toward my throbbing, aching center.

He tried to go slow. I know he did. But I've always been of the yank-the-Band-Aid-off-quick school. I thrust my hips up hard as soon as I felt that suspicious fullness at my entrance, and he slid in, filling me with a not-unpleasant sensation that felt both new and completely familiar.

There was some sort of resistance; he wasn't going in any farther, and I'd begun to feel a terrible burning sensation. "So tight," he moaned. "I don't want to hurt you."

"You already are," I said, and used my arms to yank him down so he fell onto and into me, all the way to the hilt.

It was way more painful than the romance novels had led me to expect.

Tears welled instantly as burning turned to stabbing, accompanied by an uncomfortable fullness that felt like an invasion. I went utterly still and rigid.

I shut my eyes and the tears rolled out and down my cheeks.

"I'm sorry, Ruby. It'll get better." He moved tentatively and the resistance was gone, but the burning wasn't, and he moved and moved and groaned suddenly, arching his back and pumping into me.

I'd gone stiff and frozen with the sudden and unexpected pain long moments ago, and the minute I knew he was done, I heaved him off and ran for the tiny head, sitting on the toilet, where I was sure my uterus was going to come sliding out in a welter of gore. I crossed my arms over my aching pelvic area and waited for death.

"Ruby? Ruby!" He pounded on the door in alarm.

"It hurts so much," I sobbed. "What a total drag! I can't believe I got married for this!"

A startled silence on the other side of the door.

I continued my rant. "That totally sucked. It was way worse than Shellie told me. K-Y jelly, my ass!"

"It's only the one time that it hurts, love," he said, as if speaking to a nursery-school child.

I wiped. Sure enough, blood. Lots of it. I threw open the door and held up the toilet paper. "See that? I'm wounded. Like, really wounded."

He blanched a bit. "That is a lot of blood. I've read it's different for different women. Some have hardly any pain; some have..."

"The hymen from hell," I finished. I threw the toilet paper away and flushed. I made a pad of toilet paper and stuffed it against my sore parts. "I feel so cheated. I am not in a hurry to do that again anytime soon. And to think I used to like the Captain."

The tops of his ears were red as Rafe drew my stiff, outraged body into his arms. "I'm sure it's going to get better with time."

"More champagne," I said.

I ended up finishing the bottle and puking with drunken seasickness as the mellow waves we'd been going through turned to heavy seas.

Rafe administered first aid and left me sleeping off the disappointment of my first time in a fuzz of Dramamine and alcohol, seasick wristbands in place.

CHAPTER TWENTY-ONE

I woke up in what must have been late afternoon with the seasickness blessedly abated, though the seas had not gotten smoother. I could tell we were under sail now, though, because the thrum of the engines had ceased. I turned on my side and looked out the row of portholes, enjoying the splash of the waves, the sweep of ocean and sky—and some green coastline, too.

I wanted to go right topside and see all I could see, try to get Rafe to tell me where we were going—but I realized I needed a little time alone to reflect on all that had happened.

Only a day ago, I'd been saying goodbye to my roommate and best friend.

And Sam, too. I felt a pang for how things had ended.

And now I was married and sailing away on a yacht, married to a man whom I knew so well, so intimately in some ways—but whose full name I'd heard for the first time when it was spoken by Captain Huskins during our five-minute wedding.

A man who wasn't poor after all, but certainly was dangerous —to any sense of control I might have had over my own life.

And the sex! The sex I'd been so excited about, so thrilled to finally have—had been horrible. Literally one of the most painful, disappointing moments of my life.

I sat up gingerly. I was wearing my yellow terry-cloth robe and a pair of big white granny panties with a frayed elastic waist-band Rafe had handed me from my suitcase, panties I wished not even my mom would have seen.

I thought of how Rafe had tried to check me out with the first-aid kit right after. My bruised lady parts were packed with toilet paper, all we'd been able to come up with to deal with the ongoing leakage. I'd been drunk by then and mean with disap-pointment.

"You can't put a Band-Aid on it, Rafe," I'd said. "And nothing you say or do could make that anything but the worst sexual experience ever."

I put my hands up against my hot cheeks in mortification at my awful words. I was a terrible person. He'd really tried hard to make it as good as it could be; I just had to hope, like virgins everywhere with hymens from hell, that it would be better next time.

The cabin was large and luxuriously appointed, with built-in cabinetry and the little wet bar we'd already used. While I was sleeping, Rafe had tidied everything, hanging up my wedding dress in the closet. He'd even unpacked my disreputable suitcase and filled two drawers with my clothes.

I really didn't deserve this guy. I couldn't wait to go up above deck and apologize. I dressed in jeans, my Northeastern hoodie, socks, and those preppy boat shoes that I was finally, actually wearing on a boat.

I realized as I headed up the steep, ladderlike stairs, that I was going to have to see the crew now, and they'd have no doubt what we were getting up to in that forward cabin. After all, I'd been seen for five minutes during the ceremony, then disappeared into the front cabin, where things had been noisy for some hours.

I felt like everything was written on my face, and I pulled my hood up over my head and skulked through the galley without looking up.

"You hungry at all, Mrs. McCallum?" A gruff, but kindly voice.

Belatedly, I realized I was Mrs. McCallum. I peeked sideways out from under the hoodie at a large, bald-headed dude I dimly remembered meeting up on the deck.

"Uh. Freddie, is it?" His name came back to me by some miracle. His smile was kind and welcoming, not mocking or disrespectful. I began to relax a little.

"Yeah. I'm the steward. That means I'm in charge of meals and supplies at sea. Need anything special?"

I thought of my messy situation and how I wished I had a panty liner, but didn't yet feel comfortable asking him to buy me some tampons for the inevitable monthly either. "Can I give you a list or something?"

He beamed as if it genuinely made him happy that I'd thought of that. "Great idea."

"Thank you for asking if I needed anything. I got a little sick down there. Do you have any crackers?"

He was solicitous and gave me a roll of Ritz Crackers and a ginger ale and insisted on accompanying me to the top deck.

The wind smacked my cheeks immediately, blowing away the last of the champagne cobwebs and Dramamine hangover. I gasped at the expanse of cobalt-blue horizon, the scudding whitecaps, the vast acreage of dazzling sails. I felt euphoria sweep over me as I spotted the dolphins again, leaping ahead of the ship.

"Ruby. You're feeling better, I hope?" Rafe was approaching me from the helm area at the back of the yacht. I saw Sven, one of the sailors who'd helped at my dorm, had taken the wheel, and he lifted a hand in a friendly wave.

No one was mocking me. Or if they were, I wasn't going to know it. I relaxed a little further.

I hopped up onto the deck, the roll of Ritz in one hand and the ginger ale in the other. "Freddie was so nice. He had just the thing for my tummy."

I saw Rafe nod and smile at Freddie's large, shiny pate poking up from below like a gopher checking the weather. Rafe's approval seemed to make Freddie happy, too, as the big man grinned and gave me a thumbs-up before disappearing below.

I pressed into the wind shadow of Rafe's body. "I was worried everyone would know what we were doing and... it would be embarrassing."

I felt him chuckle, and his arms around me felt like the best thing in the world. "They are really happy for me, Ruby. They've all been my friends for years. Yeah, I got a little shit for your age at first, but once they got a load of you in that wedding dress, nobody did anything but congratulate me."

"Ha," I said, and snuggled my face into his parka. "I'm sorry I was such a bitch. After. You know."

"You've got a right to be disappointed. I was, too. I've been racking my brain for how we could have gone about it differently, but I guess we can just chalk that up as beginner's bad luck."

I tipped my head to grin at him, and he bent and kissed me.

"So, where are we going?"

"Charleston, South Carolina. There's a lot to see and do there. I thought we'd put in for a few days, let the guys go home to see their families. And we can spend some time together. Alone."

"Cool," I said, as if my cheeks weren't on fire. "Hey, shouldn't I be oriented on emergency procedures in case we sink or something? Tell me more about the boat."

He obliged, showing me the lifeboats and describing the

various alarm and other systems, and talking me through an evacuation.

"She's a sailing yacht, so she can go under sail or power, whatever we need." He was clearly proud of the *Maid* and how far she'd traveled. "The *Maid* has some real miles under her belt. She's been around the world one full time now, and I'm hoping to make it twice."

"How long to get to Saint Thomas?" I asked, already worried about being back in Boston by September.

"Actually, we're going to fly out of Charleston," Rafe said. "September, not May, is the best time for the route from Charleston to Saint Thomas, and it's a long haul. I don't want to put you through that right away, especially with the way you got sick this afternoon."

"I love you!" I exclaimed, my grin huge. Somewhere inside, while I was excited to be on the *Maid*, I had also been worried. I had sailed a bit around the islands growing up, but never anything serious. I wasn't at all sure I had the stomach for a long voyage, though anything Rafe loved so much, I would to try hard to enjoy, too.

"That was a good call, then," he said, drawing me back against him, resting his chin on my head as we looked off the bow at the dolphins, gulls, and the green coast of whatever state it was we were passing. "I want this to be fun for you. After all, it's our honeymoon."

"I still can't get used to you being rich," I said. "But it actually doesn't change anything. Except I won't be worrying as much."

"And you don't have to work in the dining hall anymore."

"Hey! It wasn't a bad job. Especially when I was Juliette." I tilted my head and batted my eyes at him. "So I guess I'd better call Shellie and tell her she has to get another roommate next year. And Sam." My stomach pitched a bit at the thought of Sam.

Rafe kissed the crown of my head. "We haven't talked about

next year, but I assumed you were continuing at Northeastern. I don't mind parking in Boston during the year, and maybe I will look at an art history program. We own a house in town. It's rented out, but we could reoccupy it."

"Only now you mention we own a house in Boston," I said, frowning. "But I like how you said 'we' own it. I was worried you didn't want to wait for me to finish my degree to continue sailing around the world."

He turned me in his arms. "Ruby. What else would I want to do but see my wife fulfill her dreams for herself? While I do the same for me."

"I don't deserve you," I said suddenly, my eyes filling. "What did I ever do to deserve you?"

"It's not about deserving," Rafe said. "It's about finding the person you're meant to be with."

I put my ear on his heart, leaned against him, and sighed for a long moment as the sun set.

We went down to the dining room and had a great dinner with the guys. I didn't feel uncomfortable anymore as they told funny stories about Rafe: the time he'd got his tattoo, which apparently was just a claw to start with, "And a hideous one, too."

That time in Chile when he'd decided to leave his money and ID behind on one of his "I'm going to make it on my own" quests and had disappeared for days. Sven had bailed him out of a jail, after he'd been arrested for public indecency from peeing against a statue of the Madonna, which he hadn't recognized in the dark.

Then there was the time Rafe had come back to the *Maid* after meeting me on Saint Thomas.

"He said he'd met the woman he was going to marry," Freddie said. "'She's an angel,' he said, 'with the hair of a devil.'" They all busted up, including me.

Rafe pulled me to my feet. "On that note, we'll see you all in the morning." To their credit, no teasing followed us out.

Back in our cabin, Rafe seemed oddly withdrawn.

"Can I take a shower?" I asked.

"Of course. Unfortunately, it's not big enough for two," he said. "I'll go after you." He'd sat down at a desk area that efficiently folded open as part of the built-in furniture. He had a stack of ledgers stashed inside and seemed to immediately immerse himself in his project.

In the small metal surround, I washed briskly, keeping my hair in a pile on top of my head because it didn't dry well at night, and reflected how already the ceaseless movement of the ship was beginning to feel soothing to me, a new normal that reminded me, somehow, of being a small child held close to my mother.

Rafe went in after me, and I found a book of maps to study while he showered, trying to figure out our route. He came out wrapped in a white terry-cloth robe and resumed his seat at the desk. I got out and snuggled against Rafe in my yellow robe.

"I'm willing to give it another go if you are," I said against the nape of his neck.

"Hell, no, love," he said without looking up. "You need at least a couple of days to recover. Platonic snuggling only."

I was shocked at the stab of rejection I felt. It went straight south and throbbed there in reproach.

I snorted. "You obviously don't know the Michaels family. You fall off the horse, you get back on. Skin your knee, you keep going. Bad sexual experience? No problem. Keep doing it until it feels better."

"You forget." He turned to grin at me, an old-fashioned fountain pen in hand. "I do know the Michaels family. One of the reasons I like you so much."

I was suddenly curious about the pen. "Is this where you would write me letters?"

"Yes."

197

I felt a sudden heat, thinking of his letters, picturing him sitting here, writing me. Now that we were finally together, it had begun to feel prophetic somehow, destined, and yet at every stage I knew how fragile our relationship had been.

I knew. I'd lived through the last year without him.

"Will you read me 'First Night'? I have it in my suitcase." That love poem he wrote me in February had brought me all the way out to San Francisco to see him at spring break, a wildly reckless move on my part. That poem was when I'd begun to fall in love with him.

"Really, Ruby?"

I pulled the battered old case out from under the bed, fumbled with the zipper, and took out the topmost letter, a little fuzzy around the edges from folding and refolding. "Here."

He looked at me, and I saw a shine of moisture in his eyes. His voice thickened. "I don't know if I can read it to you out loud."

"Come to bed and read it to me," I said. And I dropped the robe.

He stood up and dropped his robe, too, and we climbed into the wide bed together with the stars and moon flashing on the ocean outside the portholes. The sound of the ocean a foot away was like the sound of blood rushing through my veins as he read to me.

First Night

She comes to me in ivory
Not white, because she's Ruby
Even the skin of her secret places
Is a tawny shade of pale
Peppered with nutmeg freckles I want
To spend a lifetime counting.
She offers herself

Abundant and strong, sweet as honey and tangy as mango
And I use my tongue to worship her.
Every inch.
Every cranny.
Every place that's never seen the sun or
Known the touch of a hand.
Nothing is hidden from me, nothing is off-limits as I make her
mine.
She's never known what can be felt and discovered, and every
place I take her
I mark it mine
I take and I own
With kisses. With my hands. With my mouth.
With all of my body I worship her.
I teach her what has always been in her to feel.
I touch the nub of her pleasure until she explodes in cries of
delight
And I'm surrounded
By her perfume
She's the garden of my delight.
Only when she's boneless and begging
Will I move into her, sliding into that tight glove
Made for me alone
I'll take that "jade gate" by storm
I'll make it so good for her
She's ruined for anyone but me
Because this is only the first night
And there will be an eternity more.

I was crying by then.
We both were.

He reached over to draw me to him, kissing me, and it was
like the very feeling of hope. He stroked me gently, and he

TOBY JANE

stroked me hard, unleashing a melody I felt like I'd always known that could be released only by him.

This time, when he eventually rose and entered me, it was a little tender but full of a pleasure I couldn't articulate except with sighs and kisses, and even a few tears, my eyes on his, a part of me still waiting for the pain, the burning.

But it never came. Instead, I found myself moving with him, rising up to meet him, our motion echoing the cleaving of the ship through the sea, something ageless and eternal about it, and yet unique. Us, only us, in this moment, in this place and time.

"Okay?" he asked, still moving slowly, but I could see the strain of being gentle in his shoulders, in the cords of his neck. That reckless daring rose up in me—the same daring that made me climb a tree, try a flip, and get on a plane for San Francisco. I wrapped my legs tight around his hips, pushed myself up against him with my arms, and bit his nipple.

"Give it to me like you mean it," I said, and he did, and I swear it just got better and better. And then he flipped me over.

"Oh, this ass," he whispered. "I need to write a poem just about your ass." He bit it, just lightly, and shivers of anticipation rippled over my body.

"I like poems," I panted, as he shoved a pillow under my hips and hefted me up. I could already feel myself bending and melting to open for him, and I wished we had a mirror so I could see it all going on. But I also felt another quaver of apprehension. The Captain was so very big.

"Consider this a poem." And he entered me. I arched and cried out as I felt whole new mind-blowing sensations, and all was a blur after that of an almost violent clashing that ended in the most glorious orgasm I'd had yet.

"I guess it does get better," I murmured, face down in the sheets.

"And we have a lifetime to practice," he said.

Knowing that filled me with something a lot like joy. And I got it suddenly, why he'd wanted to marry me. This particular ecstasy could bloom only in a protected place, where hearts were bound together.

I was glad I was reckless enough to take the ride with no seat belt.

CHAPTER TWENTY-TWO

Rafe - *Five Years Later*

God, she's beautiful, my Ruby. I can see her sleeping from where I sit at the desk, and the sun coming in the porthole is hitting her hair and turning it all those vibrant colors it goes when the light hits it—a red so deep it's like a good pinot noir. But there's cinnamon in there, and an orange like the heart of flame, and even some gold, each strand so purely metallic it seems like they were spun from a dragon's hoard.

Ruby makes me a poet, even after five years of marriage. I keep waiting to wake up from the spell she's cast on me, but it only gets stronger, deeper, and more complex.

We're on board our yacht, the *Creamy Maid*, and last night we finally got the boat in the water. She's been sitting in dry dock way too long, waiting for us to have the time for her. If we ever needed a distraction, it's now. It's the ideal time of year to take the boat to Saint Thomas from Boston, and we need to help Ruby's family pack up to move.

Ruby's father, Peter Michaels, died suddenly of a stroke. We've already flown out to the Virgin Islands for the funeral and been through that, but now, a month later, Ruby's still having a hard time getting out of bed. To complicate things further, her mother, Kate, called me to say she "couldn't handle" all the reminders of Peter and is packing up Pearl and Jade, Ruby's sisters, and moving back to the mainland United States, to her family's hometown of Eureka, California.

It didn't help that this happened just when Ruby had graduated from law school and passed the bar. She'd been looking for jobs, refusing to work for any of our McCallum Enterprises companies. She was determined to build her own career "without nepotism," which I thought was silly; I hired lawyers all the time and could genuinely use her. Now, with this tragedy, she seems to have lost all interest in the job hunt and doesn't have a good reason to get out of bed in the mornings.

Ruby's sister Pearl is seventeen now, and Jade fourteen, and apparently the girls aren't taking their father's death well. Pearl has taken to being out at all hours, while Jade has become overly perfectionistic, cleaning everything and washing her hands all the time, according to Kate.

Ruby's family needs help—help it would be good for her to give.

So we're sailing to Saint Thomas, and it's a sign of Ruby's lethargy that she didn't even ask any questions, just packed her things and got on board the *Maid* with the crew.

I set my ledgers aside and stand up, looking at Ruby, curled into a shrimplike shape, barely visible under the blankets except for that bonfire of hair on the pillow. I know her body so well that memory fills in all the places hidden by bedclothes: round tits, a deep waist with a tiny cup of navel, and that ass. *Oh, that ass.*

I want her with that painful tug of need deep in my body, a nagging ache that has had me going around at half-mast for days now; but she's withdrawn from me. We haven't made love since she got the news on the phone. That first, terrible wail she gave before she broke down was the last time I felt close to her.

But I'm getting less and less functional, constantly irritable with deprivation and missing her. It's been a month, and if that makes me a horn-dog who can't keep his hands off his wife, then I'm guilty. I'm done waiting for her to come back to me. We need each other.

Ruby

I don't sleep well since Dad died, though I constantly feel tired and want to slide into that oblivion. Rafe wakes me instantly as he gets into bed. I sense a slow-moving stealthiness in his movements that puts me on alert.

It's been a month since we made love. I know he misses me, but in my own misery, I've felt unable to reach out to him, even to draw the comfort I know being with him would give.

His hand moves up my hip as he slides in close, spooning me from behind, and I feel the heat of his naked body. He always burns hotter than me, like he carries around a little furnace inside —and right now, in this frozen place I'm in, it feels so good.

His hand, large, warm, and rough with calluses from working on the boat, circles my nipple, loose in that tank top with the skimpy straps I can never wear in public because my breasts are too big. I have a sense of how they feel through his hands by the way he hefts and caresses each of them, and he moves closer still, moving the long hair off my neck to kiss the exposed skin there and sending a shiver through me.

I feel what he feels somehow, as often happens between us.

My body tells me of his strength, his intent, his gentle but persistent waking, and at the same time, through his hand I feel how deliciously silky my body is, the softness, the velvet texture.

In the big, hot, humming restraint of his body, I sense the ache to be in me where all is slippery tight warmth and a fit that's perfect.

I let my breathing quicken just a little to show I know he's there and I like what he's doing. It feels like Rafe's thawing the ice that's surrounded me with his very hands.

I arch back against him, feeling his hard length against my butt, but he makes no move there. He slides his roaming hand under my shirt, traveling down from my sensitized breasts along the curve of my waist, tracing along my ribs, and through his touch I feel the contoured plane of my belly as he slides across it with that delightfully rough hand. He palms my plump mound, just for a moment, just long enough for me to want more of that, before he's moving again.

He circles around my thighs in the cotton pajamas, then abruptly slides that exploring hand into my pants and panties, lifting the fabric away as he presses the length of his muscular arm against my butt and penetrates my slick heat with firm, knowing fingers.

Deep. So deep. Just there, just that place that knows him so well.

I jerk and moan instantly and press back against him, but again he doesn't stay there. Quick as lightning his hand is gone and back up at my breasts, working the nipples until I'm twitching and panting, impatiently tugging my shirt off and shoving out of my pajama pants. I push my ass against his crotch and feel his hardness leap at the contact.

I feel good that I'm affecting him, too, as I slowly arch back and forth so he feels my firm, silky ass against his length in invitation, even as I turn my head to see him, up on one elbow as he looks down at me, working me with that busy hand.

I push the covers off, and the bright morning light pouring through the porthole hits my white body like a spotlight. He looks dazzled by the brightness on my skin as I roll onto my back and open my legs beside him, guiding his hand. We gaze at each other a long moment and I shut my eyes, the intimacy too much.

"I want you," I say. "I need you."

He smiles and leans down to kiss me as that clever hand slides down and between to stroke me firmly. *Again and again. And again. And again.*

I'm moaning, and he takes the sounds into his mouth as if sipping them, as if we have all the time in the world, even as I know touching me there makes him just want to pry my legs wider and dive in.

But he doesn't.

Instead, that skillful hand, so delightfully rough, slides up my belly, wanders and circles, and everywhere it goes tells me everything it touches is beautiful, beautiful.

And that makes me want him even more. My hand slides down his hard, hair-roughened chest, across the chiseled plane of his abs to circle his length with my hand. It gives a happy throb of greeting as my hand circles it and my thumb caresses the shapely head, so much like a warrior's helmet.

I've always thought so and never said it, afraid to be cheesy. But his shaft is a beautiful thing to me, as all of him is, and perfect for all we do together. Now that I have him in hand, I tug him closer and I feel him chuckle, a vibration that rumbles against me as I slide my hand, caressing, up and down the steely length.

He slides his free, roaming hand one more time up and down my body, leaving sensation stirred like the movement of bioluminescence on the tide. That expert hand comes to rest on my breast, and he pinches my nipple hard, leaning over to capture the other nipple with his hot, slick mouth at the same time, biting, and it's exactly what I want in that moment, and my body arches involuntarily off the bed as I cry out in delightful pain-pleasure, "Yes!"

He turns me on my side again, my back to his front, and he

lifts my knee and slides into me in one long, slick stroke, filling me so completely I arch back and my head bangs his collarbone in my rapture and my cries sound like seagulls flying by outside the porthole.

It feels like a key sinking hard into a lock, turning tumblers of delight. Like a plug connecting with an electric socket and lighting up with current. Like what it is, lovemaking that's an utterly perfect melding of power, connection, and pleasure.

I wonder how I lived a month without him in me.

He grabs my hip and pumps into me, so hard, so hard, and in this moment of connection, I know his loneliness, his desperate need for me, how much he missed me and needs to be in me, and it melts me further so I feel myself fragmenting in his arms, coming unglued as I reach back to grasp his ass and he hauls me closer, grasping my breast for leverage, and it's hard and sweet and exactly right, and I am on the verge of coming, pressing back for more.

But he doesn't want that yet, and he pulls out abruptly.

I moan at the coldness and emptiness of being left behind as he rises above me, his face dark and intent. I feel him want an even deeper connection with me, to be so deep in me I'm filled only with him. In some way he wants to obliterate the pain of my grief and fill it with only him, with his life, with his passion and love for me.

That shaft I've come to love juts in front of him, promising all the pleasure I'm going to feel, and he rolls me onto my back and folds my knees up against my chest. I'm open to him, tight, hot, and slick, my movement restricted, utterly vulnerable and in his power, and somehow in this mind meld we have, he knows how much I need that, and I know it, too.

"Yes. More, yes. More, yes," I breathe as he gazes at me for a long moment as if impressing the sight of me on his eyes.

I live through a long moment of anticipation until he plunges into my vulnerable slippery tightness. My eyes instantly roll back as he goes so deep it seems to touch my spine, lighting up sensation that ripples up my nerve endings, cascading me with pleasure like a pinball machine going crazy with lights and music and a pulsing *SCORE!*

And if it's possible, and somehow it is, he's holding himself above me by pressing down on my shoulders, pressed against my knees, and he's pumping, pumping, pumping, no restriction of any kind between us, and all I can see are spots of light behind my eyes, all I hear are our panting cries of pleasure, and all I know is that there is nothing and nowhere better than this long, hot, trembling pulsation...that goes on and on.

Rafe pulls my legs down suddenly, still deep in me, and the change of angle pushes me over the edge, bucking and mindless, coming around him coming, too, a long, physical crashing into each other that feels more like fighting than sex, a grappling and wrestling as we wring every bit of pleasure from each other while simultaneously giving all we have to each other.

It is messy, ugly, loud, hard, soft, generous, taking, and utterly beautiful.

He falls across me, huge and strong and as totally felled by me as if I were a woodsman who just took down the biggest tree in the forest. I feel triumphant. I own him, my great felled tree, and somehow, in that intimate sharing we still have for a little while, I know he feels exactly the same.

Triumphant possession and utter fulfillment.

I wonder, as I stroke his cooling back beside me, if we two are the only ones to know this feeling, and somehow I know we're not, but we've been lucky enough to taste this remarkable ecstasy more than most.

His back feels vast and smooth and so familiar it's a part of me and yet fascinatingly different from everything about me. There are tiny vertebrae bumps in the deep groove of his spine, and the tops of his buttocks are silky with tender fuzz, and he vibrates with the beginning of a snore.

It's chilly in the bright sunlight, and I pull the blanket up over us and snuggle against him. For all the time we were making love, I was in both our bodies, and it was everything good and perfect, and for a little while I forgot my father is gone from the world.

But eventually Rafe moves and gets up, and I sigh sadly as he does. He fetches a towel and puts it between my thighs and tucks me up in the blanket and says, "I have to go topside. We're casting off in an hour."

Casting off for Saint Thomas. Where I have to help pack up my childhood home and help my mother and my sisters get ready for a huge move into the part of all of our lives that is *after*.

After Dad.

I shut my eyes because the grief is back, like a sickness in my bones, draining and cold as I remember my father's dead ashes on the ocean and nothingness, and I nod and can't even smile.

CHAPTER TWENTY-THREE

Rafe

It takes ten days to get to Bermuda if all goes well sailing and five more to get to Saint Thomas. A week into the voyage, we're making good time. The crew and I are glad to be back on the ocean after five years of nothing but summer trips, and though most of them have families and lives now, scattered across the States, they dropped everything to come when I called. Freddie, with his big, bald head, who runs our galley; Sven, my right hand, who helps me with navigation; Fitz, an all-around sailor but who's in charge of monitoring our lines and sails on this voyage; and Ronnie, who is an engineer in his other life and the official mechanic for the _Maid_; plus an assortment of other hands who are new to me.

We're busy all day, keeping the _Maid_ shipshape, on course, and moving steady, and so far we're ahead and the seas have been good.

The only person without a real role is Ruby. She sits in a deck chair at the bow of the _Maid_ for hours at a time, watching the horizon.

I'm used to a different Ruby. Always on the go, she is usually bubbly and talkative, or serious when she's reading or studying. But whatever she's doing, it's a hundred percent. Now she stares at the far horizon, wrapped in a blanket from the cabin, her expression empty.

I am at a loss as to how to help her. All the guys are worried about how she's acting, trying to think of ways to cheer her up. We've made love a couple more times since the voyage started, but it certainly hasn't been the sex marathon I'd been hoping for. Even though being with me seems to help get her mind off her loss for a little while, it always comes back, and she hasn't initiated anything with me.

Sven asked her to play chess, which she usually loves, but she said "maybe later" and never took him up on it. Fitz tried to get her fishing, but she lost interest after five minutes. None of that is like the Ruby we know.

This morning I bring her a cup of hot chocolate that Freddie made for her in the galley. Freddie keeps cooking her little special things in the galley and asking me to take them to her; he always fixes me one, too, as if whatever it is was my idea.

Today is brisk and there's a feeling of some far-off northern storm in the air, and I'm glad of the rich, steaming chocolate to warm my hands if nothing else. I take it to her in her usual spot at the bow, and I pull up another low webbed chair to sit in beside her. Today she has a journal open on her lap. It's new, and I hope it's a good sign.

"Freddie made you some chocolate." I hand it to her so there's no argument about whether she wants it or not. She hasn't been eating much lately either, and I see the sharp wing of her collarbone in the low neck of her shirt. She takes the chocolate.

"Freddie's so sweet," she says absently.

I pull part of her blanket over my legs. The wind feels like it's cutting through my clothes, but I love it out here. The sky and

ocean are a broad sweep, as if we sail right into a universe that's
all shades of blue. There's a tiny glint of flying fish leaping across
the surface ahead of us. I'm so used to the endless rocking motion
now that it doesn't even register consciously, and won't until
we're on land again and I feel it as something I miss.

"You really love it out here, don't you?" Ruby looks at me, her
white fingers wrapped around the mug. Her eyes are a change-
able green; today they seem almost turquoise, as if they've picked
up blue from the ocean.

"Yeah, I do."

"Has it been hard for you, being a landlubber with me?" She's
been in school the last five years, and we've been living in one of
our Boston houses, just taking the boat out for short runs in the
summer.

"It was time for me to give the businesses attention. It's been
good." I don't answer her directly, because the truth is, I have
missed the ocean. When I met her, I was at the end of three years
of sailing around the world. After we got married, all that ended
abruptly—but it was good timing. I don't regret it. She had
college, and it was time for me to pick up the reins of the businesses I'd inherited.

"But you want to be out here more." She said it as a statement, and her small hand, warm from the chocolate mug, takes
mine. She tucks it under the blanket, in her lap.

I'm aware of how close my hand is to her box of secrets, but I
just hold her fingers, relishing the fact that she's reached out
to me.

"Tell me more about your dad," I say. I know she needs to talk
about him to begin to let go of the pain inside. "You know I
always meant for us to have a whole summer with your family in
the Virgin Islands."

"I know. You always said that, but we never took the time."
She sighs, sips the chocolate. "You knew him pretty well." I

worked for Peter and Kate for a whole season in their vacation-rental management company before Ruby and I married. I'd liked and respected them, my inappropriate attraction to their daughter aside.

"I did know him a bit, but not what it was like having Peter as a dad." I press her a little.

She doesn't answer for a long time. The wind fans her hair back, and I see her skin's begun to go that tender golden shade it picks up, like the beginning of toasting a marshmallow. She has new freckles on her arms.

"Dad was one of those parents who always had time for you. Whatever I had to tell him or show him, he'd stop whatever he was doing to give me his full attention." Ruby sips, her eyes on the horizon. "He was so clear about everything—what was right, what was wrong. I feel like I'm not sure about anything anymore without him here."

I squeeze her hand. "Do you think he'd want you to feel that way?"

"No. I know he'd say I'd put him in the place of God, and he was never anything but a guy who tried to live the truth as he understood it."

The fact that Peter Michaels had been a career missionary was definitely something to do with this definiteness Ruby referred to; I had always been looser in my interpretations of things, but Peter and I had understood each other.

"We never got to have that summer with them. And even though you tried to fly them out to visit us, he never accepted your help." She was still ticking over all the coulda, woulda, shouldas. I know all about that. My parents died when I was close to her age, and it had thrown me so far off my game, I'd farmed out the businesses and taken to the sea for three years.

I hope it isn't going to take Ruby so long to grieve the loss of her father, but having been through it myself, I know it might be a while.

"It was what it was, and it will be what it is," I say, as much to myself as to her.

As suddenly, as if conjured, dolphins erupt around the bow. These are little dark gray spinner dolphins, and they begin water acrobatics as they surf the bow wave, leaping and flipping, spinning as their name implies.

"Oh!" Ruby exclaims, and gets out of her chair. She goes to lie on her belly as far out on the bowsprit as she can, and stretched out there, her red hair flying like a flag, she reminds me of a figurehead.

Ruby loves dolphins. She told me once she thought they were her spirit animal. I know they'll do much more to cheer her up than reminiscing about her dad.

I stand up, and Sven catches my eye at the cockpit and waves me back to take a look at something.

His brow is knit with worry. "I know we're not supposed to have heavy weather in September, but there's a hurricane forming about two hundred miles from us, according to the weather report."

"How close are we to Bermuda?"

"Still a couple of days out."

"Let's put up all the sails and see if we can outrun it."

"Aye, Skipper." Sven got on the PA that piped into the interior of the ship. "All hands on deck. Putting up sail to get ahead of a storm. Check with me for assignments."

I glance up at the bow. Ruby is still lying on the bowsprit, mesmerized by the dolphins below. Let her enjoy them as long as she can.

A hurricane is coming, and we are in its way.

CHAPTER TWENTY-FOUR

Ruby

I've been out on the deck for a lot longer than usual without a hat. I've been doing a little tanning on the voyage, just so I don't get sunburned so badly when we are back in Saint Thomas, but I can feel my nose getting hot. I can't stop watching the dolphins.

Dolphins and I have always had a special bond. Growing up on Saint Thomas, I'd go swimming in the ocean and they'd appear, circling around, leaping over me, even letting me touch them a couple of memorable times.

Now I feel them almost trying to tell me something, send me some sort of reassurance. I could swear some of them are leaping up so we can lock eyes with each other. One is a little bigger, and she has a scar on her sleek, gray leather back. She catches my eye, and I hear something in my mind. *"Go fast."*

Did she send me a message? I must be imagining things.

I realize there's a lot more activity than usual going on behind me.

Rafe and the crew were putting up all the sails. Rafe has tried to teach me all the names and functions of the sails, but I've never bothered to memorize them. The front little one is going up, the big main one is being let out, and they've even hoisted the spinnaker, a huge balloon-like sail. It seems like they've adjusted the heading, too, so we are running downwind.

I look around, but I can't see anything to be concerned about. The sun shines bright, poufy popcorn clouds dot the horizon, and the sea is calm but for whitecaps generated by the moderate twenty-knot breeze. I am getting better at judging the wind speed, at least, and I don't usually start getting seasick until it's around thirty knots.

I say goodbye to the dolphins and scramble backward to see what's going on.

Rafe's got the tiller. He's wearing a nylon ball cap, as much to hold down his shoulder-length hair as for sun protection. Even after he came back to his companies and put on a suit, he refused to cut his long blond-streaked hair. "It's my rebellion," he said. "I won't be a corporate stooge even if I have to go to board meetings."

I love him for that rebellious streak. I have a little rebellion in me, too—it's what made me take a chance and get married at a ridiculously young age.

He's not wearing sunglasses at the moment, and his cobalt eyes are sharp on the horizon, fans of sun creases setting off those eyes. I can see we're going a hell of a lot faster than before, and the motion of the *Maid* is brisk and efficient as her aluminum hull, tapered for speed, slices the water. The sea peels up and flies back around us, and spray hits my face.

"What's going on?" I ask.

"We're trying to outrun a storm. Once it hits, I want you to stay below. It's the safest place for you. Report to Freddie and see what help he needs securing everything belowdecks."

"Aye, aye, Captain," I say, and when he glances at me, we both grin at the inside joke.

Sometimes I address his equipment that way in playful fun, and I can see the memory of it turning him on even at this inappropriate moment. I waggle my tongue at him and take off, knowing I distract him, and none of us need that during pre-storm prep.

As I go down to the galley level, I realize I'm apprehensive. I've never been through a storm on the *Maid* before, and the dolphin told me to "go fast." This is going to be a big one.

I'm nervous, but I'm also excited. We have a great ship, an experienced crew, and the fog that's surrounded me since Dad died seems to be lifting with this new situation.

Freddie has his cupboards open. He keeps his supplies in zippered bags for the most part, but he is pulling up elastic nets inside the cupboards and tucking everything inside so they don't move.

"Captain told me to report to you to help stow everything belowdecks. Thanks for the chocolate; it was delicious."

"Good. I need the help. Go do the heads and bedrooms. We have these security nets inside the cupboards and slots for everything, but we've been getting lazy with how mellow our trips have been."

"How bad of a storm do you think this is?" I ask, handing him some items he had piled on the floor.

"I believe the word 'hurricane' was mentioned. It's still two hundred miles away, so we have a good chance of outrunning it. The captain and Sven have done this route and this scenario before. It'll be a fun story you can tell your grandkids."

"Hope so," I say, and go to the crew's head. Shaving cream and a bottle of shampoo are already rolling around in the shower just from the increased motion of the ship, and I get busy stowing, tucking, and securing.

A story for our grandchildren. Now, that would be something,

I think, tucking a bungee cord around the cleaning supplies under the sink.

And then it hits me.

I stopped taking the pill after I heard the news about Dad. Just clean forgot. And then Rafe and I didn't do it for a month. And now we had, not once but several times, and I hadn't even remembered to bring my pills when I'd packed for the trip.

There is a chance I might be pregnant even now.

"Oh damn," I mutter, rocking back on my heels. "Oh boy."

And what if I were? Would it be so bad?

We've never talked specifics. I knew we both wanted a family, in that far-off "someday" that my goal of getting through school and starting my career had pushed out into the future.

A future I'd thought I'd have a lot of time for. A future I'd pictured sharing with my family, maybe when my parents were retired and ready to be grandparents.

But Rafe's parents are gone entirely, my dad has died, and now there is only my stressed-out mom, dealing with my teenaged sisters. While I'm done with school and the dreaded bar exam, I don't even have a job yet. None of this is the rosy scenario I'd imagined.

The ship lurches, and it flings me forward into the corner of the bathroom cabinet. "Ow!" I exclaim, even as the reverse direction lands me on my ass.

Oh well. Whatever is going to be with getting pregnant has already probably happened. I won't have access to more birth control until Saint Thomas, and who knows if I can get a prescription filled there. Rafe can start using condoms, but why bother?

Maybe the timing is perfect to get pregnant. I can still get a job when we got back to the States, or even do what I'd been refusing to do and work for McCallum Enterprises. Then I can make a flexible schedule.

Another heave of the ship brings me back into the present, perilous moment, and I hurry along, latching the cabinetry in the hall and ending up in our stateroom.

We've gotten sloppy. Water bottles roll back and forth on the floor, and the telescope has fallen over. I continue with the securing process in our closet, cabinets, and head.

Through the double row of portholes alongside our built-in bed in the bow, I can see the plunging motion of the ship. The portholes are around six feet above the surface of the water when we're in port on an even keel. Now we fully submerge, so I can see beneath the ocean's surface, and then lift so high I can see the sky.

It's mesmerizing, and I thank God I have a pretty strong stomach.

I go back to the galley and check with Freddie. He's sitting, strapped into his bolted-down chair, watching a soap opera on the tiny combo TV/VCR player at his work area. "All set below," he says. "Don't go above without safety lines."

"I don't know where those are."

"Here." He shows me the webbed nylon belt with its clip-on rope. "They've got safety cables all over. You clip your rope to the cable in case you get swept overboard."

"Oh cripes," I say. "Rafe told me to stay below, but I want to see what's going on above. See what the storm looks like."

"Look through the skylight." He has a big plastic skylight above the galley, and he points. All I can see is gray, and I frown. "I need to at least get a look at what's above."

And before Freddie can stop me, I grab one of the ropes and nylon belts and head up the ladder leading topside.

Rafe

The weather is hitting us now. I can see the leading edge of the hurricane behind us, and it looks like a purple wall shot through with lightning bolts. We've made good time with full sail, but it doesn't look like we are going to make it to Bermuda before we're engulfed by that thing behind us.

I still have hopes of making it to one of the atolls outside of Bermuda. There's one roughly an hour away, and if we can make it into a cove there, or even into the lee of the island, we'd be better off than bouncing like a cork in the open ocean.

The guys and I have our full weather gear and safety lines on now from the aft storage locker because, even though the rain hasn't hit yet, the spray and waves off the bow are fully engulfing the *Maid* from stem to stern every few minutes.

I spot Ruby when her head comes topside, because the minute she opens the hatch, light streams out and water streams in, and I see a gleam on her red hair. I feel something new and terrible: *fear.*

Does my wife have a safety harness on?

"Get below!" I bellow, but the wind whips my words away, and I have both hands full with the big wheel of the tiller and can't let go. Sven spots her, too, and he runs down the length of the deck to stop her, but she's already up on deck and has clipped a safety line onto the cable. I sigh with relief as my second reaches her.

She's wearing the same outfit she had on before, and she and Sven are instantly doused as a wave engulfs the starboard side. The big blond Swede has a grip on her arm and is arguing with her, but I am somehow not surprised when she yanks away and comes toward me, clutching the rail, all the way to where I hold the tiller in the sheltered hollow of the cockpit.

"Sorry, Rafe. I just had to see this," Ruby says. Her eyes are sparkling, her cheeks pink, and her hair is flattened to her skull like a drowned rat. Sven, having delivered her to me, moves on.

"You disobeyed an order," I snap, the fear I felt at seeing her replaced by anger. "This is no place for you."

"Wherever you are is the place for me," she says with perfect composure. "Don't worry. I'll go below. But I want to know what's going on." She turns to look behind us, and her eyes widen. "Oh my God. Is that the storm?"

"Hurricane Shellie," I say, still pissed, and now thinking about spanking her. She deserves it for scaring me like that. The thought makes me hard, and that's distracting, too. "You need to get below. Seriously."

"Shellie will like that," Ruby says, smiling. Her former room-mate, Shellie, has remained one of her closest friends. "But that storm looks serious."

"It is. Very. I'm hoping we make it to this atoll." I point to the location on my laminated sea chart. "We have a good chance of getting into this cove on this side of the atoll and dropping anchor."

"Then I won't distract you any more, Captain," she says, and presses a kiss on me with her wet, cold mouth, which tastes of the sea and makes me think of tasting it more. But then she's creeping along the rail, her nylon safety line trailing her, and going below. I sigh with relief as she disappears and the hatch is secured by Sven from the outside.

"She had a belt on," Sven says, reaching me, his expression apologetic in the bright yellow hood of the slicker. "She said she had to see the storm."

He's defending her, the sod.

"I'll handle my wife," I said frostily. "No thanks to you, letting her come up here."

He shrugged. "It's Ruby. What was I going to do?"

What indeed? Now, at least, I believe she'll stay below, where it is safe.

The next two hours are a blur of fighting the wheel to keep the compass heading for the atoll with all sail out and the seas, churned up by the hurricane, getting bigger and bigger while the wind gets gustier and smacks us around like a giant cat's paw.

I'm about ready to call for the sails to be pulled in, giving up our run before the storm. Sven, hanging in the rigging, spots Atoll 57, too small to even have a name, ahead. According to the charts, it has a bay on one side, really its only geographic feature. I have the guys pull in the spinnaker and tighten us up, and we tack around the islet in the waning light. Purple is the color of Hurricane Shellie, I've decided, as the sun shuts down into a deep violet gloom.

The crew is perilously hanging off the bow and sides, looking for shoals and reef, as Sven, wiping his binoculars constantly, scans the atoll for the opening of the bay.

"There!" he yells, pointing, and I can see a slight break in the tropical landscape of rugged black rocks and palm trees whipping so hard in the wind they look like feathers beating the air.

I clock it a few degrees, but I can't tell if we're coming around fast enough. "Reef all sails!" I yell, and Sven passes it on. The guys move like a well-oiled machine, dropping and furling the sails while three of them still watch for hazards in the water. "Sven! Give me headings!" I shout into the teeth of the wind, and Sven, an even better sailor than I am, calls out degree headings for the turn.

I fire the engine to counteract the momentum from the sails, and slowly, carefully, nose the *Maid* into the sheltered bay.

The bay turns out to be deeper than it at first appeared. Tall volcanic-rock cliffs rise around us, and I feel a tremendous sense of relief as we pull all the way in, and there's at least a hundred yards on every side before the rocks.

The rocks are bad, though. Black as sin and twice as jagged. But if we can just keep from losing anchor, we should ride out Shellie just fine.

Sven is already calling for two anchors, aft and stern, and I have the guys put out a couple of sea anchors off the port and starboard, too, in case we pull a chain.

Finally, I can let go of the tiller. I find myself trembling all over, my muscles locked, my hands in the shape of claws from gripping the wheel so long and hard.

Sven takes a look at me. "I'll take the first watch, Captain. Go below and get some rest."

One last look around at my crew, half of them going below to rest, the other taking the watch to keep the ship from running aground, and I go in the hatch and down two levels to our bow stateroom.

Ruby's wide-awake, sitting in bed in flannel pajamas one of her sisters sent for Christmas; they have pink pigs with wings on them. She takes one look at my face and clambers out of bed with a cry.

"Oh my God! Rafe! You look exhausted!"

"Pretty beat," I say through chattering teeth. Now that I've let go of the tiller and the effort to get us here, I am coming apart physically.

Ruby pulls off my yellow rain gear, throwing it into the tiny head. She strips off my clothes, and I'm already falling asleep as she's getting a warm washcloth and wiping down my sweaty, trembling body.

I wake up hours later. It's night, I know, by the pitch-blackness we're in, intermittently lit by lightning flashes. The wind is a terrible banshee howling outside, and the ship shudders periodically with its blows. We're moving; the sea heaves around us, but the motion of the *Maid* has a very stable feel, and I can tell our anchors are holding. I'm warm and the bed is comfortable, but I'm totally rigid and aching in my hands, arms, and neck from the battle with the wheel.

Ruby is wrapped around me like a snuggly koala. She must

have dressed me in something, because I can tell I have a shirt on, but nothing below. Must have been too hard to get underwear on me.

I think about her coming topside and feel a tremor of that primeval terror again. She's not a sailor, never has cared to become one, and if Freddie hadn't told her about the safety lines...There's nothing to do in these dark hours of the storm but recharge our batteries and pass the time, and there's nowhere I'd rather be than with my wife.

"Ruby." I have to shake her a bit to wake her, but the pain is bad. "Can I get some help? My hands are all locked up." I run the back of one of my curled hands across her soft cheek. "There's some of that muscle massage cream in the head."

"Of course. Poor thing." She gets up and pads into the head. I'm glad it doesn't seem like she's been seasick. She comes back and, in the dark lit by flashes of lightning, she works my hands with the heating cream.

I can't help groaning as she rubs my fingers with Bengay, gradually straightening and opening them, working her way down the wrists and deep into the bulging, tight muscles of my forearms. She strips off the shirt and gently rolls me over. She straddles me and begins working over my shoulders and neck.

My moans and groans of painful pleasure at the rolling touch of her strong little hands and drilling thumbs would be embarrassing if anyone heard them, but it's just me and Ruby here in the womb of storm-filled dark.

She disappears for a moment, and I must have drifted off, because the next time I wake up, she's rolling me onto my back again.

"Listen. I have to tell you something," she says. I'm pretty groggy, but I realize she's tying my hands with something silky to the handles on the sides of the bed where we have storage below. "I can't decide what to do, and it's not fair not to tell you about it. I forgot my birth control pills after I got the call about Dad. I haven't been taking them, and I don't have them on the voyage. It might be too late already, but it's too soon to tell right now. So my question is, do you want to wear a condom or not?"

I tug at my hands and realize I can't get them undone. "What the hell, Ruby?" I growl, the implications barely penetrating my fogged brain. "What are you doing?"

My erection has a pretty good idea of what she's doing, and it's been interested for a while now.

"You have Bengay on your hands," she says primly. "I'm going to be taking care of you tonight." She applies her mouth to my nipples, stroking up and down my chest and abs. I can feel the length of her hair trailing over me like feathers. Her strong thighs clench my hips, and I can feel how hot her center is, how close it is, how sweet it is.

Everything on my body rises to full alert: every hair, every muscle, and of course, my cock, but I'm still trying to process what she was asking me.

Condom or no condom? I've gotten spoiled by her being on birth control, and I'm not even sure I have any. Is she saying she might already be pregnant?

My hard-on gives a joyful leap of excitement as she gets to it with her mouth and those skillful hands. I'm groaning now, in an entirely different way than from the massage. "I'm going to get you back for this."

"I expect nothing less." She kneels between my legs, takes me deep in her throat, and reaches up to work my nipple with her other hand.

I arch up off the bed with a hoarse cry, overcome by surprise and sensation. There's nowhere I can go with all the pleasure I'm feeling, the firing of nerves intense as she works me in all the different places. I'm reduced to twitching, quivering, moaning jelly, and I'm tied up, wrestling with my own neckties and total sensory overload.

Just the thought of what she's doing to me makes my balls tighten. I'm at the very edge. She can tell I'm about done for because suddenly all is withdrawn. I collapse, gasping like a gaffed fish, throbbing painfully.

"Ruby. You witch," I moan.

"Condom or no condom?" Ruby asks again. She's rising up before me, her white skin lit by flashes of lightning, her long hair around her like a cape and black in the shadows. I can't see her eyes, but I can see her delicious curvy body in those flashes of storm. She's up on her knees, straddling me, and everything in me is straining toward her, going *yes, yes, yes*.

I finally manage to say, "No condom. Ever again."

She leans down to lick my nipples. "Good answer," she says, and sits down, taking me into her.

It feels unbelievable, as if my shaft is connected to my whole spine, and all of it's wrapped in tight, hot, tingling pleasure.

Of course I've had her this way before, on top, but she's never tied me up and tortured me this way before, and she's never been possibly pregnant before. Something about it all, and the storm, makes us both crazy.

I buck my hips helplessly, trying to get deeper into her, but she raises and lowers herself, controlling the movement, emitting little panting gasps. I can tell she's barely hanging on, trying to make it last. One of my straining arms breaks loose and then the other.

I've got her by the hips and ass now, and I'm holding her hard and driving into her. She loses all control, bucking out of rhythm, hair flying as she rides me, but I've got her where I want her—*so deep, so deep. I need only now this minute. Oh God*—and we come explosively together.

She's down across me, and my arms are around her. I'm

pretty sure I've just had a stroke, because the top of my head feels like it blew off. We both can't do anything but pant for a good while.

"I should have known you'd break those ties," she mutters.

"So you think you could be pregnant?" I ask. My world feels a little off-kilter. I've wanted this a long time, actually, but haven't brought it up. She's had goals, school, plans. She's a planner, my Ruby. For her not to plan this, too, surprises me.

"It's possible." She sits up, gets off. It feels like loss, being separated from her, but she pads to the bathroom and gets a washcloth and comes back. I look out the portholes—there's an eerie stillness of sea and sky now. She sees me looking. "What is it?"

"I think we're in the eye of the hurricane. See how calm it is outside?"

"Do you want to go topside and check it out?"

"No." I draw her down beside me after we both use the wash-cloth. "The guys have it handled. I just want a few more hours with my wife." I tuck her in against my side and draw the blanket up over us.

CHAPTER TWENTY-FIVE

Ruby

I'm at my favorite place in the bow of the *Creamy Maid* as we motor into Charlotte Amalie on Saint Thomas, under engine, as the last of the hurricane has moved on and would have left us becalmed outside that venerable old harbor.

I've felt different ever since the night of the hurricane. Sad still, but managing it better, and it's a good thing, too, because I have a sense that Mom's going to need all the help she can get packing and dealing with my sisters, each a handful in her own way.

Pearl's almost eighteen, a senior in high school, and according to Mom, has "gone off the deep end" since Dad died, partying late every night, sleeping until noon on the weekends, and barely passing her classes. Jade, the baby at fourteen, has gone total responsible and is cleaning everything, OCD-like, and trying to boss Mom around.

I glance back. Rafe's behind the wheel, and the wind picks up his blond-streaked brown hair. He has his shirt off, and the sight of his muscled arms gleaming in the sun, that eagle tattoo seeming to fly as he moves, does something to me. I feel a deep tug inside. I keep wanting to find a time to talk about maybe getting pregnant, but we haven't found it. Instead, we've gotten insatiable with each other, as bad as when we were newlyweds and twice a day was normal.

I've never stopped loving Rafe or being turned on by him, but this crazy passion since the hurricane four days ago...This is a weird way to grieve. I feel guilty that he makes me feel so good.

He sees me looking at him and quirks his eyebrow questioningly. I blow him a kiss and turn back to the view.

The town of Charlotte Amalie grew up around the harbor, and it's the capital of Saint Thomas, a mix of utilitarian modern and gracious old-world charm, all white stucco and red clay roofs. Palm trees are everywhere, and the city is immaculately groomed for all the tourists from the cruise ships that constantly line the great harbor walls. The turquoise water that makes the Caribbean so special glitters with sunshine.

Being in Saint Thomas always takes me right back to growing up here—the smells, of overripe banana and plumeria mixed with the tang of the sea and the smell of unfiltered exhaust. The cries of parrots and mynah birds, the kids running through the streets chasing soccer balls—all of it is dear and familiar, though it feels so small to me now.

We drop anchor with plenty of room around us from other boats, and Rafe and I pack overnight bags to stay at my family's house near Magen's Bay. We could easily have sailed into Magen's Bay itself, and we may move the boat there if we have to stay long, but we need to restock and the guys need to be able to go ashore for provisions and recreation, too. The ship came through the hurricane pretty well, considering, but there are definitely some repairs to get done before we try to sail back to the States.

Rafe and I take the Zodiac tender in with Sven, register the boat at Yacht Grande Harbor, and go on the hunt for a rental car.

We end up with a battered old Citroën from a guy who knew my dad and rents five or six used vehicles.

"Such a shame about your father," old Pietro says, hugging me and smelling strongly of his ever-present Gauloise cigarettes. "He's gone too soon."

"You're telling me," I say, sniffing back tears. It's my first time talking to another person who knew him since I was here for the funeral.

I make a quick call to Mom at the yacht club to tell her we're on the way. "Oh, thank God," Mom says, her warm voice cracking. "I was so worried about you during the hurricane."

"Rafe was amazing," I say, looking right into my husband's eyes as I say it. "He found us a secret harbor on an atoll, and we were fine. Do you need anything from town?"

Trips to Charlotte Amalie have always been a big deal since gas prices are so high on the island. Mom has us pick up some extra rice and staples at the market, and we're on the road. The Citroën doesn't have air-conditioning, so we roll down the windows as we drive out of town. I rest my head in the window frame, and Rafe reaches over to play with a piece of hair that's escaped my braid.

"How are you doing?"

"Okay. Sad, but okay. I feel like something changed for me the night of the hurricane." I turn to look at him. "I think I decided to let a few things go the way they wanted to. Not to try to control so much."

"Like getting pregnant?"

I nodded. "I think it's okay for it to be whatever it is. Just let nature take its course. Because we just never know, you know?" I find myself blinking back tears, and I look back out the window. We're rising into the mountainous area around Saint Thomas, and green surrounds us. It's a beautiful jungle and reminds me of that first hike I took with Rafe.

Rafe puts his hand, that long-fingered hand with its wonderful calluses, on my smooth, bare leg. "This might be our last chance to help nature along before we get to your mom's."

I smack his arm. "You're bad."

"That's why you love me."

"A little bit, yeah."

He keeps massaging my leg, igniting tingles as he slides his rough palm up and down. "God, you're so silky here," he says, exploring that area.

"For goodness' sake," I gasp. "No fair." So I turn and begin an exploration of his lap. In short order he's frantically looking for some sort of exit off the main road. We end up turning down a muddy driveway heading into the jungle, and as soon as the jungle thins enough to pull off the road, he pulls the Citroën over and hauls me out of my seat and into his arms.

We keep our shirts on in case of interruption, laughing as we bite and caress and kiss each other, mad with a crazy lust that makes no good sense. I end up on his lap, the manual gear shifter stabbing one thigh and the steering wheel in my back, totally uncaring as he spreads my ass cheeks wide and digs his fingers in, creating a brutal sweet tension as he penetrates me. I arch and cry out, then bite him and ride him hard until we're done.

Not a long time, it turns out, before the windows are steamed over and we're both temporarily sated.

He reclines his seat and I sprawl across him. "God. I needed that," he says.

"What's gotten into us?" I wonder aloud. "I mean, we were getting kind of sedate back in Boston. Couple or three times a week, like normal people."

"I think you feel better when we're together," Rafe says. "And it's my mission in life to help you feel better."

"I can go along with that. But maybe you're just trying to get me pregnant as fast as you can now that that's on the table." I've crawled back to my side and am doing my best to get my clothes back on and tidy up.

"Not gonna deny it. That possibility makes the Captain really happy," Rafe says, waggling the aforementioned appendage playfully.

"Don't do that to him. It's beneath the Captain's dignity. Let's get going, or I swear Pearl will guess what we've been up to and give me crap about it," I say. "That girl is way more sophisticated than I was at that age."

"If she's half the firecracker you were, the world's in trouble," Rafe says, and we get on the road.

CHAPTER TWENTY-SIX

Ruby

The house I grew up in is a sprawling old plantation-style with a wide, deep veranda for shade and catching the breeze. It's on a tiny knoll and has a sliver of a view of Magen's Bay, that gorgeous deep pocket in the side of the island with such a sandy bottom that the water glows as if lit from within. My mother meets us on the porch.

"Mom!" I get out of the car, running to embrace her. It's been only six weeks since I saw her for the funeral, but her tall, sturdy body feels fragile in my arms. She's lost weight, and her deep auburn hair is filled with new threads of silver.

"Ruby. So glad you're okay from the hurricane." Mom squeezes me. She smells like the lemon oil she uses for polishing. "We're getting ready for another garage sale, and Jade and I have just started on your old room." She embraces Rafe and receives his kiss, and I turn to my sister Jade, who's pushed open the screen door.

I see the source of the lemon-polish smell. Jade is holding a bottle of oil and a rag, which she sets aside.

"Oh, sweetie," I say, hugging her close. Jade is as tall as me but with a different build—long, coltish legs, a slender, short waist, and small breasts. She has big green eyes that many have said are similar to mine, but she inherited Mom's dark auburn hair. She is going to be gorgeous, but right now that promise is hidden behind braces and a pair of thick glasses. I hope it will stay hidden a lot longer. Mom doesn't need another Pearl on her hands.

"Where's Pearl?" I ask.

Mom shakes her head as she leads us back into the house. "She spent the night with a friend last night. She was supposed to be back by now."

"Why don't I go get her?" I say. I'm eager to see my little sister and eager to give her a piece of my mind.

"That would be great," Mom says. "She might even come home with you."

"I'm having a hard time imagining Pearl outright defying you, Mom," I say.

"The grief counselor we've been seeing says Pearl is grieving in her way," Jade says. "But she's awful to Mom."

"Where is she?" Looking at Mom's caved-in cheeks and sad brown eyes, I can't wait to chew a piece of Pearl's fine ass for adding to her stress. Mom gives me the address, and I know right where it is—the Carvers' house in the tiny hamlet of Peterborg.

The Carvers have a reputation. Not a good one. I knew and avoided the Carver boys and experienced their pinches on my butt firsthand.

"I'll be back soon." I give Rafe a quick kiss goodbye as he goes back into the house to help Mom move some furniture outside for the garage sale. I'm glad we took the time for that session in the car. I have a feeling privacy is going to be in short supply now that we're here at the house.

A short time later, I pull the Citroën up outside the Carvers' compound of lean-to shacks held together with corrugated roofing. As soon as I turn off the car, big loose dogs swarm around, barking. I'm in no mood to deal with the Carvers' unruly pack, and I remember how visitors get attention at their house.

I lay on the horn.

"*Beep. Beep. BEEEEEEP.*" The Citroën's horn is not impressive, but it is annoying. Pretty soon I see movement at the screen door. I wave through the windshield and honk another three times until Pearl comes staggering out, rubbing her eyes.

She's not wearing a bra, and her breasts, as big as mine, bounce distractingly in the thin T-shirt she's wearing. She's carrying the familiar black hoodie she wore the whole time when I saw her at the funeral. She pushes her feet into sandals on the porch and waves back at someone in the doorway before heading toward me, reluctance in every line of her body.

And what a body it is. She's the tallest of us, with Jade's long legs and my hourglass curves. I have no doubt at least one of the Carver brothers has had his hands all over her. Maybe two or three of them, from the glares I'm getting from the surly looking cluster of disreputably handsome Carver boys clustered in the doorway.

In lieu of greeting, Pearl opens the car door and says, "Where'd you rent this piece of crap?"

"Hello to you, too," I say, waving with mock cheer to the Carver clan. "You know where—Pietro's. Why aren't you home helping with the garage sale?"

Pearl shrugs.

I'm spoiling for a fight, and as I leave their driveway, I hang a left, away from the direction of our house, and floor it. Pearl frowns and grabs the sissy handle. "Where are we going?"

"Somewhere private where we can talk."

"I've got nothing to say to you."

"Well, I've got plenty to say to you." I scan her with a contemptuous glance that takes in her bed head, braless chest, and hickey-covered neck.

Pearl and I have always been close. Well, as close as you can be with a four-year age gap. She really hated it when I left for college five years ago and she had to become the oldest Michaels girl. She narrows bloodshot blue eyes at me.

"Easy for you to get all high-and-mighty, Miss Perfect," she says. "You have no idea what I've been dealing with here, since well before Dad died. Did you know they'd been on the verge of divorcing? Fighting all the time because Dad was getting so religious. He wouldn't let me do anything, not even go to a friend's house! I'm glad he's gone."

"You bitch!" I slam on the brakes. Pearl, who hadn't put on her seat belt, whacks her head on the dashboard. She reels back and goes for me.

"You're the bitch!" she yells at me, and there we are, stopped in the middle of the road, slapping each other and pulling hair like we used to when we were kids.

Suddenly someone's honking behind us, and I put the car in gear and we drive on. I'm taking us to the old lighthouse, a place we liked to picnic with the family when we were growing up.

We drive along, and Pearl's rubbing her forehead and has finally put her belt on.

"I'm sorry," I say. "I didn't mean for you to get hurt."

"Except where you pulled my hair out," Pearl says, holding up a handful of drifting white-blond strands.

"Well, you got me good." I show her the puffy spot on my cheekbone where she connected. "This has been a great welcome home."

"I'm sorry, Ruby," Pearl says, and suddenly her plump lower

lip is quivering and tears pop out of her eyes and roll down her cheeks. I know how that feels, because I'm crying, too, now.

I turn into the deserted, sandy parking lot of the lighthouse. "Let's take a walk."

Pearl puts on her discarded sweatshirt and I find Rafe's Windbreaker in the backseat. We walk into a fresh wind off the late-afternoon ocean, which tumbles our hair. It's a beautiful color out on the sea, but having been on the ocean for close to two weeks, I enjoy seeing it from a distance.

Pearl's sniffing and wiping her tears on the backs of her hands as she walks. "I don't want to go to that armpit town, Eureka," she says. "I would sooner die."

I know Eureka, a small logging town in the ass end of California, is hardly sophisticated. I had to visit Grammy and Grandpa there with the family once a year before I went to college and married Rafe.

"Have you told Mom you feel that way?"

"Of course. She says it's my fault we're going." Pearl sobs now, putting her hands over her face.

I loop an arm around her. "Well, she called us about you. She's obviously not doing too well after Dad, and she thinks you're acting out because you're grieving. She thinks she needs to get you away from 'bad influences.'" I make air quotes. "What's really going on with you, Pearl?"

Pearl looks up. She's the only one of us who got Dad's blue eyes, and seeing them now, so much like his when he was upset, gives me a stab of fresh grief. Crying makes those light blue eyes, fringed in dark spiky lashes, even brighter. Unlike Rafe's dark nautical blue, hers are a light crystalline turquoise, shot with white like chips of ice, and there's an indigo circle around the iris. Pearl is seriously beautiful and has always been a magnet for trouble. I fear the darkness I see in those light-struck eyes.

"It's always been too late for me," she says. "I just wanted to feel better." She holds out her arms, and I see the thin raised lines of scars from cutting herself interspersed with needle tracks.

"Oh God, Pearl." I pull her into my arms. "It's never too late. But I don't think you should go with Mom to Eureka. I think you should come home to Boston with us."

CHAPTER TWENTY-SEVEN

Rafe

It's been a rough ten days getting the house closed up and Ruby's mom and sisters packed, but finally it's all dealt with. Turns out they never owned the house. Kate has a little money from the sale of their possessions and Peter's life insurance policy, enough to have a cushion when she arrives in Eureka, but no security blanket. She takes Jade, who is frighteningly self-contained—and we take Pearl.

I'm braced for a rough voyage back to Boston in more ways than one as I guide the *Maid* out of the Charlotte Amalie harbor. For now Pearl and Ruby are in the bow, sitting in deck chairs, and it's all good because our favorite school of spinner dolphins have come to see us off and the girls are watching in delight, exclaiming and pointing.

They really are cute together, though I'm worried about Pearl. Ruby told me about her drugs and promiscuity, and we have a rehab place set up for when we get back to Boston—but in the meantime she's bound to have some withdrawal symptoms on the trip, and I've already seen the way she's looking at the guys.

And they're looking back at her. It would be hard not to. Pearl's one of those girls you can't ignore. Tall and bold, with a mouth on her that promises all kinds of sin and a body that won't quit. I already had to issue a "hands off, she's a minor" dictum, which was fine, as most of the crew is older and married, but there's still Pepe from Brazil, who's only twenty-two and can't take his eyes off her, and Jesse, who's twenty-five and should know better but clearly doesn't.

Only hours later, Pearl's below decks puking, and the ship's barely got any big motion. This does not bode well. Ruby's taking care of her, but when I have Sven take the helm and go down to check on them, Ruby's looking bad, too. I find her seasick bands and an extra pair for Pearl and put them on her.

Ruby's skin is bleached-looking and her hair is stuck to her forehead with sweat. "I was trying to help Pearl." We can hear Pearl heaving in the tiny head attached to her stateroom. "And it seems to have made me sick, too."

"Go topside and get some fresh air. I'll look out for you and have Freddie look after Pearl."

Ruby is green around the lips, but she manages to smile. "I think Pearl would rather Jesse looked in on her, though I'm sure she doesn't want him to see her looking like she does right now."

I hook an arm around her shoulders. "Don't worry. I'll deal with her. And Jesse, too, if that's who she's got her eye on."

I give her a little squeeze and push her gently toward the ladder.

In the galley I find Freddie. "Pearl's seasick. And I think maybe a little something more. She was doing drugs in Saint Thomas, so she might be having some withdrawals."

"We need to keep her hydrated," Freddie says, immediately opening his cupboards and looking for supplies. He rode with a motorcycle gang in his younger years, and he's seen his share of people dealing with addiction. He also completed a two-year nursing degree so he'd be able to be our shipboard medic.

I leave Pearl in Freddie's capable hands and head topside.

Ruby's sitting in the bow again, wearing one of my billed hats, and she already looks better. "The smell of puke has a way of spreading," I tell her, sitting down beside her for a moment.

"Ew. Don't remind me." She wrinkles her nose.

"You know, we didn't have much time to talk about Pearl and what we're doing with her. Technically, we have no authority over her."

"I think she's going to be fine. She wanted to get off Saint Thomas as much as I did at that age. I don't think she's been doing drugs long enough to be really hooked, but those Carver boys are bad news. She hasn't told me anything really about what she was getting up to with them, but getting her away was essential." Ruby looks at me, her green eyes luminous. "I love you for taking her on, no questions asked. I won't forget it."

I lean over to kiss Ruby. "She's family."

In the coming days, Pearl finds ways to test that resolve from both of us. She's seasick and miserable for days at first, complaining and driving Freddie nuts. Then she finally begins to feel better and spends most of her daytime hours in a white bikini on the deck, trying to get the guys to talk to her and causing Pepe to almost fall off the rigging. The old married guys like Sven try to avoid the whole section of deck she occupies like the queen of Sheba, untying her top and lying there like a centerfold.

I'm sure this is only the beginning of what she's going to put us through, and it doesn't help that Ruby seems to have succumbed to seasickness. Even the bands aren't helping as she lies around, limp as a dishrag between puking bouts.

It takes me longer than it should to realize there might be some other reason she's so sick, and the night it finally dawns on me, I pull her into my arms in our bed. I've told the guys I want this voyage to be as short as possible, which they're all in agreement with, so even at night when the wind is light, we've got a lot of sail out and are moving at speed. The moon tracks along the water beside us, silvery and bright, and its reflected light gleams on Ruby's pale skin.

"Do you think you might be pregnant?" I whisper to her, holding her close but platonic, as we've been since Saint Thomas. "Could that be why you're so sick? I mean, you made it through the hurricane without puking."

"Oh God," she moans, as if this is the worst news ever. "I kind of forgot about it with all the drama with Pearl. I didn't think of buying a pregnancy test in Saint Thomas. We'll just have to hope for the best."

"What is hoping for the best?" I'm not liking this new attitude. I thought we'd decided to let nature take its course and that this was as good a time as any to start a family. "I thought you were okay with this."

"That was before we got Pearl, and now I have to help her get adjusted here, set up in school, all that."

"I don't see how that has anything do to with being pregnant and, nine months from now, having our baby," I argue, feeling something incredibly hopeful and excited as I say the words. I pull her head against my chest and stroke her hair. "Pearl's a big girl, as she is fond of reminding you and everyone else. It might even be a fun thing for you two to share."

"I hope so," Ruby says listlessly. "Maybe I'll be ready when the time comes. We'll know soon enough." Gradually, her breathing changes and she falls asleep. I feel alone with her in my arms for the first time.

And I don't like it.

Ruby

I haven't been able to show Pearl our house in Boston because Dad would never let us pay for the family to come visit and they never had the money to, so it's a treat for me to lead my little sister, gleaming golden with shipboard tan, to the door of our lovely old brownstone in the Back Bay area.

Two sandstone lions perch on the broad rail areas leading to the front door. I insert the brass key into the lock as Pearl looks around at the quiet, leafy street and exclaims in excitement. "How close is this to the high school?" she asks.

"I don't know. I never had reason to wonder about that before," I say, getting the door open at last. I hear the sound of a vacuum, and we step inside to the familiar smell of lemon polish. "Seems like Mrs. Knightly is here cleaning."

Pearl grins. "Wow. I know you told us Rafe had money and all that, but we only ever saw you on Saint Thomas, slumming on your yacht. This is sweet. How'd my nerdy sister nab a hottie who's rich, too?"

"Shut up," I say, smiling. "I didn't know he was rich. And honest to God, by the time we got together, it didn't matter to me. I was fully prepared to live in a boardinghouse and see him a few months of the year."

I lead her into the house and startle Mrs. Knightly, who clutches her chest in fright. "Oh, Mrs. McCallum! You're back!"

"We are. Rafe's still down at the docks, but this is my sister Pearl. She's going to be living with us for a while. I was thinking the pink bedroom for her?" We both turn to look at Pearl, who's turning in a circle under the gigantic crystal chandelier in the foyer. She looks like an angel with her creamy blond hair hanging to her waist and her glowing tan, even in cutoff shorts and a ruffled gingham top tied beneath her breasts.

"Wow, Ruby," Pearl says. "I think I'm going to like it here."

CHAPTER TWENTY-EIGHT

Ruby

I leave Pearl getting settled in with Mrs. Knightly's excited help and tell them I have to go pick up some food at the grocery store. Really, I need to buy that pregnancy test.

My stomach does a flip at the mere thought, and I need to stop on the sidewalk and lean against a building to breathe, gulping down the little bit of granola I ate this morning that's trying to come back up on a wave of nausea.

Finally, I can go on and walk to the corner market. I do pick up some fruit, vegetables, and food for dinner, but also the pregnancy test. I feel as self-conscious paying as I did the first time I bought tampons as a teenager. I hurry home and meet Rafe pulling up to park on the street in his disreputable old truck. He gets out and slams the door.

"Went to the store already?"

"Had to get some food. And another thing," I say. I see his eyes widen in comprehension, and I need him suddenly. I put down the bag of groceries and hug him, putting my face into his shirt. "I'm scared," I mutter into his collarbone.

His arms are around me and he rocks me close. I hear cars honking in the background and people talking and walking by, but we just stand together beside the bag of groceries at the foot of the stone steps.

"It's going to be okay," he says into my hair, brushing a kiss on the top of my head. "I know you're not sure how to feel about it, so I'll be happy for both of us."

"Okay." I smile at him, and he brushes a kiss on my lips, a kiss that turns into a conversation, a long exploration that gets us a wolf whistle from a passing car, and I break away and pick up the bag.

"I put Pearl in the pink room. She and Mrs. Knightly seem to be hitting it off."

"Good. I hope she doesn't get too comfortable before she has to go to the rehab place."

"It's an outpatient treatment program. She's going to be here in the evenings."

Rafe looks down at me ruefully. "I'm missing our privacy already."

"She's going to be gone a lot. Can you take this stuff into the kitchen? I have to go to the bathroom."

"Want me to come?"

I smile. I still like privacy in the bathroom, but Rafe's never had any such hang-ups. "I'll meet you in the bedroom and we can look together."

"Sounds good. Any chance we can get rid of Pearl for a while?" Rafe waggles his brows as he takes the bag after I've removed the pregnancy test from it.

"I heard that," Pearl says from the top of the steps. "No problem. I want to explore this town. Give me a map and I'm out the door."

It's a mark of how desperate we are to be alone that we give her the map and dismiss Mrs. Knightly for the day. Rafe finally takes the groceries to the kitchen and I go to the bathroom for my appointment with the little white stick that turns blue if you're pregnant.

I'm sitting on the bed in our big, sunlit bedroom, holding the little stick, afraid to open it, when he comes in from his bathroom wearing nothing but a towel. Even in my state of nervous anticipation, I appreciate the sight of his bronzed chest, muscular arms, and the sculptured abs disappearing into the towel wrapped around his hips. He's all power and utility of form, but when I meet his eyes, the only thing I see in them is tenderness.

He sits beside me and takes hold of one side of the little plastic holder.

"Ready? Let's pull it open on three."

"One, two, three," I say. We each tug on our ends, and the middle section opens to show the chemical strip.

It's blue.

I feel like I can't breathe, but at the same time my heart gives a giant squeeze, and I feel my eyes fill with tears. "I wish my dad were going to be here for this," I say.

"I wish my parents were here, too. But it is what it is, and they will live on in our child," Rafe says. I shut my eyes, and the tears roll down my cheeks.

He kneels in front of me, takes my face in his hands, and kisses the tears off my cheeks. "I'm so very happy about this," he says. "I'm happy enough for both of us."

"I'm happy, too," I say, and realize it's the truth as the words leave my mouth. "I'm really happy, too. I'm scared, but happy. I can't wait to see our baby."

"God," he breathes into my mouth. "I sometimes think I can't contain how you make me feel."

"Likewise," I say, and then he drops the towel and sits beside me on the bed. I turn and perch astride one of his thighs as I kiss him. Those long arms stroke up and down my body, squeezing hard. He takes hold of my ass, his hands rough on me through my pants as I rub up and down, up and down, moaning with the furnace heat of want he's ignited in me with just a look and a kiss.

He pushes me off and back onto the bed, kneading and biting my breasts through my shirt, nuzzling between them, an expression of ecstasy on his face as he touches them, and I moan with the pleasure of it as he pulls my shirt and bra off and does to my round, full, achingly tender breasts what I see others wishing they could do to them: rolling his face between them, massaging and toying and mouthing. Because they are luscious, these breasts of mine, with their pointy blush-pink nipples that will someday nurture our child.

Then he takes my nipple deep into his mouth and sucks hard, and I throw my head back and cry out at the sweetness of his mouth on me, feeling the heavy sucking all the way to my spine, opening everything and making it ready for him.

He pays homage to the other breast, as I'm still rubbing against his heavy, muscled thigh as he leans over me, and by then I'm almost ready to come and my clothes aren't even all the way off. He keeps sucking my breasts and slides his hands down to my waistband and unzips and tugs my pants and panties off, his busy, hungry mouth never leaving me.

He turns me away from him, though, and I know it's so he can see and touch and play with my ass, his other favorite part of my body. He pushes me down in front of him across the end of the bed, and I know he's gazing at my butt, each cheek smooth and silky, firm and shapely, lightly freckled like a plover's egg. He strokes and explores me, driving me mad, and finally he tests my readiness with a skillful hand, and I cry out for him. "Yes! Yes!"

And then he drives into me from behind so deep and hard my head snaps back and I let out a wail of fulfillment. He's grasping my hips and surging into me, watching and controlling everything that feels utterly wild and abandoned. I'm right there with Rafe, in his body, enjoying the hell out of his conquering of mine, and at the same time I'm in my body, reveling in the heavy, deep strokes of his conquest.

I want even more sensation, so I pull my legs up and kneel on the end of the bed before him. He gives a husky groan at the sight of my folded body with him so deep in me it's as if we're one. He grasps my waist, and all is a pinwheel of colored light and inarticulate sound and overwhelming pleasurable sensation as he cleaves me again and again until I'm boneless and melting around him.

When the sensations have abated a little, he leaves me and I moan at the loss but don't have time to really feel it before he pushes me down on my back now, puts my legs up on his shoulders, and enters me in one long stroke.

I gasp with the shock, with his sure and confident handling of me for maximum pleasure. My hands grasp his muscular buttocks as he gazed into my eyes, the intimacy almost too intense.

More.

More and more and more.

Just when I think I'm going to fly apart, broken on the anvil of his desire, he comes, arching like a hawk flying above me, his arms tight and body vibrating with the release of a hoarse and triumphant shout.

The depth and heft tips me off the ledge. I spasm in his arms, my whole body rippling as waves of pleasure surround the rock that has fallen into the lake of my being in one long endless *now*.

Whatever else happens to us, there was this moment in time when I lived in two bodies and almost died of the pleasure of it. If I have to go, this is how I want to—death by pleasure in the arms of the man I've come to love beyond life.

CHAPTER TWENTY-NINE

Rafe

Ruby's feet are up in the stirrups finally and I'm clutching her hand. It's been a long nine months of life, work, Pearl, and other travails, and eight hours, so far, of labor. I totally get why they call it "labor," and I'm exhausted. Ruby's exhausted, too, but I think we're finally in the home stretch of this arduous adventure. She's looking at me, her vivid hair stuck to her face with sweat. Her eyes are round and scared and so very green.

I'm scared, too, but I'm smiling to hide it.

She's been telling me she thinks she's going to die for an hour now. Her belly, that great heaving mountain, looks enormous to both of us. The fact that somehow, any minute now, she's going to push whoever's in there out still seems totally unrealistic to me, but everyone assures us things are going well and nature is cooperating.

"I don't want to die this way," she says to me, dead serious. "I want to die having an orgasm with you."

The doctor, a woman who looks way too young for the job, is

checking around down there under the sheet, and she snorts with laughter.

"Think of this as the biggest orgasm you've ever had," she says. "One that actually produces something. You can push on the next contraction."

We see the contraction begin before the pain hits. Ruby's vast belly seems to pull upward into a teardrop shape; then it goes square and harder than stone.

I know because I've felt it happen under my hand a hundred, maybe a thousand times now. Those muscles would put a world-class weight lifter to shame.

She's still looking at me when the pain hits, and her eyes widen with the shock that, no matter how many times it's happened today, never seems to get less terrible.

I squeeze her hand hard. "Go for it, Ruby! It's time to push. You can do this!"

She seems to gather herself and sit up past even the inclination of the table, and she bears down, turning bright red, and damn if I don't see something emerging between her legs.

"Go, Ruby! Go! The biggest one ever!" I yell.

She sucks a great big breath and bears down again. Our child slides out into the world after three massive pushes.

"Fastest first baby I've delivered in a year!" the doctor exclaims. We're both crying and laughing and trying to get a look at the baby and see what it is.

Ruby says, "I didn't die!" in some astonishment, and they hand him—he is most definitely a boy—to me first.

He's crying a bit, covered with that white stuff, flailing his long arms as the nurse helps me tuck a thin blanket around him. I hold him close against my scrubs and angle him so Ruby can see his face. I can feel tears pouring down my cheeks, but I'm grinning so hard it hurts.

"Oh, hello, Peter," she says, and I swear I see him recognize her voice. He goes still. His eyes open and they're dark blue. His hair is dark like mine, and I can hardly bear to part with him for a second, but he needs his mama now.

Ruby's putting our son, Peter Kane McCallum, named for both our dads, to her breast, cooing in a soft voice I've never heard from her before.

Ours is an ordinary story, really. Girl meets boy, they fall in love, they get married, and they have a baby. He's rooting around and getting hold of that tasty nipple, and he latches on so hard she yelps, and we laugh. We look down at him together, amazed at this miracle that happens to people every day.

And it happened to us.

Turn the page for a sneak peek of *Somewhere in the City*, Book 2 of the Somewhere Series.

SNEAK PEEK

SOMEWHERE IN THE CITY, SOMEWHERE SERIES
BOOK 2

It's dangerous to be too beautiful.

I know. I've lived it. Right now I'm sitting on a hard metal folding chair in the recovery meeting, enduring the way guys scope out my body and girls judge me. I've dressed down for the occasion, too—I'm no threat to anybody in my ratty hoodie, the hoodie that's been a kind of security blanket for the last six months since Dad died and everything changed.

I have on baggy jeans, and my hood is up to hide my hair. I'm thinking of dying it. Some mousy color, like muddy brown. My hair draws way too much attention.

In fact, that's what I'll do, right after this stupid meeting.

The leader gets us going with the Serenity Prayer, and then we are supposed to go around and share our "experience, strength, and hope."

I don't have much of any of the above, at eighteen, just moved here, and my biggest hope is to get everybody off my back as soon as possible.

I endure the stories. Sad ones, really. Kids ripping off their parents. Guys giving other guys blowjobs in parking lots for a few bucks to get high. I was never into any of that shit or did anything radical like that. In fact, I'd have been fine, would never have had to come to this meeting, if it weren't for the Carver boys.

But who could resist the Carver boys? The only thing to do in that pothole in the road, Peterborg, on Saint Thomas. Yeah, it all started with Connor, but then there was Keenan. I shut my eyes and indulge in a little memory starring me and the Carver boys.

Someone elbows me. "Your turn."

I sit up. The leader, a chubby lady with one of those soft do-gooder faces I'm too familiar with, gives me a hairy eyeball.

"Welcome to our meeting," she says. "Is this your first time with us?"

I nod. "Hi. My name is Pearl."

I'm supposed to say, "and I'm an addict," but I don't. I can't. It would be a lie. I just barely got going with some hard stuff and everybody freaked the hell out, and now here I am enrolled in this "day treatment" daily meetings routine. It sucks. But at least I'm not in Eureka, Armpit of California, with Mom's tears and Jade's compulsive cleaning.

The group leader narrows her eyes a little that I haven't said the catechism. I remember she has to sign my attendance sheet, though, as she says, encouraging, "Would you like to share your experience, strength and hope with us?"

"Not really, no. But thanks for asking."

A titter goes around the circle, and the leader moves on.

There's a guy across from me, long thick legs extended into the circle, his jeans just the way I like them—broken in, with split knees. He's wearing black boots and a leather motorcycle jacket that looks like it's the real deal, like he got here on a Harley or something. His arms are folded on a chest I wouldn't mind getting a closer look at, and dark brows are pulled down over eyes that look black from here.

I stare back at him, and touch my tongue to my lower lip.

Then, I shut my eyes very slowly, and open them again, so he can see how blue my eyes are, how long my lashes. I uncross and recross my legs, so he can appreciate that mine are almost as long as his.

His face doesn't change and he looks away with such a bored expression I feel heat rise up my chest under my hoodie.

Well, getting him to notice me will make the meeting a little more interesting. I push my hood back so my naturally curly blond hair tumbles out like Rapunzel sending down her ladder.

He doesn't so much as glance at me, and I spend the rest of the meeting trying to get him to.

When it's finally over, I get up from my chair, unzipping the hoodie so my black turtleneck showcases my curves, but he's already walking out without talking to anybody, picking up a helmet from beside the door.

Well. That gives me something to look forward to tomorrow when I come here again, same Bat-time, same Bat-channel. And maybe I'll keep my hair blond for a while longer.

Unfortunately my antics have attracted someone else's attention, one of those lumpish hockey-player types that think they're God's gift—not that I would know a hockey player from a pole vaulter, since we have nothing but soccer on St. Thomas.

"Hi." He actually reaches out and picks up one of my curls, rubs it between his fingers like he wants to smell it or something. "Pearl."

I yank my hair out of his hand and bundle it into my hood and zip it up again. "Howdy, fellow druggie."

That puts him back a bit, rubbing his rash-roughened chin with a hand. "Need a ride somewhere?"

"No thanks."

"I'm Steve."

"And I don't recall asking." I turn and walk out. I can feel his eyes burning holes in my back, and I can feel the other girls hating on me. Everyone judging me, like they always do.

Well, if they'd walked a mile in my boots they wouldn't envy them, I can tell you that. Not that I'm complaining. I'm not in Eureka, California, after all. Instead, I'm living in Boston with my sister Ruby and her hunky husband Rafe, and they're pretending they have some idea how to deal with me.

I don't need anything but to be left alone.

That's what I tell myself as I walk home from the meeting. It feels lonelier and more pathetic than I ever like to feel, the wind cutting through my jeans and the last of the fall leaves rolling along the sidewalk. There's a sharp wind off the Charles River, only a few blocks away from my sister's sweet old Back Bay neighborhood. I go up the stairs of their brownstone with the sandstone lions that guard the door. I've nicknamed the lions Beowulf and Odin, and I pat their heads as I get my key out and go inside.

Yeah, every time I think I'm lonely or sad or get tempted to drink or hit someone up for a line or a hit, I have to think: *EUREKA*. I don't have to go there. And I need to be grateful.

Up in my girly-pink bedroom, I turn my radio to the rock station and flop backwards on the bed, listening to the Top 40 of 1989.

I really am grateful to be here.

Rafe and Ruby didn't have to take me in, make me the third wheel to their two-person googly-eyed love fest, especially now that Ruby's pregnant. Right on cue, Ruby knocks on the door and then opens it. "How was the meeting?"

Ruby's so pretty. She has green eyes and long dark red hair, and the kind of heart-shaped face with blushed skin that makes guys want to protect and take care of her, when nothing could be further from what she's really like: stubborn as a mule and smart as hell. She just got her law degree, and the only person who can sometimes beat her at an argument is me.

"It was fine."

"Where's your paper?"

I got so distracted I forgot to have the leader sign my attendance sheet. "Dammit, I forgot to have it signed. But Ms. Betsy can sign it next time."

Ruby comes all the way into the room. She's about three months pregnant and just beginning a little pooch of belly. "Pearl, come on. You promised. Let me see your arms."

I push up the sleeves of my hoodie, biting down on all the ways I want to tell her to back off. She and Rafe trying to lay down rules is really kind of funny, when Mom and Dad never could get me to obey anything.

I'm the original rebel without a cause. I don't know why it's always my first instinct to do the opposite of what everyone wants.

She sits next to me. "I hate this, Pearl. I hate having to hold your feet to the fire like this. But I just don't think you get how serious things are."

"Oh, I get it." I pull my legs up under my stretched out, comfy old hoodie. "I do what you and Rafe want or you ship me back to Mom."

"I guess that's the bottom line, but that's not what I'm talking about. I just don't think you get how worried we are about you. You have a problem."

I can't take it anymore, and surge up off the bed in a waft of anger.

"You don't get how it's really not a big deal and never was."

"Mom and I talked. She said she's thought a lot about how things started going bad with you and traced it back to a Christmas party two years ago that you went to at the Carvers' house. Did something happen there? Something bad?"

Yeah, I remember that party. What I remember is that I don't remember.

"You know what? If I'm too much trouble, send me back already. I'm sick of the inquisition, of nothing I do being right."

I slam out of the bedroom, feeling tears at the backs of my eyes.

If only Dad hadn't died because of me.

I could have still turned things around if he hadn't died when he did. How he did. I jump on the smooth walnut railing and slide down the long curving stairs to the entryway.

I'm not a total nutcase. I grab a coat. Boston in November is pretty damn chilly at night.

Out on the street it's quiet. I head for one of the walking bridges that crosses over the freeway to the park that runs along the Charles River. I just want to walk, to clear my head. I'm not looking for trouble.

But trouble has always seemed to find me.

Download and continue reading *Somewhere in the City* now: tobyneal.net/SSCwb

ACKNOWLEDGMENTS

Dear Readers,

I hope you enjoyed this story of a deep and fateful love filled with life's layers of complication. *Somewhere on St. Thomas* is the story of a young woman's awakening sexuality with the man she loves, an incredible time for anyone lucky enough to have that experience. Continue reading for an excerpt from *Somewhere in the City*, Ruby's sister Pearl's very different story, but an equally thrilling path to love.

Special thanks to Eden Baylee, a romance/erotica writer I particularly respect for her classy handling of some of the stickier parts, who read my earlier drafts and said, "You've got a nice way with this!" Believe me, I needed the encouragement.

Yes, I'm a hopeless romantic that believes in Big Love.

Much aloha,

Toby Jane

FREE BOOK

Join my newsletter lists and receive free, full-length, award-winning novel *Torch Ginger, Paradise Crime Mysteries Book 2*.

tobyneal.net/TNNews

TOBY'S BOOKSHELF

ROMANCES
Toby Jane

The Somewhere Series
Somewhere on St. Thomas
Somewhere in the City
Somewhere in California

The Somewhere Series
Secret Billionaire Romance
Somewhere in Wine Country
Somewhere in Montana
(*Date TBA*)
Somewhere in San Francisco
(*Date TBA*)

A Second Chance Hawaii Romance
Somewhere on Maui

Co-Authored Romance Thrillers
The Scorch Series
Scorch Road

Cinder Road

Smoke Road

Burnt Road

Flame Road

Smolder Road

PARADISE CRIME SERIES
Toby Neal

Paradise Crime Mysteries
Blood Orchids

Torch Ginger

Black Jasmine

Broken Ferns

Twisted Vine

Shattered Palms

Dark Lava

Fire Beach

Rip Tides

Bone Hook

Red Rain

Bitter Feast

Razor Rocks

Paradise Crime Mysteries Novella
Clipped Wings

Paradise Crime Mystery
Special Agent Marcella Scott

Stolen in Paradise

Paradies Crime Suspense Mysteries
Unsound

Paradise Crime Thrillers
Wired In
Wired Rogue
Wired Hard
Wired Dark
Wired Dawn
Wired Justice
Wired Secret
Wired Fear
Wired Courage
Wired Truth
Wired Ghost

YOUNG ADULT

Standalone
Island Fire

NONFICTION
TW Neal Pen Name

Memoir
Freckled

ABOUT THE AUTHOR

Toby Jane is the romance pen name for author Toby Neal, a mystery author who can't stop putting romance into all of her books! Toby Jane is the place where she gets to indulge her passion for happy endings, big families, and loving pets..

Toby also writes memoir/nonfiction under TW Neal.

Visit tobyjane.com for more ways to stay in touch!

or

Join my Facebook readers group, *Toby Jane's Romance Readers,* for special giveaways and perks.

Made in the USA
Columbia, SC
20 May 2021